BLACK WARLOCKS PROWLING

WILDE WITCHES - BOOK 2

ERIN RICHARDS

Midnight Muse
PUBLISHING

BLACK WARLOCKS PROWLING
Erin Richards

Digital ISBN: 978-1943800179
Print ISBN: 978-1943800186

Cover Designer: Book Cover Artistry by Heather Hamilton-Senter

Editor: Jessica Meigs @ Edits by Jessica

PRAISE FOR
ERIN RICHARDS' BOOKS

"I loved this book [*Chasing Shadows*] and it never faltered from its action and suspense." ~*Night Owl Reviews* (NOR 5-Star Top Pick)

"The suspense will keep you turning the pages... The characters are complex and well-developed and there is never a dull moment in the story [*Chasing Shadows*]. If you love your romance with suspense, this is one book you need to read! 5 stars all the way!" ~*The Romance Reviews*

"*Stealing Twilight* by Erin Richards is completely enthralling with its addicting characters, unique plot, and satisfying ending." ~*Amazon 5-Star Review*

"*Seducing Darkness* is fast-paced and action-packed. It is well-written with vivid imagery that allowed me to get lost in the story. It offers drama, intrigue, and romance with a hint of humor that kept me entertained throughout." ~*Amazon 5-Star Review*

"Full of adventure, romance and two wonderfully heroic characters. The descriptions of the island are beautiful and the passion between Morgan and Ryan leaves you turning the pages to see if they can finally come together. A great book [*Wicked Paradise*]." ~*5-Stars, Paranormal Romance Guild*

"Perfect for fans of Julie Kagawa & Alyssa Rose Ivy. Loved this book [*Forbidden Thirteen*]! The plot was unique in a genre where everything has been done before. Just the perfect balance of action, supernatural and hot romance. Bring on book 2!" ~*5-Star Amazon Review*

BOOKS BY
ERIN RICHARDS

Psychic Justice Series
Chasing Shadows, Book 1
Twilight Rising, Book 2
Stealing Twilight, Book 3
Seducing Darkness, Book 4
Tempting Midnight, Book 5

Forbidden Legacy Series
Forbidden Thirteen, Book 1

Wilde Witches Series
Igniting the Witch, Prequel
Black Magic Rising, Book 1
Black Warlocks Prowling, Book 2
Black Curses Brewing, Book 3

Wicked Paradise

Young Adult
Vigilante Nights
Dragonfly Nightmare
Bittersweet Wreckage

See updated book list at:
www.erinrichards.com/booklist.htm

BLACK WARLOCKS
PROWLING

Chapter 1

Sage adjusted her blouse, revealing the top half of her breasts. A scowl traversed her warlock's face, and a low-throated chuckle escaped her. She knew how to work her feminine wiles—and status as a powerful witch— to her advantage. She shivered and pulled down the hem of her short black skirt, wishing she'd worn leggings. So much for exposing her skin. Unfortunately, duty and an invited guest dictated playing dress-up that afternoon. Despite the furnace running at turbo speeds to fight off the late winter chill in the Santa Cruz Mountains, her witch-fire wasn't doing a stellar job at keeping her warm either.

Snow, one of her bonding owl familiars, lifted off her right breast and flew to her left. Her skin re-absorbed the living tattoo, tickling her flesh. After Evan Ravenwood broke their bond a couple of days ago, the owl had returned to her. Shock still tingled through her gut after learning that Evan held the ability to break a bond previously only broken by the witch who'd bonded him. Namely Sage. Nudging aside her blouse, she stroked the owl. Its wing lifted off her skin and twined around her finger for a second.

"What are you doing?" Rafael scowled again, oh so cute. A subtle draw from her magic resulted in a tiny flame extending from his right pointer finger.

She blew the flame out rather than use her air magic, which he'd use to fan the flame, playing his usual games. "Really?"

Caerwyn, the snowy owl she'd bequeathed to Rafael when she bonded him, fluttered its black-spotted, white wings and cooed at her from the opening of his dress shirt. Caerwyn, an Irish name, meant white fortress. Rafael Reyes, the warlock she adored beyond reason, and her main bonding familiar were her fortress. The familiar's name wasn't coincidental.

She reached across the desk and stroked Caerwyn, giving the owl love as well. "You love me in sexy, revealing clothes." Grinning, Sage fluttered her eyelashes at Rafael.

"Not for this meeting. And you don't get to have sex with every warlock you meet. Not now." He skirted the desk and pressed his lips to her neck, trailing scorching kisses to her mouth, teasing his tongue across her lips. "Leave it alone." He pulled her blouse over her breasts. Snow pecked at his fingers, and her main owl familiar Gwyneira cooed at him. She had two other bonding familiars attached to two warlocks who remained bonded to her to use her magic. Otherwise, the warlocks contained no magic of their own.

As High Priestess of a coven of witches, she required three bonded warlocks for protection. The other two warlocks were free to find another witch of their own to love. Only then she'd break her bond to them. If they were to find a love match with a human woman, she'd maintain the bond if they continued guarding her. They'd need her magic to do their jobs. Tired of stringing Rafael along, she'd sowed her wild oats and emptied the silo. Time to get real.

Stroking her familiar's white chest, she fake-pouted. "You're no fun."

"Not what you said last night and again this morning," he said in his slightly and only sometimes nasally voice.

Ah, sex. Sex with Rafael pretty much made her day... every day. Sage loved his raw power and magnetism, both in and out of bed. She loved being held in his arms, feeling safe and loved.

Easing away, he positioned himself close, magic simmering on his skin's surface, drawing from her fire magic. A warlock's tug on her magic wasn't usually noticeable, but they both teetered on the edge, and all her magical elements played havoc inside her. Rafael's layered dark hair, tanned, angular cheekbones, and Roman nose over his full pouty lips occupied her and minimized her jitters.

A knock thumped the door, and Sage's middle sister Aspen entered, earbuds stuck in her ears. Faint rock music wafted across the room. The myriad scents of Aspen's herbal potions swarmed the room, and Sage crinkled her nose at the perpetual odors accompanying their coven healer.

"The man of the hour's here," Aspen said, swiping the front of her blouse. Crushed rosemary floated in the air. The dust motes sparkled like tiny diamonds in a sunlight beam glinting through the large picture window overlooking the gardens. Coastal fog didn't reach into the hills every day, and she welcomed sunshine on a potentially ominous day. As if sunshine alone could solve her problems. *Le sigh.*

"Send him in. Are Willow and Evan on their way?" She straightened her blouse and plumped up her boobs, avoiding Rafael's frown.

"Yep. On their way like good little minions." Aspen left the door open, hightailing out of the thick tension, and waited in the hallway with Sage's other two warlocks standing guard.

Sage sat in her mother's old chair behind the black walnut desk, another relic of the coven's past, and awaited her youngest sister, Willow, and her new consort. Rafael positioned himself to her right, her ever stalwart wingman, consort, number-one warlock, and guard. The calming influence in her chaotic life. A life made more troublesome the past week after rescuing Willow from Andre Charlemagne. The Black Tide leader ruled an ominous group of black warlocks, which forced the Ravenwood family to swear allegiance to Andre or bite the literal bullet.

The Witches and Warlocks War had decimated black warlocks over a hundred years ago. But somehow, some way, the Charlemagne, Ravenwood, and a few other bloodlines had survived, and they'd flown under the radar. Until now. It rankled Sage to no end that long-dead black warlocks were rising to power.

Light glowed at the end of the tunnel, and she intended on embracing that light. If it meant bonding one last warlock, so be it. Rafael would have to suck it up. A High Priestess had the right to bond multiple warlocks and use them at will. Except in her case, she was done with the sexy times.

Ethan Ravenwood, a Black Tide lieutenant, and head of his family's coven of black warlocks, entered the large office. Sage took in the fiercely magnificent warlock from his dark, cinnamon-brown hair to his black loafers and about melted in a puddle of molten lava. Snow tingled across her breasts, wildly beating its wings, then sinking below her skin. The blasted familiar wanted Evan's older brother, it seemed. Sage exerted mental control over the über-excited owl. *What the bloody moon is that all about? Later...*

Ethan was even more scrumptious than Evan. The brothers shared the same dark, neck-length hair, chiseled, aristocratic face, and muscles to die for, all contained in a towering height. All male brawn. Her gaze raked down Ethan's wide chest encased in a dove-gray dress shirt and arrowed in on the impressive bulge in his slacks. She licked her lips. His allure slammed into her, flustering her usual cool composure.

Growling like a dog staking his territory, Rafael hulked behind her chair. Magic floated in the air. Not dangerous, but calming.

"Something to drink?" Aspen asked Ethan.

He rejected Aspen's offer and perused Sage. Male perfection in his well-cut designer suit showed off his thick arms and thighs. And that ass. His ass rivaled Rafael's perfect ass. An ass to grab on to.

Ethan approached, and Sage rose from behind the desk, a welcoming smile breaking across his oh-so-handsome face. A brilliance sparkled in his intense gray-blue eyes, and his tan challenged Rafael's natural swarthy complexion. *Well, hello. Everyone knows I like them tall, dark, and studly.*

"Ethan Ravenwood," he greeted. He skirted the desk, took her hand, and pressed his lips to the back of it. "A pleasure to finally meet you, Sage Wilde. I've imagined this meeting for eons." He nodded at Rafael, and Rafael grunted low in his throat, his hand gripping her shoulder from behind, possessive and a bit irritating.

Ethan's voice spread warm, silky chocolate through her veins, reminiscent of Rafael, as if brothers from another mother. Sage's mouth dried to dust. "No doubt," she managed to squeak out, idiotically defying her natural commanding voice of the Wilde West Coven High Priestess and High Priestess of the entire western region. She eased her hand from his and clasped it to her middle as if to hold on to his touch. Snow slithered to her hand to wallow in the feel of Ethan. *What the living hell is he doing to me?* She didn't sense glamour magic, and bottom line, her attraction was a natural response to any sinfully sexy man or warlock. Was she fooling herself by believing she could give them all up for one man?

Right after she'd agreed to Rafael's numerous demands for exclusivity, in walks sex on a stick. From her intel, Ethan wasn't bonded to any witch nor attached to any woman. *Stop! Why do you care? He's a black warlock, a potential enemy, not yours to take. Not yours to bond and screw his brains out. Not now. Not ever.*

Evan barreled into the room, helping Willow hobble in on her crutches, their laughter rippling at something, infectious and hopeful. Despite breaking her left ankle during Andre's capture, a happy-go-lucky attitude erased Willow's usual seriousness, and Sage gave her sister an affectionate smile. She'd waited a long time to witness her sister gain her witch wings. Sage never considered Willow would also gain a black warlock, considering Willow had decried the ways of witches and warlocks forever.

The magic in the air electrified in the presence of two black warlocks who held their own power. Twenty-first century warlocks didn't possess their own magic. Or so everyone believed. Little had Sage known, the group of power-rich, black warlocks known as the Black Tide had hidden in secret, growing their ranks and rising to power. The Ravenwoods were one of the ruling families under their leader Andre Charlemagne, the world's most powerful warlock. Powerful in position, maybe not in magical ability. Time would tell. And Sage held the man locked in her basement. His punishment for dumping a black spell on Willow and attempting to kidnap her this past week. Hence the reason for her present parlay with the Ravenwoods.

Sage returned to her chair behind the desk, the cool leather upholstery tempering her inner fire. "Everyone, please take a seat." She gestured to the guest chairs and the black leather sofa against the far wall. Willow cuddled against Evan's side on the sofa, resting her head on his shoulder, while Ethan filled an overstuffed wing chair in front of the massive desk. In reassurance, she feathered her fingers over Rafael's wrist, felt his pulse level out.

"Let's cut to the chase, shall we?" Ethan's smooth baritone echoed up to the high open-beam ceiling.

"By all means." Sage tramped down the sinful chocolate his voice caused to flow in her veins. "I have something you want, and a Ravenwood has sworn fealty to my coven twice now. First to me last summer, and second, due to the mutual bond with my sister." She nodded at Willow and Evan.

"We'll discuss what I desire in a moment," Ethan said. "I'm sure you know that Evan and Willow can rule your coven. Together they hold four elements of magic, not just one element like yourself."

Sage glared at Willow. At least he didn't know she possessed aether, which allowed her to use all natural elements in her witchcraft. "So I've learned," she said. Willow met her glare and upped it with a triumphant smile. "And what magic *elements* do you possess? Willow and Evan can rule the Ravenwood clan as well."

"*Touché,*" Ethan volleyed.

"Hey, leaders of the free world, we're not here to yak about ruling the Wilde and Ravenwood clans." Willow rose off the sofa and paced the room, her crutches and one sneaker squeaking on the hardwood floors. "We need to figure out how to use or get rid of a certain fungus growing in our basement and prevent the Black Tide from destroying every coven from California to Mars."

"Bro, don't pretend like you care for Andre and want

the Black Tide to succeed," Evan piped up, lounging back on the sofa, more delectable than Sage remembered. She'd never had sex with him since she'd recruited him after she swore off sex with any other warlock—or man—except Rafael. Wistful, Sage almost wished she'd partied down with him before she bonded him, despite discovering Evan had tricked her to infiltrate her coven. Despite the ruse, he'd paid his restitution after helping Willow escape Andre's clutches.

Ethan held up a hand, attempting to reduce the sudden excitement to a simmer. "To answer your earlier question, I hold the sole element of air. Yes, Willow and Evan can rule both covens since their magic surpasses mine and yours combined. They're admittedly not ready for leadership. Maybe in the future." He shrugged. "For now, we need to combine forces to halt the Black Tide's rise to power. And determine what to do with Andre. Are we agreed on these two objectives?"

"Of course." Sage sniffed disdainfully. "I want what's best for my coven and the western region. I don't want my witches or warlocks harmed. We've worked too long and hard to maintain our position as the West's leading coven. I refuse to jeopardize it or allow anyone to usurp my leadership."

"Then we're stomping on the same page." Evan stood and took Willow's hand in his. "Willow and I renounce any claim, rightful or not, as leaders of either coven. But only if the Ravenwoods and Wildes work together. If you don't reach an understanding, Willow and I will seek command."

Willow pinned another smug look on Sage, and Sage nodded, accepting her collegiate sister's position. *Over my dead body will you rule this coven. It's mine by right. I'm the oldest daughter of the Wilde High Priestess.* Her sister knew better. Willow's magic was too new, barely tapped. She'd sink herself and the coven if they had to rely upon her while she learned how to use her newly minted magic and wound her way around her new bond to Evan and his black magic. Willow was the only witch Sage knew of bonded to a *black* warlock.

"We done here?" Willow asked. "I need to hit campus, and Evan needs to go to Stanford."

Sage waved Willow and Evan off and waited for the door to close behind them. Rafael's fingers tangled soothingly in the hair at the nape of her neck. She leaned against his hand for a second, seeking his comfort, bolstering herself to confront Ethan again.

She straightened. "If we're in agreement, Ethan, let's discuss how to diffuse Andre," she said. "I can hold him for a long time, but not forever."

"Hold on." Ethan smiled like a Cheshire cat. "We're not done sealing our alliance."

His beguiling grin set off a new flood of anticipation washing that silky chocolate through her bloodstream again. She squirmed in her seat, pressing her legs together.

"What's left to seal?" Rafael dropped a crumb in the conversation, his voice deep and powerful. Another flame danced on his finger for a second.

"I want a true alliance. I want what you have, Rafael, friend."

"Friend, huh? Not sure I'd go that far, considering we just met. You want Sage to bond you? You don't need her. You have your own magic."

"You know as well as I do the extra power a bonded witch and black warlock possess. Look at Willow and Evan."

She'd made a pact with Rafael. No more warlocks bonded to her, except the bare minimum required by Council rules. Licking her lips and fighting off a twinge of regret, she said, "Wasn't part of our bargain. There's no need to bond you. I can find you a wonderful witch in my coven who'd be thrilled to bond you." Snow remained hidden, accepting it may never belong to Ethan. The owl quivered against her upper arm beneath her sleeve.

"We're not done bargaining. And that's not all I was referring to," Ethan purred.

Rafael gasped, rolling Sage's chair aside. "You're not serious!" He pounded his fist on the desk, knocking an empty mug on its side. The mug clunked on the thick wool rug, a brown stain of coffee spreading as if to diffuse Rafael's anger.

No such luck. His anger vibrated his body against Sage's arm. She'd never seen her First Warlock exhibit such fury. Heat stormed her again, and his jealousy thrilled her. She crossed her legs against the double sensations *both* men caused in her body's nether region.

Ethan towered over the desk, hands flat, leaning forward. "Oh, but I am serious. If you want the Ravenwoods in your pocket, then Sage becomes mine. In *all* ways."

Masking the astonishment speeding her heartbeat, Sage twined her fingers and rested her chin on her hands. She wasn't used to taking orders or demands from others. The offer Ethan Ravenwood presented was more than an alliance demanded between the two covens. It spelled insanity on a silver platter.

Sage had never bedded an equal or dominant. She ruled her warlocks with an iron fist, following the rights and traditions of witches. They took her command and gained their magic from her and her coven's witches, giving the warlocks the tools necessary to guard and bolster the protection of her witches. No one questioned who maintained control. Yet Ethan may have suggested equality between witch and warlock in his casual and intriguing offer, totally against modern practices. *Did Willow and Evan enjoy the same?* Was Ethan suggesting one night or a lifetime?

"Sage!" Rafael clenched her shoulder, his fingers biting her flesh. "Are you buying this extortion? You don't need the Ravenwood coven under these bogus terms."

She caressed his hand over her shoulder, and he loosened his grip, massaging her tender skin. "Put it on the line, Ethan. What are your exact terms? And why should I agree to them?" She had to take care or Rafael would walk, the last thing she wanted. He was too valuable to her coven, to her. The first and the only warlock to earn her heart and her complete trust. The first warlock to make her surrender all the others. In the order of their coven, he was her First Warlock. Her right hand who called the shots when she was unavailable.

Ethan sat, crossing his ankle on his other knee, as edible and comfortable as a fire-breathing dragon. "You're a smart woman and a dangerous and formidable witch. Bonded to me will grant you more power if you recall your ancient warlock history. Black warlocks can extend their magic to any witch, like you extend your magic to your bonded warlocks. We'll recruit other covens and become the largest in the world. We'll end any idea of war between black warlocks and witches. Willow and Evan are already an impressive couple or will be once Willow learns how to use her two elements along with Evan's two elements. Why don't we join ranks as *the* most powerful couple?"

Rafael's fist tightened on her shoulder. No one had to tell her he wanted to knock Ethan and his offer six ways to Sunday. "Is this your attempt to screw Sage any time you fucking want?"

Sage patted his curled hand, twisted her head to the side to speak to him in a low tone. "Let him finish. We'll weigh his offer together. Maybe we'll have a counter for him."

"Actually, yes, it includes all privileges a coven leader

gives her warlocks." A sinister smile kicked up the corners of Ethan's lips.

Unable to stand still any longer, Rafael stormed around the desk, electricity streaming off his fingers pointed at Ethan. "Get out and shove your offer up your ass. Sage is no longer offering *privileges* to other warlocks, least not you."

Ethan raised a gust of wind and blew Rafael's lightning bolts to the floor, singeing a jagged slash across the rug covering the dark hardwood. Air sizzled, Rafael shot more flares, and Ethan deftly deflected them away from his body. Smoke and burned wool scents rose, clogging Sage's nostrils.

She jumped up and slammed her palm on her desk. "Enough! End your ridiculous tug of war." Her voice took on the deep, commanding voice of the most powerful High Priestess in the West. Her natural magical element of aether gave her the ability to use fire, water, air, and earth magic. However, fire was her kryptonite, the element she spoon-fed her warlocks to use for defensive purposes. *Thank the goddess, Rafael only used her fire or he'd go* loco *on Ethan.*

The gusts Ethan stirred up softened to a gentle breeze. Rafael's magic fizzled, and both warlocks returned to their positions. *As they damn well should.*

Ethan continued speaking as if he hadn't entered minor combat against another warlock, albeit not as powerful as a black warlock who had his own innate magic. "I have no illusions Sage and I will ever marry. Maybe never love one another. Nor do I have a beef if she marries you, Rafael. I don't attempt to assume your claim. However, our covens will expect us united in *all* ways, including bonding during sex to solidify our alliance. You know how important that act is, how it strengthens the bond between a witch and black warlock using the old spells." He stood and skirted the desk, approaching Sage and Rafael. "Makes our combined magic more powerful. For all three of us."

Standing to Sage's other side, Rafael molded Sage against his body, protecting her from the ogre Ethan represented. His body burned from his power display and his consuming wrath. Sage wanted to soothe him and reassure him that he'd always remain her number one. However, she refused to display her vulnerabilities and Rafael's weaknesses to Ethan. Until that week, a black warlock represented the enemy, especially those on the Black Tide's side. She'd never get used to black warlocks prowling the world again, let alone her coven... and herself.

The closer Ethan approached, the more her body reacted to his power, his lethalness, his absolute charisma. Her nipples tightened painfully. Sage gauged Rafael's reaction, beseeching him along their bond to remain calm. Rafael's eyelids drooped as if Ethan had spelled him. Maybe the idea of gaining power from Ethan intrigued him as well. Rafael always wanted more power, always asking her to give him full use of all her magical elements.

Ethan reached her side of the desk and solidified his offer in the press of his full, soft lips against hers, teasing the tip of his tongue past her parted lips. She melted into the kiss, so different from Rafael's expert kisses, so very new and exciting. Ethan drew aside, leaving her flustered. "My offer stands for forty-eight hours."

Rafael grunted and rolled her chair out of Ethan's bubble of space.

Sage touched her fingers to her lips. "If I don't accept?"

"My people may never align with yours. Willow and Evan will be adrift, never able to side with either coven in any authentic way. The Black Tide will destroy both covens under this dissension. We will never dominate them alone without the other and without other covens joining us. If you kill Andre, the Charlemagnes will murder every member of your coven." He walked toward the door, stopped, and turned on his heels. "My offer extends to you, Rafael Reyes. You will also have full use of my power."

Caerwyn beat its wings against Rafael's chest beneath his dress shirt. Snow flew off her fingers, landing on Ethan's arm for a second before merging back onto her skin, a white owl tattoo, a slight contrast to her pale skin. Sage mentally tamped down her other bonding owls who all wanted to join the dance of desire permeating the room.

"Forty-eight hours," Ethan reiterated. He left Sage and Rafael behind the desk, invisible magic arcing in puffs of air hissing through the room.

The moment the door closed, Sage unbuttoned Rafael's pants and slipped her hand around his growing erection, soft skin gloving a thick rod of steel. He groaned, thrust back his head, and eased her hand off him. "Now, Rafael. I need you inside me."

He hauled her into his arms and nipped her lips with his own. "And you'll get me. Not like this. Not with you lusting after *him*." His mouth landed on hers, possessive and blazing, and his kiss erased the last hour. A hint of mint met her tongue, and fire met her desire.

The kiss couldn't erase the excitement building in her chest about leading the most powerful coven to rule the United States. With that supreme power came an alliance with *black* warlocks. And Ethan Ravenwood. Who would've thought?

Chapter 2

Piercing sunlight poked Sage's eyelids, blinding her for a moment. Rafael had left with not a word, nor a kiss. He'd never split in the morning without at least kissing her, and her familiars always knew. They remained excited, tickling and churning over her skin. Not at all calm and content like normal after making love with Rafael... all night. Since she'd quit having sex with anyone but Rafael, her familiars seemed happy. Until Ethan Ravenwood and his compelling offer stepped into her orbit.

After Ethan left and they had dinner, Rafael carried her to bed. Not one word spoken about the offer. They didn't want his insanity to mar their night. Ethan's offer changed their lovemaking into something fierce and possessive. And it was all Rafael in her bed. He always made her feel special and like the only person in the universe. Such a strong and beautiful man and lover. Sore between her legs, Sage pushed off the bed and headed to the bathroom to start her day.

After she'd eaten a strawberry yogurt parfait, Sage found Rafael in his office. More handsome than ever, he wore a new suit. Dark chestnut hair slicked back, clean-shaven, he smelled scrumptious of the sandalwood, citrus cologne she had created for him. She breathed deep, infusing his scent in her senses to last her through the day.

Sage smoothed down a tousled lock of his hair. "The new suit is impeccable. You look divine. Should *I* be jealous?"

He caught her hand and kissed her palm, the touch of his lips shooting a frisson of warmth up her arm and to her heart. Rafael played with her magic, and sparks tingled against her skin. She eased her hand from his and shook off the magic.

"I'm meeting the museum people today about a new security contract," he said.

Caerwyn peeked out the neck of Rafael's suit, snowy white against his clothing. The owl eyed her, made sure she was in one piece, then hid beneath Rafael's collar to snooze the day away.

Once a witch developed an affinity with a familiar, when a witch's magic first manifests around eighteen years old, the familiar transforms into protection mode. The main familiar creates bonding familiars that transform to blood and bones when called forth. The main bonding familiar becomes a love and protection familiar, meant for a witch's lover.

Sage wandered the room loaded with computers, monitors, and security devices. She feathered her fingers over several magic-detecting wands Rafael had been testing for years, to no avail.

He managed a top-notch security firm from the covenstead. His clients never let on if they realized how much witchcraft Reyes Security used in securing their buildings and priceless property. His expertise earned Reyes Security one of the best reps in the business, and from a man a mere twenty-nine years old.

Sage tugged down the shoulders of her loose blouse, exposing the tops of her breasts. Rafael grimaced and tossed stars off his fingers until she straightened her blouse. Their daily tango.

Pride and love swelled Sage's heart. How could she jeopardize the life they'd built? But could she forsake the safety of her witches and warlocks and plant them at the mercy of the Black Tide? Though she ruled the Western Witches Council—the Council which ruled both the Pacific and Mountain west regions—it was a tenuous rule. With the Ravenwoods in her back pocket, she'd stabilize her position and boot the dissenting covens off her back and fully under her authority.

Rafael handed her a black folder. "My intel on the new warlock who hit our radar. Lucky Lorenzo."

Sage opened the folder. "The supposed warlock Aspen discovered in the new compounding shop?" Her healer sister, Aspen, was always searching for new herb shops and apothecaries for supplies. Aspen was all too happy to rocket off the covenstead, dare-deviling her motorcycle along the twisty mountain roads, hunting for all matter of healing herbs and apparatuses. Sage swore it was the only action her sister got between her legs.

"Yeah," Rafael replied. "He's twenty-six, practices alchemy in his father's compounding pharmacy. Aspen sensed his magic, but he appears unbonded."

Sage blinked up a breeze. "What? How? Aspen's not strong enough to sense an unbonded warlock." A warlock possessed no magic until a witch bonded him, at which point he wielded his witch's magic element. An unbonded warlock possessed an aura of magic about him, which made him discoverable by a powerful witch. Like a receptacle waiting for a witch to fill his emptiness. A powerful witch could usually tell what element of magic the warlock could master with the right witch. A bonded warlock exuded witchcraft most any witch noticed. "Well, hell. Do you think he's a black warlock?"

Rafael drummed his fingers on his desk, his impatience growing thin. "Who knows, since they're now crapping on our turf."

"How lucky is Lucky, I wonder?" Sage flipped through the three-page dossier. "Or he's a master at alchemy." She tapped her lip. "We can use another alchemist. Plus, I need to replace Evan since we're no longer bonded."

The mere mention of a Ravenwood caused a rumble to rise from Rafael's throat. "You don't need another warlock. I can protect you better than four warlocks."

"Excuse me? You're not always here, and I'm down to three, the bare minimum. It's my decision," she said, not unkindly.

"Assign him to Aspen. They'd make a good match, since they both snort herbs."

"Hmm... Aspen does need a permanent warlock. Flake Marty can't even protect his own dick."

"Let's not count our ducks in a row yet. The dude may not want to join your coven or any other. Maybe he already belongs to a coven." Rafael stood and adjusted his blue-and-purple-striped tie. "If he's unbonded, there's a reason."

Your Coven. She didn't miss his Freudian slip. "Who can resist a Wilde witch?" Sage trailed her fingers over her lover's smooth, chiseled cheek.

"He may not know he's a warlock." Stiffening, he wheeled away and gathered his smart phone and tablet.

"Rafael," Sage commanded in her magic-infused pitch. "Shall we kick around the elephant in the room?"

Following her command, he rounded on her. "Later," he rebuffed the rest of her command and tapped his smart watch. "I need to hit the road."

"Love." Sage sidled closer, feeling insignificant next to his six-three height and gym-toned body, despite her five-nine stretch. "We'll figure another way to align with the Ravenwoods."

"You know exactly what I want to hear," Rafael said, as cold as the kiss he feathered across her mouth. "You always do what you always do."

Before he stalked off, she grabbed his hand and tugged him against her, molding her body to his in the perfect way they fit together. "You are and will *always* be my First Warlock, my number one forever, my soulmate, my heart. I love you beyond reason, and I will never give you up." She kissed the dimple centered on his chin, swept her tongue across it, the salt of his skin mixing with his citrusy aftershave.

"You may not have a choice." He gave her a half-assed hug, lacking any warmth.

Sage returned to her office alone and confused. Had he seriously threatened to leave her if she accepted Ravenwood's offer? Give up everything they'd accomplished? Give up the power he derived from her? He'd leave their coven behind and never experience the exquisite bond they shared with another. Would *she*?

Framed photos sat in a row on a white marble-topped credenza to the side of her desk, and she stared at them. Her thoughts returned to a dark time and how Rafael had almost single-handedly flipped it into the light.

The moment she'd sensed Rafael in the woods at a regional coven gathering almost six years ago, she'd felt his innate magic tug on her fire and something more. As if he'd reached inside the core of her aether and connected to her, where no other warlock ever had. As if he possessed magic of his own that complimented hers. Now she granted him access to her magic like all witches conferred upon their warlocks. But it was different. No one wielded her magic better than Rafael, their bond unique and irreplaceable. The incredible sex and the way he loved her had ultimately encouraged her to choose monogamy with him. Her bio clock also ticked, and she didn't want to miss its last tock. She didn't think she'd ever love a man more than she loved Rafael. He'd make the perfect father to their future brood. Together, they made the most powerful witch and warlock couple among the western covens, even if others didn't know it.

Sage buried her face in her hands and rubbed her eyes. She promised him exclusivity. *But this indecent proposal! Ethan Ravenwood?* He was no slouch in the charismatic, drop-dead-gorgeous department, but they'd have to find another way to partner with his coven. She refused to let her people suffer at the deadly hands of the Black Tide. Nothing good promised to come out of black warlocks prowling the Earth again after they'd died off during the Witches and Warlocks War.

"What does Ethan Ravenwood think he's doing?" Thoughts swirled chaotically in her brain. The warlock was right. Sex made a stronger bond between a witch and warlock, when their barriers were thin and they were the most vulnerable. Oh, goddess, the extra power she'd possess with his air enhancing her own aether-tainted air magic. Could she risk losing Rafael for such power and the chance to keep the Wilde Coven secure? To protect the West from a potential attack by the Black Tide? *Hell to the no!* They were powerful enough. They didn't need Ethan's bond. "Why such a ludicrous offer?" she mumbled.

Sage sat for the longest time at her sparse desk, weighing and agonizing over her options. A bang on the hallway wall preceded the double doors bursting open, sending her pulses racing. Sparks dripped off her fingers, and witch-air bubbled around her. Her sister's red hair gyrated above her head, and Sage dropped the magic.

Aspen flounced in, flustered, clasping her healing bag to her side. "That jerkwad Charlemagne is self-mutilating.

He's threatening to bleed out if you don't talk to him." She did air quotes with her free hand, slanted her head to the right. "What's up with you? You're pale." Aspen approached, already opening her herbal tote. Echinacea wafted strong from her clothes among the myriad scents billowing from her herbal cache. "Take an energy potion." She shoved a vial in Sage's hand.

Drained, fire erupted off Sage's fingers, and she accepted the concoction, heating the vial to a boil.

Aspen hauled her hand back. "Whoa, sis, what's got your panties twisting in the fire?" Aspen rubbed her hand. "You never lose control. Did that hotter-than-sin Ethan Ravenwood get you all hot and bothered?" She fanned her face. "I wouldn't mind a piece of his pie. He topping the alliance off with a hookup? I'd love to dump dumb-as-a-placebo Marty."

"Sorry." Sage downed the vial and chased it with water from her flask.

An idea whacked her upside the head. What if she offered Ethan to Aspen? Aspen, the middle sister of the three Wilde sisters, contained water magic more potent than a witch twice her age. Her innate healing abilities made her a major catch. They'd certainly enhance each other's magic. Sage had no experience partnering black warlocks and witches. The smart thing to do was match warlocks and witches with complimentary magic to enhance each other's skills with a second element. Although Aspen was a few years younger than Ethan, she always wanted to hook up with an earth warlock to enhance her healing abilities. *No. Lame idea.*

"Are you serious? But he's an air warlock," Sage said, her hope deflating from her myriad thoughts.

"Air's not a terrible combination with water." Aspen grinned. "But a black warlock?" Her nose crinkled. "I was kidding. No matter how fine or strong he is, I don't want a black warlock in my wheelhouse. I felt nothing toward him, anyway."

Sage patted Aspen's arm. "Don't fret, my little water nymph. I may have a new warlock lined up for you. Later. We need to deal with Mr. Psycho."

"Talk about nymph." Aspen whacked Sage's arm. "I'm not the one who swam with every warlock with an erect pole for the last ten years."

Sage plucked her sister's sleeve. "It's my right as High Priestess. Sampling the merchandise is my job." They headed toward the rear staircase, the dark paneling on the hallway walls lending a double dose of darkness to her mood. Two warlocks guarding each end of the hallway closed ranks behind them.

"Not now, right? I mean, Rafael's smacking down dicks left and right that point to you."

"My First Warlock *is* territorial," Sage mused. "I've practiced monogamy for two years, if you must know."

Sage faced the retinal scanner, punched in her code, and the door locks clicked open. She gripped the doorknob to the basement, and fire ignited, flames flickering, singeing the wooden door.

"Sage!" Aspen yelped and jumped back, stumbling against their warlock guards. "What the holy moon has taken hold of you?" She flicked her hand, and water doused the flames. "Maybe you shouldn't be in the same room with Dark Dick Warlord."

Yanking her hand to her side, Sage inhaled a deep breath, the apple-and-cinnamon scents wafting out of the ventilation system calming her. "I'm fine."

"Define *fine*?" A familiar male voice sounded behind them. Concern danced along the edges of his amusement.

Her nipples pebbled upon hearing the smooth, sexy baritone. Dampening her buzzing lust, she spun around. "Ethan Ravenwood. A pleasure to see you again." More pleasure than she cared to admit. "What brings you back to my domain?" She glanced behind him. "And who let you in without an escort?" The two warlocks stood at attention, grumbling between themselves. "Ryan, please explain this breach of protocol."

"Rafael approved it. We have witches following him." Sage peered beyond Ryan at the trio of witches trailing behind Ethan.

Ethan chuckled. "I asked Rafael to allow me to get to know your warlocks and survey your covenstead. I hope you don't mind."

Shock suffused her. Why had Rafael granted the allowance? She sniffed and slipped the top of her blouse down in defiance. "I mind." Well, hell. How'd she miss the boat on those facts?

He took her hand and brought it to his lips, where they lingered in the longest kiss. Then he bowed to Aspen, taking her right hand in his and pressing a kiss to the back. "It's my pleasure to stand in the presence of another lovely Wilde witch. I've admired your skills from afar. I hear you're an amazing, up-and-coming healer and alchemist."

Inappropriate, white-hot jealousy inundated Sage, propelling her against the wall to prevent herself from stepping between Ethan and her stunning and *available* sister. Fire magic crackled, meeting two swirling gusts of wind emanating off Ethan.

Amused and sensing her jealousy, Ethan contained his air before he fanned the flames of Sage's fire festering close to the surface. "Andre wants to talk to us both. Didn't Rafael brief you?" Ethan opened the door for Sage and Aspen. Sage brushed against him, accidentally skimming her hand over his crotch and an instant hardness. Pulsating shockwaves zinged to her core.

"I haven't changed my mind," he whispered. "I want you. I want everything you can offer me. Plain and simple.

And I'm a man who gets what he wants."

Sage's knees weakened, her confusing alternatives becoming more difficult to manage considering Ethan's irresistible allure. Goddess, she wanted this man touching and kissing her. More than that, she wanted Rafael's mouth on her body, whispering the words of love her sexy soulmate was so expert at. *Holy moon. Two men at once? Never in a million years.* Rafael would rather bail than allow another man in his bed, or in her bed again. *And I'd die without him, my fire dwindling to ash.* All her sacrifices for Rafael's love would shrivel up into a wasteland of Andre Charlemagne and Ethan Ravenwood's creation.

"Sage?" Aspen waved her hand in front of Sage's flushed face. "Hello. Earth to Sage."

Marty, Aspen's tow-headed warlock, bounced up the stairs at a running leap. He skidded to a halt, his slender shoulders shaking, color-changing hazel eyes sparkling, the same unfathomable eyes that'd lured Sage to him a year ago. How such an ordinary young man used Aspen's witch-water was a mystery. One warlock she'd never desired to sample, much to his dismay. Fortunately for Aspen, the two never connected on a romantic level.

"You better hustle," he sputtered. "That sucker's threatening to poke his eyes out with a mattress coil." Grinning, he rubbed his hands together.

Did her witches and warlocks crave a fight between the covens and the Black Tide? Despite the bickering among the local covens, and half-hearted attempts to rid Sage as High Priestess of the West, too much complacency led to a great eagerness to change the status quo. Andre Charlemagne, in their midst, provided way too much fuel, at least for the Wilde Coven. The other covens had yet to learn of his capture, even of his rise from the ashes of a long-ago war. Or was Sage deluding herself?

Chapter 3

Sage sprinted down the stairs leading to the magic-deadened cell holding her nightmare. The Wilde Coven captured Andre two days ago after he'd spelled Willow and tried to kidnap her to use her as a conduit for his magic and as his forever plaything.

"No freaking way. Not before I snag intel out of that black-ass warlock," she grumbled.

"Sage!" Ethan trailed her so close his body heat assaulted her. "He's baiting you." Air whooshed off him, blowing through her hair, his magic prepping for a fight.

"No shit, Sherlock." Aspen's sandals click-clacked on the cement floor behind them along the brightly lit hallway. "He's tried to lure me in the room all morning after using himself as a pincushion. Dumbass is bleeding all over his bed and the floor."

"Not enough to bleed out?" Sage reached the doorway to the coven's dungeon, a fancy name for a heavily warded, indestructible basement.

"He knows what he's doing," Ethan replied. "He won't kill himself."

"Yep. Enough to piss me off," Aspen spat out. "He'll get me in the room to treat him and try a lame-ass black warlock trick on me."

Ethan cringed. "Not every black warlock is Andre Charlemagne. And if he's in a warded cell, his magic's dead, right?"

"Yes. But so is ours." Sage knocked once, twice—her signal—on the door to the dungeon and used the retinal scan to unlock it. Gwyneira launched off her arm and flew ahead to scope out danger.

Two witch-and-warlock pairs guarded the cell twenty-four-seven, rotating every four hours to keep their magic fresh. Sage approached the bulletproof window, and the warlocks surrounded her. Ben, her aunt's one and only warlock and husband, called for backup for Sage's protection against the fierce black warlock who may possess more magic than all her witches combined. Bleeding or not. If not for the wards. Satisfied, Gwyneira returned and perched on Sage's shoulder.

Sage was still adjusting to the discovery that warlocks holding their own innate magic roamed the world again. She hadn't known the extent of their existence until Black Tide traitor, Evan Ravenwood, snared Willow's heart and confessed how the strongest black warlocks had survived the aftermath of the Witches and Warlocks War for over a century. The Black Tide could mow down the Wilde witches under an onslaught of fire, air, water, and earth magic if Sage didn't tie their hands soon. According to Evan, the Black Tide was a pinnacle of strength, and Andre had been gathering warlocks to his side for decades. They were raring to control the witchworld. Further, factions of the warlocks, like the Ravenwoods, wanted alliances with witches and a return to the old ways, witches and black warlocks living in harmony. She wanted *those* black warlocks on her side.

Bumps and valleys paved the road ahead. The bumpy ride also included witches from other covens who've vied for her position since she'd inherited it from her mother. The first major speed bump sat on a blood-smeared mattress in his prison cell. She'd deal with the other covens later. Maybe a task made easier with the Ravenwoods on her side. Andre held answers, and she'd snag them one way or another along her bumpy ride.

The warlock in question had stripped to his black skivvies, his scrawny arms and narrow torso covered in rusty and bright red scratches from the mattress spring. Her guards had already confiscated the makeshift weapon and removed the box springs from the room. They'd left his foam mattress for his accommodations. No one could ever accuse her of being a poor hostess. He could stuff foam up his ass to his heart's content and not bleed out all over her floor.

Unfortunately, her guards missed a short length of spiraled metal clenched in Andre's hand. He'd shoved his long, dark hair behind him and created a knot of hair to contain the mop.

Mattress stuffing littered the cement floor in little white clouds. Hand on the doorknob, Sage knew her witches had already captured his familiars in tattoo ink form, unless magic-resistant panthers hid up his ass. She muffled a snort behind her hand.

"You can't go in." Ethan grasped her arm. "Not without me and magic wards for your protection."

Gwyneira hissed at Ethan. "Your offer of protection is admirable. However, this is my domain." Sage contemplated her next move. "Our wards are active, and he's in a warded bubble. He can't hurt us."

"You'll have no magic, and he can *physically* hurt you."

"Zip tie him," Ben cut in, bristling at Ethan's insinuation the Wildes didn't have matters under control.

"He may try more self-harm." Ethan refused to let up.

"I doubt he'll kill himself." She stroked the wing of her owl familiar until the owl vanished under her blouse, dissolving into ink spreading across her skin. "If he does, so be it. We'll have rid the world of Mr. Smarmy Evil."

"Ms. Wilde," Andre greeted through his cell's thick walls. "Dear Lieutenant Ravenwood. I'm glad you joined my party. Care for a pint?" He wanded his left hand down his bloodied right arm.

"What do you want, Andre?" Crossing his arms over his chest, Ethan positioned himself in front of the cell's viewing window.

"Have you so cavalierly flipped to the other side already, Ravenwood?" Andre trailed the mattress spring's jagged edge above his left eye, dripping blood down his temple.

"You're a smart man. You do the math," Ethan said. His magic whipped the air, whizzing and whining and more potent than any Wilde Coven air witch.

His air magic could magnify my own not-so-insignificant witch-air. Sage snapped back to her senses. *Nope. Not going there.* "What do you want, Andre?"

"To make a deal, of course." The prisoner guided the spring across his left nipple, a smile quirking up the corners of his lips. "If I die, my family will exact a deadly revenge upon the Wilde and Ravenwood covens. If you don't release me soon, the consequences will be disastrous." He paused and grimaced. "I'd like to talk without yelling through the walls." His dark-eyed gaze scanned the room, his eyebrows lowering and pinching together. "Wrap another cocoon around me, and let's discuss in a more accommodating environment."

"Strip down to skin," Sage commanded, fire simmering beneath her skin's surface. Rafael would kill her once he learned she'd exposed herself to Andre without him guarding her. But Ethan had proven himself an equal and reliable wingman. It wasn't an unwelcome idea to have another powerful warlock in her rear pocket. Maybe the rise of black warlocks wasn't such a bad deal if she swayed them to her coven. The Wilde West Coven could be the strongest in the States, maybe even the world. The idea of ruling such a coven buzzed excitement through her chest.

"You're not serious." Ethan rounded on Sage. "The man's sneaky. He's got something up his sleeve."

"He's not wearing sleeves," she said wryly.

Stone-faced, Ethan advanced upon her. Sage warmed from his nearness, and she had a sudden craving to touch every inch of him. She wagged her head to clear her crazy-ass and ill-timed visions.

Andre slipped his black briefs to his ankles and slowly spun in a circle to prove no more tattoos existed on his body.

Sage's eyes widened at the impressive size of his penis and his foot size. Proved the old saying about small men with large feet. "Thank you. You can put your clothes back on."

She faced her witches and warlocks. A gaggle now crammed the dungeon, normal practice when a High Priestess planned to challenge an enemy. Not that it happened often. She liked to think she'd hold her own in combat against a black warlock, but this new warlock breed mystified and alarmed her.

She murmured, "When I say go, drop the wards. Three witches wrap him in a warded circle, three more secure me and Ethan in a circle, surrounded by your warlocks, and the rest guard the doorways." She elevated her tone for Andre's sake. "If he tries to escape or attacks anyone, kill him."

"How will I treat his injuries?" Aspen shuffled her feet.

"You won't," Ethan replied. "Kick your medical supplies inside the room, enough for him to doctor himself up. Nothing sharp. He's not stupid. He wants to live."

"Agreed." Sage glowered at Ethan. She wasn't used to others ordering about her witches. Equality wasn't a word in her mental dictionary when it came to leading her coven… or dominating her warlocks in bed. A vision of Ethan storming her body with his large, powerful hands, his lethal appendage assaulting her, caused a flush to creep up her neck.

"Sage? Hello, space cadet. You listening?" Aspen stomped her sandal on the glossy cement floor. "I swear to the goddess, I'm gonna give you a full medical workup later."

Irritated, Sage chopped her hand through the air. "I'm fine." Andre put on his grubby, long-sleeve dress shirt and wrinkled slacks. He sat sedately in the single chair and buttoned up his shirt. "Move in position. Ben, open the door. Drop the wards. Go."

The witches spun a protection circle first around Sage and Ethan. The wards protecting the room fell at once, the magic slithering into the atmosphere. Air witches cocooned Andre in a bubble of air, thick and touchable. He wavered in and out of focus. Ben shot the bolts on the steel door and opened it. Aspen slid a plastic bag filled with antiseptic, alcohol wipes, and bandages inside the doorway and skedaddled out of the way. Sage and Ethan stationed themselves inside the open doorway for easy access. The coppery scent of blood, male musk, and sweat rode the air. Sage added an extra padding of air over her nose to minimize the stench.

Ethan at her side lent her confidence Sage didn't normally lack. But Andre Charlemagne scared the crap out of her. Entering the room presented a tough task she never thought she'd ever entertain. Nor did she believe she'd meet a black warlock in any lifetime until she'd confronted Andre, Evan, and now Ethan. At least the Ravenwoods had retained their common sense and the aspiration to return to the old ways where witches and black warlocks lived and ruled in harmony. *Whoa. Since when did I want to return to the old ways of equality? Did Ethan Ravenwood truly want the old ways? Equality is Willow's thing, not mine.* She blinked rapidly as if to blink the thoughts away like specks of dust.

"Well met again, Sage Wilde. I've been a member of your admiration society for a long while. In fact, I met your mother several times. Delightful creature. My belated condolences on your parents' unfortunate demise."

Andre ended her meandering thoughts. *Ethan and his offer are too distracting. Get your freaking act together, idiot witch. Or lose everything witches have gained after a hard-won victory.*

"Yes, well, theory holds that a mere drunk driver didn't cause their deaths." Sage cocked her head. "However, we're not here to place blame, are we?" Neither police nor family ever completely concluded that the drunk driver caused her parents' car to veer off a road and down a cliff in the Lake Tahoe mountains seven years ago. Foul play remained a major plausibility. Had the Black Tide caused the accident in their domination plan?

"*Touché*, sweetling. *Touché*." Andre clapped once, a loud smack reverberating up to the ceiling and dispersing in a long pause. "Well, perhaps you can tell me what *you* want from me."

"Simple. I want your family and its allies to back off from any threats or harm to *any* witches or covens worldwide. I want the Black Tide and allies to sift out of the shadows and live in peace among witches."

"Ruled by witches even though we possess our own magic and aren't dependent upon trifling witches for thimblefuls of power?"

"It's the way of our world now, the pact we signed to

end the Witches and Warlocks War," she replied.

"After you witches destroyed us. Alas, pacts can be broken, rescinded, revised."

"Apparently, we didn't destroy you." The thought of failure chased a shiver of dread up her spine.

"What do you really want, Andre?" Ethan crossed his arms and spread his legs in a defensive stance.

"Ah, my lieutenant, you well know what I covet."

"To rule every witch and warlock on Earth. Not gonna happen. Not now. Not ever."

"Is your defection completed now?" Andre asked slyly. "Have you plowed the witch and made her your own?"

Fire bristled to her skin's surface. "No one makes me *his*," Sage tossed back. "Obviously we have much to teach you about modern witches." Ethan side-stepped closer, his natural heat drawing on her innate fire, his air magic fanning her flames. Magic hissed in the circle as her witches reacted to the eruption of Sage's fury. Water spritzed the circle's interior, dousing the flames undulating along the invisible walls. Sage gave her cousin Brianne, a water witch, a grateful, tight-lipped smile. Excited, Snow flitted above her breasts, teasing one of Ethan's tiny ravens scurrying across the back of his neck in a black ink blob. Interesting that both Ethan and Evan had bird familiars, like she and Aspen did. Willow had a butterfly, of all things. Birds made good familiars and were everywhere. Someday, she'd love to see a dog, or the traditional black cat familiar join her coven. And again, her mind had a will of its own.

"No need for a history lesson." Andre meekly perched on the edge of his chair. The unfurled mattress spring lay forgotten on the padded chair arm, and rusty spots of blood dried on his cheeks.

"Talk." Ethan tapped his foot on the cement floor. "You called us here."

"Of course." Elbows on the chair arms, Andre steepled his fingers under his chin. "Let's make a deal, shall we?"

"Go on." Sage narrowed her eyes. "We're listening."

"Release me, and I'll withdraw my threats to both your covens."

Ethan laughed, a rich, robust sound. "Your word is as deceptive as shit in quicksand."

"Well, if you two form your intended alliance, why are you threatened?" Andre gloved his right hand over the mattress spring. "What do you really want from *me*?"

"I want the names of every Black Tide member. I want full transparency. I want every black warlock in the world to sign a covenant signifying peaceful coexistence. I expect all black warlocks to agree that witches will continue to rule, but we'll grant them Council and voting rights... if you all play by the witchworld rules."

Andre emitted his wheezy snicker which sounded like a pig snuffling in its trough. "As your minions? I think not. We don't need witches for magic." He stroked the spring like it was a crown jewel. "Plus, there aren't enough witches in the world to accommodate a pet black warlock."

Startled, Sage bumped against Ethan and whispered, "How many?"

Spine tense, Ethan leaned closer, his arm sliding around her waist. "Andre has secret alliances across the globe. I don't know the numbers."

"Is he bluffing?"

"You'll find out soon enough if I'm bluffing," Andre replied, his ears and mind equally keen. "The longer you keep me here, the more time we have to amass a full-frontal attack against every coven in the world. Starting with the Wildes, of course."

Anger and panic seized Sage in a vise, inciting sparks to fan the circle. Brianne doused them with another sprinkle of water.

The moment the air cleared, Sage knew for certain that Andre was scamming them. He nudged the bloody end of the mattress spring toward the air shield gloving him. The shield fractured. Blood on the metal created a conduit of residual magic. The three witches who'd built the circle raced to plug the hole. Instinctively, Sage sensed they hadn't captured all of Andre's familiars, despite their concentrated attempt to do so when they'd first snared him. Andre was deflecting her attention to the stupid metal curlicue as he prepped to release a hidden familiar.

"Out! Everyone out!" Sage shouted.

Too late.

Black tattoo ink dripped to the floor off Andre's fingertips. Before Sage blinked, a life-size black panther formed and pounced through his shield, shattering the magic in drops that sizzled and puffed into nothingness. Chaos ensued, and the witches tried to reform a circle to encase the panther familiar. From their earlier attempt to capture his familiars, they'd learned the felines were impervious to protective circles. This wasn't the cat familiar she wanted to see. Far from it.

Ethan propelled Sage toward the door. Dark and lethal earthen magic soared, battering down the last stitch on the ward holding Andre. Magic deluged Sage and her people, causing their defensive magic to go awry. Andre's earth magic expanded until it dominated, smothering and suffocating anything in its path.

The panther lunged and crashed through their protective circle, lugging Andre's magic with it, nullifying Sage's fire in a breath-stealing surge. The feline landed on Ethan's back, driving them both to the floor. Ethan and the panther's weight smashed her onto the cement, air whooshing from her lungs. Fire detonated off her, fueled by a torrent of Ethan's air. White, blinding glimmers permeated Sage's vision, and emptiness met her lungs.

Chapter 4

Sage awakened on an unfamiliar bed in an unyielding embrace from behind. "Rafael?" She pressed on her aching temples, puzzled by her throbbing knees and arms. "What happened? Where are we?" Despite her uncertainty, strong, protective arms represented peace and refuge, and she sank into his embrace. Feathers ruffled her arm. Black feathers, not the white feathers of her familiars. A raven?

"I can be Rafael if you accept my offer." Ethan's baritone startled her stiff.

Reality pounded the back of her eyes, and she struggled out of his arms, falling half off the bed in her mad scramble. Hair hung across her face in a blonde tangle. Combing the tangled locks behind her ears, she scoped out a guestroom in the east wing, far from her suite. A glowing moon painted on the black ceiling cast a swathe of pale light across the bed. Twinkling stars created a colorful kaleidoscope dancing on the gray walls. Ethan wore a short-sleeve T-shirt plucked out of his pants. Other than Rafael, she'd never experienced this exhilarating rush of adrenaline for another man. No other man ever looked at her like he wanted to lick her up and savor her on his tongue. The day's events snowed her in a rush.

"Is everyone okay? Is Andre contained?" She tidied her skewed clothes, invoked her little-used witch-water to dampen her ridiculous and ill-timed lust. "How did my witches miss another familiar?"

Ethan propped his head on his powerful arm, his eyes sparkling. "He knocked Aspen to the floor and injured a guard. Both are okay. We subdued Andre, and your witches set an extra ward on the room. The panther familiar was invisible under his skin. Aspen tranqed him, and I used a black magic detection spell to find any other hidden familiars. Not something Evan can do, or he would've done it when you first captured Andre."

Shock slammed into Sage. Andre held more magic than she imagined if he could hide familiars beneath his skin *and* behind warded walls. "How many familiars?"

"Three." He trailed a finger across her thigh. "How do you feel? Sorry I shoved you to the floor." A breeze uplifted the tips of her long hair.

Sage waved her hand, dismissing his concern, and slapped his hand off her bare thigh. "Thanks for your help." She rubbed her arm where his raven familiar tickled her flesh.

"I thought you only had witch-fire. I saw you use air magic," Ethan accused, stroking his familiar's extended wingspan until it disappeared beneath his shirt.

"You don't know as much as you think." Twisting away, she flinched from pain in her upper torso and spied a pain potion on the nightstand. She downed the concoction, and it immediately went to town, making mush of her already languid muscles. Facing Ethan, she scrutinized her situation from scalp to toes... a very delectable situation. His vanilla-spice cologne and natural male musk hit her senses, and she reeled under its potency. A pheromone potion or charm, maybe? Right? Nothing else explained his magnetism. Or her brain had lost a cell or a dozen.

"What do I win for my protection?" He winked.

Sage noticed his shirt hanging in threads from his right shoulder where Andre's panther attacked him. "Roll over." She sat on her aching knees to inspect him for injuries.

"Your wish is my command." He rolled on his stomach, exposing his shredded shirt. "Aspen already doctored me up."

Sage feathered her fingertips over the deep scratches, the reddened wounds already healing. She wrangled her emotions and padlocked her internal gates to his allure once and for all. She couldn't afford the risk and distraction he was peddling. A tapeworm of guilt wound through her belly. If Rafael learned of Ethan's presence in this bed *with her*, he'd go ballistic.

Ethan's raven familiar fluttered its wings at her, spanning them across his back, folding its wide wingspan around Ethan's chest as if to protect him. "Aspen could teach my healer a thing or two about her gummies. My healer's excellent but set in the old ways."

Dazed, Sage rested against the headboard, and he rolled on his side again, head propped on his bent arm. "Is your familiar okay?" she asked.

"Balthazar pecked the panther's eyes out before your witches subdued the feline. He's fine. Now, about my offer," he said, his voice as soft and enticing as a whisper.

"Your tenacity is admirable, like your warlock services," she mused aloud, adopting a business demeanor to avoid his charisma.

Eyes drifting to her breasts, he roared in laughter. "After what just happened, do you think you can go this alone?"

"If I don't accept your offer, what happens?" She patted her hair down and wrenched her blouse up over the top of her breasts.

"Am I such an awful man, so horrible to look at? Is my offer so repulsive you'd sacrifice your coven?"

"I love Rafael." Sage chewed on her bottom lip. "He'll never accept me sleeping with another warlock again."

"Who said anything about sleeping?"

She whacked his arm, sparks scorching his shirt. Invoking a gust of air, he lifted her on top of him with just a finger, rolled her over, and pinned her beneath him in one sinfully slick move. Shimmery flames shot off her, fanned by his air magic, frolicking above the bed.

"Tell me why," she begged, unable to prevent his fingers from inching to the hem of her knee-grazing skirt.

"Simple. You're gorgeous, smart, and powerful." He sniffed and nipped at her neck. "Plus, I've admired you from afar for years."

"Stalker, much?"

"Yes." His grin lit his eyes, mimicking Evan's sparkling gray-blue orbs. Evan's eyes had drawn her to him from the jump. His expert wielding of her magic brought him to her coven in a ruse to infiltrate the Wilde Coven on Andre's behalf. The plan backfired in a million pieces. All to Sage's gain. What would she gain from Ethan?

Ethan cupped her cheek. "I won't hinder you and Rafael from having relations. Marry the man and bear his children." Air magic funneled, wreaking havoc on a bouquet of pink-and-red silk flowers in a large vase on the dresser, a tiny exhibition of his magic. Foliage landed and scattered across the floor like autumn leaves. "Think of the power we'll have, the covens we'll lead. We'll command more power in our combined coven than any others on the planet. My people want this. Yours will too. Other covens need us."

Sage gasped. "You two will fight like starved wolves over me. Not that Rafael will ever agree." *Oh Goddess, he'll bail for sure. How can I accept this mad-crazy deal?*

Pain dulled his eyes, and he rubbed them as if to erase the pain. "I'll prove my loyalty and eventually my love a million ways under the sun. I want a powerful witch to create powerful children with me." He grinned his devastating, soul-stealing grin that Sage wanted to bottle up. "And two guards are better than one."

"You toss the word love out as if you own it." Sage struggled beneath him, but his body pressed her to the bed. He was intensely hot for an air warlock, or the reaction to her witch-fire affected him.

"Do you doubt you can ever love me? Or two men at the same time?" He trailed his hand beneath the hem of her skirt and danced his fingers up her bare thigh, his calluses rough against her skin. "I can love a woman who loves another. I share well."

He kissed her, his mouth hot, his lips soft, just the right amount of pressure. Just the right kiss to prove his point.

A tiny bonding raven soared off Ethan's arm, flew onto Sage's neck, and waited for her acceptance. Sage stroked the bird's feathery head, and it pooled onto her skin, joining her own tattoos. The tapeworm of guilt assaulted Sage again, and she pressed away from him.

"That's Ravie, my first bonding familiar," Ethan said after catching his breath. "Damn, witch. You about set me on fire."

"Never kissed a fire witch?" she asked.

"Never kissed a witch, period."

Sage gaped. "You're not serious."

"Never found a witch I wanted."

"So I took your witch cherry," she kidded.

His grin brought out the silver flecks in his gray-blue eyes. "You will. Soon."

"You know, once you've gone fire witch, there's no going back." Inane ideas floundered in Sage's mind as she avoided the big picture.

"I'm counting on it." He tipped forward and playfully nipped at her lips. "Once you go black warlock—"

"There's no going back?" She rolled her eyes. Ethan's cologne clung to her like a life raft, waiting for her to grab hold.

Snow flew down her right arm in tattoo form, tingling her skin. When it spied Ethan, it zoomed back under her sleeve. Once a familiar left its tattoo form, it became real to the naked eye. On her skin, an outsider saw a tattoo. They might even see the tattoo travel from one spot to another. Sage stroked the owl's head, taking comfort in its return to her. Snow tended to push its boundaries.

"How did you gain a rare snowy owl familiar?" Ethan asked.

Unconsciously, she pushed her blouse down to expose the tops of her breasts. Reality slammed her, and she re-adjusted her blouse into a semblance of propriety. She kicked her mind out of the gutter with her story. "One night in the gazebo, a couple owls hooted and flew around the woods, driving my senses crazy with their noise and movement. I had just gained my magic at sixteen, earlier than most witches. But when my magic refused to cooperate, I was too young and lost." She stared up at the ceiling, not at all shy about telling him her familiar story. "Gwyneira landed on the gazebo's railing, as lost as I felt. The other owl had flown off and deserted her. I'm not sure it knew what had drawn us together. White owls symbolize change, transformation, and inner wisdom." She shrugged. "Maybe she sensed my crossroads."

"The color white also symbolizes purity and innocence,

spirituality, and illumination. It's good luck if you cross paths with a white owl," Ethan added.

"Good luck came." Sage stroked Gwyneira's wings feathering her neck. "We found each other. We grew together and focused on our destinies. My magic began to make sense when I beckoned Gwyneira that night."

Pain thumped her chest and radiated to her battered knees. The other vial on the nightstand drew her attention. "Is that a muscle relaxer or sleeping aid?"

"Yes. Aspen said to take both when you woke up and to chill the rest of the day."

Sage grabbed the vial and downed the cherry-flavored potion. At least it tasted good. Aspen had that going for her, mostly. The potion warmed its way to her stomach, killing the insidious tapeworm. Her eyelids drooped, but her brain hadn't closed the iron gate.

How could she forgo the protection Ethan offered, combining their covens into one mega coven? Rafael was no slouch, but he was safe and loving, whereas Ethan teetered on exciting and edgy. Ten pounds of insanity bogged his words. She bit her bottom lip, drawing in a coppery taste. *Idiot. Doesn't matter now. Rafael will split, leaving you alone with Ethan. No! I'll never make the ultimate sacrifice.*

Yet, to protect her people, it was no sacrifice to accept Ethan in her coven, her life, and possibly her bed. Would Rafael hold the same view? Languor filled her, her arms locked around Ethan, holding on as if she feared he'd rescind his offer. Feared he'd force her to accept it.

Before she lost herself to sleep, Sage turned her back on him and hugged the edge of the bed. In a prickling wash, Ravie lifted off her skin and returned to Ethan. "You need to leave," she slurred before sleep claimed her.

Chapter 5

Rafael waited in the foyer of the Ravenwood home, located too near the Wilde covenstead in the Santa Cruz Mountains. Too similar to the Wilde covenstead. "How convenient," he muttered. He slipped off his suit jacket and loosened his tie. The suit constricted him, an evil necessity when wooing a large client to his security business.

Two small wing chairs occupied a corner of the foyer for waiting guests. Too wound up to sit in a dinky-ass chair, Rafael needed to remain alert and on his feet. After all, until a week ago, the Ravenwoods had been enemies of his coven. They'd never crossed paths. Until now. How'd they miss the Ravenwoods on their radar all these years?

The front door opened, and Evan Ravenwood barreled through. "Dude, sorry. Rush hour on seventeen was a bitch." He dumped his backpack on the floor, the Stanford University logo prominent on the flap.

"How often do you drive to the Bay Area?" Small talk... avoiding the inevitable. Rafael had called to meet Evan before he went home to confront Sage and her decision. If anyone held sway over Ethan, it'd be Evan.

"Couple days a week for labs. I do most work here."

"Masters, right?"

Evan nodded. "Computer engineering."

Evan led the way down the front hallway, sneakers squeaking on the hardwood floor, reminding Rafael of Willow's squeaking sneakers. A sound he'd grown accustomed to over the last couple days as she'd finally joined the coven. Regardless, the house was silent, so very different from the constant bustle of the Wilde covenstead. Evan pushed open a door to a front office. Five monitors on a wall-length counter overlooked the overgrown front yard and the thick and formidable perimeter woods. The blinds were half closed to curtail the late afternoon light.

"We can talk in private here," Evan said.

Rafael shut the door, a definitive click grating on his nerves. "How long have you lived here?" If they were such a stellar coven, where the hell were all their people?

"We lived in Monterey until ten years ago. My dad settled us here for proximity to the Black Tide." He flinched, seeming to hate the closeness to Charlemagne. "Stand, sit, whatever." Evan leaned against the center desk. "Water? Coffee? Whiskey?"

Rafael slung his jacket on a rolling desk chair. "I'm good." He faced Evan, neither man backing down to sit, not wanting to grant more power to the other. "Do you house your warlocks here?"

"Not in the main house. The ones who live here have cabins on the grounds. Kinda like the Wilde covenstead, but on a smaller scale." Evan twisted to the right, picked up a framed photo, and handed it to Rafael. "My parents, two brothers, and two sisters."

Rafael accepted the photo. The family appeared happy, not the forced happiness for a photo shoot, but a genuine affection and joy. He recognized the dark resemblance of

Ethan and Evan to their father and the lighter complexion of the middle brother, Eli, to their beautiful blonde mother. He scratched his jaw, unable to make sense of the photo. "Who's the other man next to your mom? He resembles your dad. Uncle?"

Evan scrutinized Rafael for an expected outcome. "Like I said, those are my parents."

"Oh." Rafael scratched his cheek, unsure what to say. "I didn't realize he's your stepfather."

"No, he's Ethan and Eli's biological father. My uncle, my dad's younger brother."

Confusion crinkled Rafael's eyes. "Sorry. Didn't know your mother... had an affair. Not sure I'd have your father's *cojones* to take a photo with the man, brother or not."

"You're missing the *picture*, Rafael." Evan's mouth pinched tight, and he crossed his ankles. "My mother, father, *and* Richard were *together*."

The words took a moment to register. Rafael's jaw hung, and a muscle ticked in his neck. "I'm not following." The framed photo swayed in his hand.

Evan took the photo from Rafael before it crashed to the hardwood. "Honestly, it's a strange threesome, but arranged for a purpose. Plenty of love involved." He motioned to the chair. "Sit. I'll tell you a story. It'll explain Ethan's offer."

Rafael sat in the desk chair, leaning against his jacket, not caring about wrinkles that Sage would chastise him for. She'd chosen and purchased the expensive suit and had a say in how he treated it. *Shit... was he a kept man?* He booted the question to the back of the bus and opened his mind for story time.

Evan planted his butt on the desk for the long haul. "My mom and dad hooked up to bind two powerful families. Black warlocks and a strong witch. Even though they loved one another, the families expected them to solidify their union by having a brood. Turned out my mom couldn't get pregnant. They did all the infertility crap and still *nada*. It devastated both families who'd rallied behind the marriage."

The strange family history sunk into Rafael's head. "So your mom had an affair with Richard?" He scratched the nape of his neck, trying to wrap his head around the story.

"A consensual affair," Evan replied. "My dad suggested it. Richard was divorced and strong in magic like my dad. He and my mom always got along well."

"They shared your mother?" Rafael stuttered, his heart pounding against his ribcage.

"Well, not in all ways." A deeper flush rushed up Evan's neck. "I don't know the inner workings of their relationship behind closed doors. But they brought two covens together and bolstered the Ravenwood ranks. Their way to extend the Ravenwood family."

"Then Ethan and Eli were born." Rafael wanted to laugh at the congruity of the Ravenwood history. *Desperate times call for desperate and freaky-as-shit measures.*

"Yep." Evan returned to his story. "A year after Eli was born, my mom finally got pregnant with me. By then, she'd quit sleeping with Richard." The flush extended over Evan's cheeks. "I was born, and Mom died shortly afterward. Complications caused her heart to stop."

"I'm sorry, man." An uncomfortable warmth suffused Rafael. A sad and strange but illuminating story.

"What about your two sisters?"

"They're Richard's from his first marriage to a non-witch. They have no magical abilities. Even though we're cousins, we grew up like siblings. Their mother took a hike to Europe and never looked back."

"Pity. Why didn't he marry a witch if your family was hot to build its ranks of magicals?"

Evan frowned. "He let his dick and heart rule his

head." He stared at the photo in his hands, then set it aside. "Now do you understand Ethan's offer?"

Ire clawed up the back of Rafael's throat. "Ethan's carrying on your traditions?" *Freakass stuff.*

"The arrangement worked for them, for us. They instilled comfort and happiness in our family. We grew up with a boatload of love. Richard and Erick still live here. As brothers. Nothing more."

"Why does Ethan think it'll work for anyone else? I mean, come on, this is insane. We don't live in old-school Utah. The U.S. is anti-polygamy."

"My parents, Erick and Mariah, were married. Richard was—"

"Still polygamy." Rafael's fists balled at his sides. He didn't think he'd be able to watch another man touch Sage again. Nor did he think he'd ever give her up.

Evan took a looming step forward. Water spritzed off him—water he now derived from Willow's newly emerged magic—ready to douse Rafael's fire magic igniting from his fingers and dying before it hit the floor. "My mother was a High Priestess; she had two powerful black warlock guards. She would've died ten times over without their protection. And you well know a High Priestess can screw all the warlocks she wants. It strengthens their bonds. Married or not. Will Sage change her ways for you? Or can two warlocks keep her happy, keep her from returning to her old ways? Or can *you* alone keep her happy?"

The crux of the matter. Rafael slumped in his chair. He raked his hands through his hair, contemplating raking them through his skull to claw the confusion out of his brain cells. Evan grabbed a manila folder off the desk. He rolled a gaming chair closer and sank down.

Contemplative silence competed with songbirds chirping outside the window. A tabby cat streaked across the front yard, chasing a squirrel into the woods, the place

Rafael wanted to bury his thoughts. Finally, he asked, "Why Sage? It's not the same situation. Why does Ethan think this is right for us? Why's he bargaining for my position in Sage's life?"

"He doesn't want your position. He admires Sage... and you. You two represent a powerful alliance for the Ravenwoods, an opportunity to strengthen our future with powerful witches and warlocks. Plus, Sage needs stronger warlocks taking up her wings. You know that as well as the fog's gonna roll over the bay tonight. War's coming with the Black Tide. Are you ready to handle it alone?"

More silence smothered the room, killed the air in Rafael's lungs.

"Look, man." Evan shoved the folder at Rafael. "Here's evidence we've compiled on the Black Tide and the other families allied with Andre, everything we possess toward taking the Charlemagnes down. It's not a lot, but it's all we have. Our good faith for this alliance. Do what you will with it. But do the right thing, man."

C⋆C⋆C⋆

The right thing? The Ravenwoods were asking him to give up his heart and soul or engage in an unnatural sharing of both. He didn't share well. Not when it involved the love of his life.

Sage had pulled Rafael from the brink of despair the night she'd met him, lured by his warlock potential and a hollowness within him. Captivated by his loneliness and internal turmoil. He'd always known he differed from others, although no one had ever expressed why. He'd grown up without his biological parents and had no intel on them. Foster families couldn't deal with his desperation to fit within the human world. He'd lived in group homes until booted out at eighteen with a hundred bucks and his life's possessions stuffed in a duffel bag.

A suspecting friend—a young warlock—invited him to a Summer Solstice festival at the western coven gathering one June, sensing he might find answers. He didn't understand it at first but willingly went to the party. At least alcohol and food flowed freely. Then he'd met Sage Wilde and tumbled into her web of love, home, and happiness. It took time, but he'd found his salvation in her and her family, belonging to a world far greater than his miniscule life for the first time. She'd brought out his magic in all the ways that mattered and taught him how to master his skills, the way she did with every other witch and warlock in her coven. The most selfless, giving person he'd ever met. And he strived to please her in everything he did. The day she confessed she'd loved him from the moment they met, before he'd mustered up the nerve to tell her how much he cherished and loved her, he vowed to love her till death.

"I'll be damned if today's the end," Rafael muttered. He passed by a couple small tables on the patio between the garage and kitchen door and lit the candles from a flame he'd produced on his finger. Filling his soul, he sucked in the clean mountain air, strode to all the tables, and lit the candles, needing to display his power in his natural habitat, his home.

He jogged the last few steps to the back door. Home was wherever Sage was.

Famished, he entered the Wilde mansion through the French doors to the kitchen, the shortest path from the garage. The moment he stepped over the threshold, the stinging air of foreboding bowled him over and churned his empty stomach.

Aspen glanced up from the stove where she clanged copper pots on the stainless steel, involved in potion-making. "Rafael!" She rounded on him. "Didn't you get my dozen texts?"

He'd put his phone on silent at his client meeting and forgot to turn the ringer on. "In meetings. What's wrong?" Ice formed around his spine, inching toward his heart. "Is Sage okay?"

"She'll *be* okay."

Rafael bolted, impeded by Marty standing in the doorway to the great room on the first floor. "Outta the way." Flames danced over Marty's head, preparing to flare down upon the young warlock. Realizing he was endangering members of his coven—his family—he dropped his magic, and the flames dissipated. He took a physical and mental step back. "What did fuckwad Ethan do to her?"

"It wasn't Ethan, you prick." Aspen slapped his arm. "It was the real *wad of fuck*, Andre." Aspen regaled him with the dungeon incident. "Ethan saved her. She's resting now. I think he hit the road." She brushed green powder off the front of her blouse, touched a purple bruise forming on her chin. "Go to her. She needs you."

He elbowed past Aspen and Marty and raced across the travertine stone floor to the curved staircase. Guilt and dread fueled his race to Sage's suite upstairs. He should've sensed the breakdown in magic and her agitation in their frazzled bond. Hell no, he was too screwed up in the head to concentrate on what mattered most... the one who mattered most.

Rafael stormed to the master bedroom, banging the door open against the inner wall. Frantic, his gaze raced from each corner of the empty room, the made bed, not one of the dozen earth-tone pillows out of place. Her coconut-tinged, gardenia perfume lingered with every step he took. "Sage!" he shouted and darted into the spa bathroom, the humongous walk-in closet. Empty.

Standing stone-still, he focused on their bond.

Microscopic but active, her magic towed him to the east wing. The wing closest to the back staircase leading to the basement.

Marty jogged into the suite. "Sorry, dude. Queen bee's in the east guestroom."

Rafael nodded his thanks and sprinted to the guestroom, the lure to Sage's magic strengthening with each step. Staggering against the wall outside the door, he gave in to his momentary relief and slowed his roll.

The second he entered the room, his relief slid off his knotted shoulders. Until he realized Ethan Ravenwood was spooning her on the rumpled bed... as if she'd made her choice. One stinking day later. At least they were both fully clothed. Still drove an ice-crusted nail in his heart. Despair and turmoil snared every other emotion in his body. *Screw. Me. Now.*

Gullies creased Sage's forehead, and Rafael recognized her guilt even in sleep. Blonde hair fanned out like spun gold over the pillows, mating with Ethan's dark locks, the way her hair twined around his own chestnut hair.

Gratefulness for Ethan's protection booted his guilt and jealousy to the wayside. Rafael had never seen Sage so beautiful, so sexy and enthralling. Had she really made her decision?

Rafael needed to touch her, needed her gloved around him.

Ravenwood stirred on the bed and nearly brained himself clambering off it. "Sorry, man. I fell asleep. Sage ordered me to leave, but Aspen forced a potion on me." He staggered, proving his point, and righted himself against a carved wooden post of the four-poster bed.

Rafael gave him a moment to shake off the potion's effects. "Now I'm ordering you to get the hell out. Go home." Five seconds later, the door shut on the black warlock's ass, and Rafael's gaze feasted again on his witch.

Silent, he stripped off his clothes, tossing his expensive suit in a heap on the floor. His hand brushed his iron-hard erection, and he stifled a groan. Without jiggling the bed, he perched on the edge, rolled on his side, and spooned Sage. Her camelia perfume filled his senses to the brim, and he began to relax.

"Umm... Rafael?" Sage's sleepy words drifted to him, and she rolled over, her brilliant green eyes landing on his face. Rafael guided her hand to his throbbing erection.

Her sleepy gaze scanned the room, as if searching for Ravenwood. "Where are we?"

"I need to know you're okay." His trembling hands framed her cheeks.

Her face darkened with emotion and realization, and her bottom lip quivered. "Oh, goddess, I'm so sorry." Her fingers drooped off him, and her guilt smothered his lust. "I screwed up. Rafael, I love *you*, and I don't want to lose you. I'll make it up to you. But I have to save our coven. Love, please don't leave me over this." Sobs shuddered through her.

Shock suffused Rafael. Sage *never* cried. He wished she would once in a while, to exhibit deeper emotion than her usual stony façade. He understood her reasons for the cold veneer, saw firsthand how she'd let her vulnerability kill her guard.

Rafael kissed her forehead, her eyelids, her nose, his mouth landing on hers, wet and salty. Never fully grasping the intensity of her feelings for him, he'd gotten used to her domineering and noncommittal ways. A part of him wondered if she'd ever marry him and make good on her commitment to go exclusive.

Her hands twined around his on her face, and Sage pressed her lips to his. Her tongue tangoing with his melted him, and he lost himself in her web, in her hands now tangled in his hair, moving to his chest, staking her claim to his heart and body. And he fell into his soul. Damn the consequences.

Chapter 6

Morning landed too soon after Rafael carried Sage to their own bedroom. He'd never told her about his conversation with Evan, refused to let it mar their night just holding each other. Evan's story didn't add up, and he wanted to explore it further. He'd left Sage half asleep to start his morning routine checking the covenstead's security, walking the grounds from ward to ward, and checking in with each witch who maintained the wards.

Although he preferred the outdoors and loved his morning patrols, watching the sunrise, he now sat rigidly at his desk, so rigid his back ached, and he stretched through the knots. His mind reluctantly drifted to Ravenwood's offer and the circumstances behind it.

"Offer my ass. It's pure blackmail." Rafael slammed his fist on the scarred wood desktop, sending a framed photo of himself and Sage embracing in the backyard gazebo clattering forward on the desk. He caught the photo and righted it where he always had Sage in his sights. "And what did the asshole mean by including *me* in his idiotic plans?" The whole deal smelled of insanity. "He can't seriously think I'd agree to a threesome like his own parents." Their situation was entirely different.

When Evan helped the Wildes capture Charlemagne, he'd assured Rafael and Sage that the Ravenwoods would ally with the Wilde Coven. No one said word one about strings. In fact, Evan assured Sage that the Ravenwoods would do anything to escape the Black Tide intact, with a goal toward permanently dismantling the group.

Could the Wildes quash the Black Tide without the Ravenwoods? And learn all of Andre's secrets without insider information the Ravenwoods profess might be available to them? The information Evan gave Rafael wasn't enough. They needed more to dismantle the group.

Rafael tipped back, his hands clasped behind his head, mind spinning a million miles a minute. "Terms and conditions, my ass. Not even gonna say offer anymore. It's a damn condition," he grumbled to the room.

His office was a quarter the size of Sage's office. He didn't need the space. Just needed a place to run his security business, govern the coven's security, and escape for peace and quiet. He swiveled his worn leather chair to peer out the large window facing the lush lawn and gardens surrounded by the Santa Cruz Forest behind him. Off to his right, a tiny blue wedge of the Pacific Ocean smoothed the rough edges of his jagged mood.

He booted Sage and her conundrum to the pits of his mind. Their basement rat took priority. They couldn't keep the man locked up forever. Sage had tried a trial binding spell on him to bind his magic, but it never took, probably because his black magic reversed it. They planned to use another archaic binding spell and a truth spell to suck the man dry of information. Then what? Release him into the wild without his magic? Although not permanent, a binding lasted as long as the binder maintained the spell.

Rafael scratched his head. If he called the shots, he'd annihilate the black warlocks. They jeopardized the life of every witch on the planet. Just like the instigation of the War. On the flipside, Rafael was all about peace, love, and freedom.

He chuckled. To an extent. He was also all about monogamy and equality, a way of life Sage slowly climbed aboard. Until dick-on-a-lollipop-stick strolled through the door.

"Son of a bitch." Just when Sage had promised him exclusivity. He was done sharing her with every good-looking warlock Sage sensed in the wild and recruited into her coven, even if the sharing was temporary and necessary evil. Could he take a hike if she agreed to Ravenwood's terms?

Before his mind tortured him another moment longer, his door pushed open and banged against his overflowing shelf unit. He spun his chair around and leaped up. Electricity zinged to his hands, and sparks formed on his fingers.

Aspen's skin was pale. Rosemary wafted off her, along with a healthy dose of alarm. "Rafael!" she yelled, barreling through his door, her red hair haloing her head.

"The wards are falling." She waved her hands, pointing to all compass points. "All over the covenstead. The eastern point where the ley lines are the strongest is the only one still intact."

Five wards protected the covenstead, making a pentagram pattern for double protection. He sprang around the desk. "What the hell? They were fine during my morning rounds. You told Sage?"

"Yep. Meet her in the great room."

"Did the witches change rotation since my security check?" Rafael led the way along the hallway to the front room.

"No. The usual suspects. Nothing changed in the schedule. All the witches and warlocks made their usual perimeter checks."

He racked his mind for anything magic related affecting the wards. He didn't want to worry about a Black Tide attack, a very obvious culprit. "Any ley line disturbances?" Rafael asked. He reached the main staircase and jogged into the circular great room centered on the mansion's first floor. All available coven members who lived or worked on the property surrounded Sage standing in the center of the room. Groupings of cushioned chairs, an eclectic mix of occasional tables, and two large L-shaped sofas surrounded them. The creams, grays, and greens of the room fostered comfort and relaxation. He felt anything but as everyone stood, magic at the ready and palpable in the air.

"I felt a blip on the ley line that crisscrosses the fault line running toward the ocean. Then a draw of magic about fifteen minutes ago on the southern wards. Not an earthquake. The disturbance moved south, then north, bypassing the two lines to the east," said Marina, Sage's youngest cousin. Their strongest earth witch communed with the natural ley lines beneath the Earth's surface. Because of her affinity to the earth and her expertise, Rafael placed her in charge of the perimeter wards.

"Are all the wards down?" Sage captured Rafael's hand in her own and squeezed.

"Not completely. Enough for intrusion, though," Marina replied. "We've tripled the guards at all ingress points and are monitoring from the lookouts. Cameras are dead."

Rafael had turned the covenstead into a virtual (witch-style) and physical fortress. Even with the wards down, at least a half-dozen witches would know if another witch trespassed. The cameras picked up most visible activity, unless spelled.

Rafael turned his attention to Sage. "Can you sense black warlocks? Are we in game play with the Black Tide?"

Sage closed her eyes, something she did to concentrate on sensing magic. Since she possessed aether magic, she had the ability to sense all the elements of water, air, fire, and earth magic. Now she was learning to sense black magic, which also relied upon the elements, but with a distinction—at least to Sage. Rafael sensed minor magic, but more than he should, according to Sage.

"Not black magic. It's regular old white magic." Marina twined her long black hair around her fingers.

Not good. Rafael didn't like when the witches grew nervous. Especially Marina, who managed the property's safety, next in command to him, master of all things security.

Sage opened her eyes, rubbed her forehead. "She's right, it's not black magic. It's three very distinct witches."

Shouting and scuffling arose from the front entrance. Rafael bolted toward the foyer. "Guard Sage!" he shouted unnecessarily over his shoulder as three warlocks surrounded her. Sage may rule in most other areas of life, but she deferred to him when it involved security.

He came to a dead stop in the foyer. A round marble table centered in the circular entryway separated him from three witches—from three separate California covens— under guard from the Wilde warlocks. Magic pervaded the room. Rafael didn't need to sense it. Witch-air and witch-fire roiled in the air, beating each other in to submission, a show of force between the two covens. The witch in the center of the trio stood immobile, a dour mask on her furrowed and pallid face. Her silver-threaded black hair hung loose, spilling down her back. She wore a flowing black dress and cape and pointy-toed black boots. *Where's the stupid, clichéd pointy hat?*

"Imelda Helwig." He tipped his head at the High Priestess lording it over the small Scotts Valley region among the hills between the Monterey and San Francisco bays. She'd taken control of the Helwig coven a year after Sage inherited her role over the Wilde Coven. He dipped his head at Clarissa to her right, the High Priestess of the Central California region, and to Nella on her left, the High Priestess of the Sacramento region. Both witches, in their fifties now, earned the High Priestess badge from their mothers. They ruled larger covens than Imelda's tiny coven, and that alone gave Rafael pause. "To what do we owe this honor from three distinguished witches? Sage didn't call a Council meeting." How dare they meddle with the covenstead wards and cameras? And how the hell had they accomplished it?

"What did you do to our wards?" Marina blurted out, pushing her way past Rafael.

"Well met, Rafael." Imelda ignored Marina. The other two witches nodded once at him, also ignoring Marina.

"What gives you the right to screw with our wards?" he repeated Marina's question his way.

"What gives you the right to harbor a potential war criminal without full Council approval?" Imelda asked. "Now take me to Sage." Sparks shot off her fingers, ineffectively landing on the floor, tiny orange glowing pinpricks against the grey-veined, white marble. The six Wilde warlocks surrounding the three intruders tightened their ranks.

Imelda held up a hand. "Stand your guards down, Rafael. We came to have a healthy discourse from one witch to another... or three. As you can see," she wanded her arm, "I brought no warlocks inside your house."

"Bullshit," he ground out. "You instigated an act of war against the Wilde Coven this morning. Sage doesn't *discourse* with intruders. You should have set a mutual appointment *without* the magic display."

"Who needs an appointment among friends?" The oldest witch in her position dominated the other two High Priestesses despite the size differences of their covens. Their silence was too telling. In all actuality, Sage ruled them all as High Priestess of the West, limited by the Western Council's rules and procedures. But she allowed autonomy to all regions... only if all covens obeyed the Council rules. Today, obeying had flown the coop.

"Let them in," Sage said from behind him. He hadn't heard her or her entourage approach. "Imelda, Clarissa, Nella, well met. I wish it was under mutually acceptable terms."

Sage moved abreast of Rafael, and he growled at her, wishing she'd waited for his signal. But she knew him too well, knew his next action, which was to invoke binding spells against the three powerful witches. An action geared to instigate an even bigger feud.

"Love," Sage clamped onto his taut forearm. "Please escort our guests to the forest meeting room. I'll be there soon." Sage left the foyer, her witches and warlocks trailing behind her.

"Forest meeting room" was code for a heavily warded meeting room for outside witches. The first-floor room faced the forest and a strong ley line. The wards were so discreet, thanks to Marina, most witches couldn't discern them until they tried to raise magic. Rafael wasn't stupid to think Imelda and others hadn't caught on. But it provided a haven for all witches to talk without magical consequences. The wards also prevented the Wilde witches and warlocks from using magic. Other hidden weapons the Wildes relied upon outfitted the room.

"No magic from this point forward," Rafael addressed the three witches. "Do we have an understanding?"

"Of course," Imelda said, adding a snooty sniff.

Clarissa and Nella agreed with simple nods.

One could normally trust a witch's word—or nod—when on another witch's covenstead. Rafael didn't trust these three any farther than he could throw them toward the firepit. They'd already lied about screwing with the wards. He motioned for the warlocks to guide the witches to the forest room.

The foyer cleared, and he craned his head to Marina's ear. "Keep working on the wards. Bind any witch or warlock who doesn't belong on our grounds until this meeting's over."

Her face screwed up, the freckles smattering her nose almost enticing him to connect the dots on her beautiful face. "We're trying. We haven't yet determined how these bitches hit the kill switch."

"They're working together. Did they bring an entourage? Are they near the wards?"

Small green leaves wafted down the hallway like tumbleweeds. "Sorry," Marina said, kicking at the leaves dripping from her fingers. "Not a soul."

Ignoring Marina's magic mess of distress, Rafael's eyes rounded. "Three High Priestesses came alone. No warlocks, no nothing?" A High Priestess always traveled with a gaggle of warlocks.

Marina jerked the cuffs of her hoodie over her hands. "I know. Another rule they broke."

"No way they'd travel without an entourage." Rafael dug his hands in his pants pockets, contemplated the floor. "Hunt for invisibility spells. Put our best air witches on this," he snapped his fingers, "including Eden. Get them investigating any air spell shielding them. Use whatever Aspen's got in her alchemic arsenal."

Marina gave him a two-fingered salute. "On it."

He squeezed her shoulder. "I'll escape the meeting as soon as I can."

"No. Stay with Sage. We'll handle this."

If not for Sage's strength, Marina might've been the next Wilde Coven leader after her mother forfeited. Sage's mother and Jessica were twins, Jessica the youngest by three minutes. Marina's earth and ley line magic almost rivaled Sage's use of all the elements. Sage's aether kicked her squarely over the finish line.

On the way to the meeting, Rafael grabbed his gun and shoulder harness from his office and strapped it on.

No imperceptible magic shift met him in the forest room. Sage sat at the head of the long rectangular table and eased her hand beneath it to check two tasers on a hidden shelf, her non-magical weapon of choice. Rafael stood behind her, his customary position, his hand on her tight shoulder. He tried to rub the stiffness from her neck, without success.

Imelda regally sat in a chair at the foot of the table, as far from Sage as the room allowed. Her traditional seat when the California Council gathered at the Wilde covenstead. Still silent, Clarissa and Nella flanked her in the nearest side chairs. Rafael watched their every movement. The faces of the two wing-witches remained passive, so disconcerting, hackles rose on his scalp. Imelda's gaze slid from the murals on the wall where the forest from outside extended a small meadow and meandering creek in the middle of tree groves invitingly into the room.

"Ladies, how can I help you?" Sage splayed her fingers on the tabletop in a show of good faith. "Care for a beverage? Do you want to bless our meeting in a prayer to the goddess?"

Imelda tapped her plain, blunt-tipped fingernails on the table. "No thanks. We can dispense with the formalities."

"Why the visit without formal notification?" Rafael

demanded.

"Rafael," Sage said under her breath before he stuck his foot farther in his mouth. It wasn't his place. But a feeling of doom roiled in his gut.

"Where are your warlocks?" Sage asked.

"They're close." Imelda stretched her lips in a slight smile. "We didn't think we'd require them on the Wilde hallowed grounds. Do we?" Her eyebrows arched, mocking Sage.

"Not unless you plan on causing trouble." Sage tilted slightly over the table as if to press her words upon the three witches. "Do you plan to cause trouble?"

Rafael's phone dinged Marina's text tone, and he shucked it out of his jacket pocket.

No sign of external magic or intruders. Wards still down. Oh, wait.

Rafael sat erect, and his hand vibrated on the phone as he waited.

"Depends. We understand you're holding Andre Charlemagne." Imelda sifted her fingers through her thin, board-straight hair.

Rafael's back nearly splintered from the strain of checking his emotions. How was Imelda in the know already? They'd just captured the black warlock leader two days ago. *Marina?* Texting her, his thumbs pounded the screen.

She texted: *3 empty black SUVs a mile down road. Black magic flows around them. Gotta go. Something going down at Northwest ward. Lines are weird.*

He wanted in on the action, but he'd never leave Sage alone with Imelda.

"We do have Andre here," Sage said. "Where he'll remain indefinitely."

"It's not for you to decide his fate," Imelda ground out. "This is a Council matter."

"I rule the West," Sage intoned, low and lethal. "Not you. You best remember your place, Imelda."

"It's a Council matter," Imelda repeated as if spitting out the letters between her teeth. "Are you saying you will not give him a Council trial and allow us to determine his fate?"

"He's a black warlock. No rules pertain to him." Rafael's eyes bore into Imelda's face as if to imprint his retinas on her skin.

"I want access to him." Imelda ignored Rafael. "It's my right, then we'll decide his fate via Council."

Clarissa coughed a message into her hand. Rafael squinted at the other witch, peering between her fingers covering her mouth. Her mouth didn't budge with the cough, and Clarissa *never* coughed into her hands. She always did the inner elbow thing, total germaphobe.

His gaze bounced to Nella. Not one feature of her face faltered. Her eyes didn't even blink. Were they glamoured? No, impossible. The wards were strong and tamper-proof.

"May I have a moment, Sage?" he asked. "I'd like us to discuss Imelda's request. Outside." He needed to get her to safety.

"What? No. There's nothing to discuss." Sage's eyelashes flapped rapidly. Standing, she addressed Imelda. "When I'm ready to parade Andre to the witchworld, I'll let you three know." The last words rolled out, and the air before Clarissa wavered.

Rafael drew his gun out of his holster.

The air surrounding Clarissa and Nella churned, and the witches disappeared for a few seconds. Two unidentified warlocks took their place. Black warlocks.

Black magic killed the wards in the room, along with the glamour spells hiding their true identity.

Chapter 7

Sage sprang from her chair, a stun gun in each hand. The wards in the room faltered and disintegrated. She released her right grip, and a zapper clattered to the tabletop. A ward shielded Imelda, and one of her warlocks blocked the door, trapping Sage and Rafael in the room. They both shot lightning bolts at the two warlocks, electricity sparking in the air. The men retaliated with their own bolts, and the air sizzled with fire and magic above the table. Neither side gained an advantage, the magic merely exposing their power and magic element.

"Imelda! Call your dogs off," Sage gritted out between clenched teeth. "How dare you use magic to sever my wards? You know this is a neutral meeting place."

"How many rules have you broken today, Imelda?" Rafael's rage quaked through him and up Sage's arm. "The Council will have your crown for this."

Imelda hadn't shifted a muscle. Now she lifted off her chair, slow and deliberate. "I asked you to give up Andre. You refused. The Council's on my side. We're all aware black warlocks and the Black Tide exist. We all know about your unlawful detainment. Every High Priestess in our region knows what's happened."

A sour taste bloomed in Sage's mouth. She'd known black magic was rising. Yet she hadn't anticipated that the western covens knew so many black warlocks existed. No one mentioned it during the Summer Solstice or the Autumn Solstice festival council meetings. To think the entire West was ready to kiss the Black Tide's feet was ludicrous and insane. "Are you saying you want Andre released because you're on his side? That all western covens want to work with the Black Tide?"

A slow and radiant smile transformed Imelda's face. "The western covens want black warlocks working *with* and *for* us. We have no intention of allowing the Black Tide or any organized warlock coven becoming a power force in our witchworld."

Relief slid into the tight knots in Sage's shoulders. *At least there's that.* Rafael placed his hand over hers on the table, a bare touch, fire to fire. Sparks flickered off their skin, and he removed his hand, clenched his fist at his side.

"Why Andre? If you transfer him, you risk his escape or the Black Tide targeting *you*. Right now, he's safe from escape or harm. We have wards to prevent intrusion. We've doubled our guard," Sage explained, trying to back up the bus on crazy town.

Imelda smiled her all-knowing smile again, and she laid her hands on the table, her cheeks rosy against her pallid skin. "Have you now? My warlocks just decimated a powerful ward in this room. How can you assure me your wards will survive a black magic attack?" Her eyes twinkled perceptively.

Black magic already shot their wards to shit outside. The West never needed such powerful wards. Until now. Sage had always believed her wards powerful enough to thwart any magic. How'd she fail her people? She squeezed her eyes closed for two seconds. "We already know what you did."

"What did I do?" Imelda fiddled with her moonstone pendant, as if it was a spelled charm she was prepping for blastoff.

"Aren't you the queen of obvious? *Your* black warlock minions killed our perimeter wards." Her hands shook in thinly disguised fury. "Did you do it to prove a point?"

Rafael's phone dinged in sync with a muffled stomping of feet. Commotion arose from the basement below them.

"Son of a bitch." He stared at his phone, then at Imelda. "What did you do?"

Sage assessed the distance to the door, the two behemoth warlocks blocking it. Imelda employed witch-fire and her warlocks the same from what she'd already seen. They also might wield other magic elements not exhibited, considering they were black warlocks with their own power.

Imelda hooted. "I merely decimated your security, Mr. Security Guru. We'll take Andre now. I have black magic securing my covenstead. I can hold Andre without risk of attack from white or black magic. Don't worry, we'll grant Sage the right to talk to him. In due time."

The second Imelda and Andre stepped off the premises, Sage's control would fly off down crap highway. She'd lose her position as the western coven head when Imelda blabbed to the witchworld. With the information Andre held about black warlocks around the world, Sage would have the clout she needed. They also needed to leverage his magic for the coven's good. A few truth spells and she'd have it all. *Damn sure not gonna give it up without a fight.*

The house rumbled from the attack in the basement. Sage's spine crawled with the need to help her witches and warlocks, to end Imelda's blatant assault on her home, her life, her coven. Rafael's phone kept dinging message after message. They were being summoned and also stuck in a catch-22.

"Something got your tongue, Sage?" Imelda asked, a smarmy grin accompanying her words.

"You're breaking Andre out of my dungeon? How dare you? Do you know what this will do to your standing in the Council, your coven's standing in the West?"

Imelda wanded her hand. "We all do what we must." She reached in an inside pocket of her cape, drew out a sealed envelope, and placed it on the table.

Rafael clamped Sage's wrist to stop her from going medieval on Imelda. Sage recognized the Western Council's insignia in the old-school wax seal: the sun, moon, and stars over the Pacific Ocean. A Council mandate, absent Sage's blessing. It meant the region's majority had gone behind her back and forged a proclamation against her. Fury struck a nerve in the aether trying to emerge. She forcibly dampened it with the power of her mind before it took complete control of her.

"You broke the rules, Sage. The Council agrees that you'll remain in power. For now, with restrictions." Imelda pushed the envelope closer to Sage. "The Council decrees you are to release custody of Andre to me. For the good of the West. All the covens. Not just the Wildes."

"Blackmail's not a suitable color on you, Imelda." Sage wanted to strike down Imelda with lightning bolts. The witch must've coerced several Council High Priestesses to vote with her. No way those witches would ever rule against Sage. Unless they truly believed Sage had broken protocol, their decrees, *and* put the West in jeopardy. Had she risked them all by capturing Andre? Her palms grew damp.

"It's all spelled out in the envelope. Signed by the required majority." Imelda sat again, enjoying herself more than the situation warranted. But then, she probably assumed she'd win Sage's rightful claim as the West's leading High Priestess. *As if awesome made up her teeny tiny coven.*

Another rumble rocked the house on its foundation, knocking sense into Sage. Tapping her right finger on Rafael's hand gripping her left wrist, she tapped their secret "go" sequence. *Time for a smackdown.*

A firestorm exploded from Sage and Rafael. Fireballs and lightning bolts lit the room over the table. Sage invoked a ward around the witch circle. Air cloaked them to protect from a retaliatory attack. Imelda screamed bloody murder, and her two warlocks sandwiched her between them, blasting ineffectual witch-fire. Or warlock-fire? Sage didn't know. She had a lot to learn regarding the nature of black warlocks. Regardless, fire met fire and once again ended in a draw.

She withdrew her magic, sparks dripping off her fingers, expelling the power surging within her. Rafael toyed with the fire sparking from his hands, rolling fireballs into the air. "How much more can you withstand, Imelda? I'm in a circle," Sage challenged.

Gasping, Imelda screeched, "A circle my warlocks can destroy in two seconds. Do you want to test them? Try me."

A magic war erupted in the compound, fire against fire. Water spouting against the ceilings, war cries, grunts, and an onslaught of pain and agony. Wind whistled and flying objects clattered and clunked against walls and floors.

"Release Andre to us and the deed will lessen the death toll." Imelda held her ground, a blank mask descending over her face.

Prickly horror attacked Sage's middle. She needed to rescue her people. Needed to finish this ridiculous fight. "Call off your people."

"Sage!" Rafael threw up his hands. "Don't give in to

her."

"Call them off now." Inwardly wincing, Sage put her First Warlock on ice. "Let's talk a truce."

Imelda weighed the authenticity of Sage's words, then signaled the warlock on her left. He left the room, the door closing, a loud click radiating in the silent and ominous room.

"Good. You've come to your senses." Imelda pushed the envelope closer to Sage. "The Council has decreed I take control of Andre. You're on probation, and any decision you make requires full agreement from the Council. Then we'll discuss if you're worthy of leading again."

Sage was dying to know who'd signed the decree. Dying to smack down the defectors. They had to know her intentions with Andre were for the good of the region. She never gave them reason to doubt that she always maintained the western territory's best interests in every action or decision she made. Mentally, she tallied the usual suspects, but the numbers didn't add up to a majority. Surely, her allies—or former allies—should be happy she'd captured a powerful black warlock and removed him from the streets. What lies had the hag told? What did she promise the other covens? This defection was no way to end the growing dissension amongst the covens. It only ratcheted up the infighting. And all the covens understood the Wilde covenstead was the safest to hold a treacherous and powerful witch or black warlock. She owned the only covenstead with active ley lines. Her stomach dropped. Until the moment a gaggle of witches and black warlocks breached the property. *Son of a goddess bitch. Everything I've maintained and built after Mom died is heading to hell in a black warlock hand basket.*

Seething inside, Sage waited. Imelda's lips curled up ever so slightly at the corners. Finally, the covenstead quieted, giving way to Imelda's back-stabbing coup. Or had her own people taken control?

Her air ward dissolved. Inching her fingers toward the envelope, Sage gripped it between thumb and forefinger. Rafael's hand encircled her wrist.

"Let me," he gritted out. "She probably spelled the contents."

"It's official Council documentation." Imelda jutted out her chin. "Spelling official documents is against Council rules."

Red rage stiffened Sage against Rafael, and she wrenched her wrist out of his hand, enabling her to use her magic again, if needed. "Screw you, Imelda. Like anything you've done here today is *official*." She did air quotes. "You're just a gift that keeps on giving."

"Tsk, tsk, your mother wouldn't approve of how you've handled things, of your predilections toward your warlocks to the detriment of your duties." Imelda's eyes shot daggers.

"You have no clue what you're yakking about. My witches and warlocks are content, well cared for. Unlike your round table of turnover. And leave my mother out of this. She wouldn't approve of *your* actions, like she didn't approve of the Helwig priestesses in your lineage before you. Reasons the Wilde witches have been in charge."

Imelda shrugged, sat down again. Her warlock stood as stiff as a stone pillar, barely blinking. "*In charge* is relative. And you're done being *in charge*." She smirked, an ugly, face-twisting expression, giving definition to hag.

Gwyneira hooted and flapped along Sage's shoulders, raring to engage in a fight. The familiar's wings prickled but also soothed Sage's fraught emotions. A silent command to the owl stilled its movements. She snatched the envelope out of Rafael's tenuous grip, tore it open, and read the decree. Imelda spewed the truth. Sage was on probation. All decisions for the western covens would be by majority rule. And Imelda now owned the majority. *Shit on a stick.*

Sage handed the document to Rafael, who perused it and flung it in the trash can to his right. "Means nothing," he said.

Sage lowered her voice. "You can never hold Andre as well as we can here. You'll sink all of us."

Imelda pushed off her seat, her legs shaky as if the witch had fought a long, hard battle. Maybe she had. Witchcraft took its toll on all witches. The witch hag hastily gained solid footing. Sage noted the pain knotting Imelda's features before a stony façade and her perpetual smirk veiled it.

Imelda leaned a hip on the table for support. "I will take Andre. I have the numbers, the strength. We will destroy your entire coven if you don't surrender your rights. Do you want blood on your hands?" She paused, sucked in a needed breath. "Your entire compound is surrounded by black warlocks who hold allegiance to me *and* Andre. Don't even attempt to follow us or you'll never see the light of day. No Wilde will ever hold the rank of a regional ruling priestess again."

Rafael's phone beeped, and he showed the message to Sage. Marina verified the coup, and Imelda's people trapped all Wilde witches and warlocks within warded circles.

Sage's throat felt like it was clogging up. She lunged halfway across the table at Imelda, checked herself, and eased back into Rafael's arms. Safety for her coven overruled her lethal intentions.

"We'll release your witches and warlocks the moment we're off the grounds with Andre," Imelda said.

Sage wanted to smack the smile off the bitch. "You hurt them, you die."

"Oh, I'm sure you'll find your retribution. Just

remember who I have in my back pocket now." Imelda turned her back on Sage, stepped toward the door, froze. Her black warlock kept his gaze locked on Sage, not moving a muscle to follow his leader.

Helplessness tore through her rage, dispersing it, igniting the aether inside her. Rafael steadied her, his hands on her hips calming, soothing, infusing her with capitulation. A temporary defeat. Her coven couldn't fight a tide of black warlocks with unknown powers. That they'd cut through the covenstead wards, powerful wards locked to ley lines beneath the Earth's surface, was truth enough of their immense power.

The older witch slowly rotated around. "I'll give you credit, Sage. You took this better than expected. I respect that you recognize the power of your foes. Might help you regain your crown. When I'm gone."

"Screw you, Imelda," Sage lashed out. "You'll be gone sooner than you think."

Imelda cackled, turned back to the door. Before she touched the handle, the door swung open and air magic blew into the room, encapsulated the witch and the black warlock within a bubble. A humongous black raven flew inside, squawking and cawing over their heads.

Chapter 8

Ethan and unidentified warlocks filled the entryway to the forest room and the hall beyond. They were barely visible through the thick, swirling air circling Imelda and her guard. Air bands muffled the bound pair. The room plummeted into a mineshaft of silence.

Relieved, Sage sagged against Rafael for a millisecond. Unable to allow herself to show submission and reliance upon her warlock, she stood erect.

Ethan shoved his way around the bubble encapsulating Imelda, perspiration dotting his forehead, his layered hair in a blown tousle. He took care not to pierce the shroud. A pinprick handed Imelda an opening to break through the protective casing. Who knew what magic the black warlock beside her possessed?

"I can't hold her for long," Ethan said, a singed citrus scent wafting off him. "I depleted my powers on helping to secure your perimeter. Your witches are warding the covenstead again." He gestured to his raven now perched on a tall bookcase housing random books and trinkets. The raven dove and circled the bubble, squawking each time Imelda or the warlock touched the shroud from inside. Balthazar flew above the air cage and tied knots in the glowing magic threads Ethan weaved to enhance his magic.

"Thank you." Appreciation spilled from Sage's voice. "What about my people downstairs? Apparently, Imelda's people captured them."

Ethan blanched. "We didn't get that far." He flicked a hand, and one of his warlocks jogged away.

"How many warlocks do you have?" Rafael asked.

"Not enough if your coven's under siege." His glare met Imelda's fuzzy but triumphant gaze. "Well met, Imelda." He gave a sharp incline of his head. "What's the ask?"

"Andre," Sage responded.

"I figured when I recognized his black warlocks surrounding your property. Didn't know who was calling the shots." His gaze bounced over Imelda's blurry form, and he grinned at her ugly grimace.

He rocked the bubble, withdrew a fraction to avoid touching his own magic. "Witch, you know what you're in for, right?" He didn't wait for an answer. "He'll kill you and everyone you love before he lets you call further shots."

Imelda tried to point at her mouth. The movement appeared as if she were dragging her hand through thick mud. The raven landed on Ethan's outstretched arm and dove under his shirtsleeve, transforming into black ink.

"Let her cry her river." Sage knocked her fists on the tabletop. "Rafael, please check on our coven downstairs."

"I'm not leaving your side." He inched closer.

"Go. I'll watch your witch." Ethan kinked his head to the left, wagging it as if flinging off fleas. Pain dulled his eyes and they were almost solid gray.

"I'm not leaving her here alone." Rafael stroked the gun in his shoulder harness. Sage nearly stomped her foot on top of his boot to end the he-man play. *Jeez, he forgets who brings magic to his picnic.*

"Better with me than these two." Ethan released his gag on Imelda. Her hand jerked from her waist to her neck, and she sputtered. "Sage is safe with me. This hag won't touch her."

Sage tapped two fingers on Rafael's wrist, tapped Caerwyn's pointy, tattooed ear poking out from his sleeve. "Remember, I hold more magic than you." Her lips quirked up to soften the blow. Rafael hated the reminder. His sandalwood cologne drifted toward her, and she breathed him in deep, imprinting his scent on her nostrils. "I'll be fine. Imelda's done here." Rafael still didn't budge.

"Sure, I'm done here," the witch croaked as if Ethan's air gag dripped sand down her throat. "I got what I wanted."

"You won't leave the compound with Andre." Ethan folded his oh-so-delectable muscular arms across his toned chest.

"You sure about that?" Imelda grinned, a wicked-witch-of-the-west stretch of her mouth. Her smile, distorted by witch-air, sent ants crawling over Sage's skin.

Ethan's warlock errand boy shoved his way through the knot of waiting warlocks into the room. "The Wilde Coven members who were inside the house are caged in a warded circle. Imelda's people have left the covenstead property with Andre." The report was matter-of-fact, just not the facts Sage wanted to hear.

"Where is he?" She landed a death-ray glare on Imelda.

The witch glanced at her old-fashioned wristwatch, tipped her head back. "Long gone in the care of my witches... and *black* warlocks," she crowed. "Now let me go, or the ward on your coven will raze this goddess-forsaken place to your so-called hallowed ground."

"Aspen Wilde said the ward's set on a trigger. The old

bat's telling the truth," Ethan's town-crier warlock said.

"Release me now, and I'll let you all live." Imelda managed a half-assed attempt to wand her arm around the bubble's circumference. "My freedom or your coven's demise. You pick."

Fire sparked off Sage's fingers. Ethan's air magic ignited the tiny sparks. The fireballs evaporated the second they hit the tiles, threads of rippling smoke rising to Sage's ankles.

A long reflective moment passed, well past the time for brainstorming. Sage said, "Release Imelda and escort her off the property. Make sure every last one of her people are off my grounds."

"You made the appropriate choice." Imelda pushed an arm against her air shroud. "Although the other choice would've been... fun."

"When will my house wards dissipate?" Sage invoked an earth spell, splattering Imelda with tiny mud balls, using her own witch-air to pierce Imelda's shroud.

Imelda glowered at the spots of mud stuck to her black clothing. "When I'm off your covenstead."

"How do we know you're not sandbagging us?" Eyes flinty, Rafael pounded a fist on the table.

Imelda's shoulders lifted a fraction, then wilted. "You'll have to trust the process, *boy*."

Imelda hit a risky trigger. No one had called Rafael "boy" in a long time. "Boy" was a not-so-endearment one of Rafael's abusive foster fathers always called him. Sage seized his tight fist, fire joining fire, drizzling to the tiles like mini fireworks.

All was not lost, merely a reset in the game of witch roulette. "Ethan, please release her and kick her ass off my property," Sage commanded.

"I'll check the perimeter. You check on your coven." He bowed his head at her.

Air fluttered the ends of Sage's hair, ruffling the paper decree from inside the trash can. Gwyneira peeled off her skin and lifted off her shoulder, snowy wings pulsating, directing the air magic enclosing Imelda.

Imelda swatted off the air as if sweeping the mud from her clothes. Her black warlock linked their arms, and she took wobbly steps toward the door. Again, Sage noticed time and magic use had taken a faster toll on Imelda than her age dictated. The old bat had used her witchcraft for too much evil throughout her years, and now the heat was on. Was she sick? An idea to leverage when Sage salvaged her birthright and retrieved the most dangerous man in the world.

Ethan's warlocks surrounded Imelda. He stepped around the table toward Sage and whispered in her ear, "This is why you need me."

A frisson of heat fanned her internal fire. Before she absorbed his heat and its implications, he stalked away, a confident swagger in his stride. Rafael growled like a male lion staking a claim on the sole lioness in the pride. Gwyneira flew from atop a tall bookcase and landed on Sage's right shoulder, wings tangling in her loose hair.

Once the room cleared, leaving Sage and Rafael alone, she counted to ten, turned to him. "I'm ready. We need to survey the damage." Gently, she pushed against the boulder of his unmoving body.

"What did he say?" he demanded.

Knowing Rafael's question was inevitable, she replied in a flat monotone, "This is why you need me." No time for his jealousy, not when her coven was suffering from the attack. A shiver worked across her shoulders as her familiar transformed to a tattoo and unfurled its wings across her shoulder blades.

"He's an asshole." Rafael gave way to Sage's gentle shoves and led her out of the room.

At first sight, nothing appeared amiss. The house looked as they'd last seen it, but way too static. Residual magic lanced the air, and magic tingled through the soles of her leather boots, rising off the floor, latching onto the first bodies to absorb it. Warlocks didn't feel magic the way witches did, but Rafael's back went steel-rod straight and sweat dusted his upper lip. Tendrils of air shifted her hair, tickled her cheeks. A puddle of water here and there on the floors revealed evidence of witchcraft gone wild.

An ache bloomed behind Sage's eyes, and an acidic taint gushed in her intestines. She dreaded the damage to her witches and warlocks. They could rebuild the house, reset the wards, heal wounds, yet they held no capability to resurrect the dead.

The scent of witch-fire, earthy, sunshine on a rock in a hot desert kind of way, filled the kitchen and dining hall. Food, pots and pans, and cooking utensils littered the kitchen floor. The covenstead's chef and kitchen staff had vanished. As lower-caste witches, they didn't traditionally engage in much witchcraft, unless they used magic to create scrumptious dishes. No one worked for the coven who didn't possess magic, or a bonded warlock who wielded a witch's magic. Even then, a normal warlock held magic in his soul and his aura, untapped until a witch bound him.

Lethal magic coiled inside Sage, her elements competing for dominance. She stumbled, righted herself, signaled Rafael to step away. The ache blazing behind her eyes now traveled to the back of her skull, down her neck, and across her shoulders. Only a few times in her life had the precarious signs arisen within her. Only one other person she'd crossed triggered the uncontrollable chaos, when she normally kept a handle on her aether. She struggled to quell the magic and bit back a frustrated scream. Gnawing her bottom lip to remain silent, she hoped against hope she was mistaken. Lightning twinkled off her and dispersed a couple feet in front of her. Stars dotted the air above their heads, floating and discharging in tiny explosions. Blue fireballs rolled off her fingers and died on the tiles. Fearing the aether, Gwyneira froze on Sage's upper back, so unnaturally static, the owl felt dead.

"How much magic?" Rafael asked, his voice gruff as he absorbed the magnitude of what happened.

Sage hated that Imelda caught them unawares. Hated that she let her coven down. She'd sooner face the end of the world, especially with the storm she was about to unleash. "More than I've ever experienced in a room, or house for that matter." As well as inside her.

"Then it's bad."

"It's bad," she echoed, fisting her hands against her sides as if to block the magic from escaping. She felt her eyes changing color, cloudy emerald to the darkness of night, silver blistering away the green, radiating around the black of her pupils into her irises. Transformation complete, the fog cleared, and her twenty-twenty vision returned.

They trod along the rear hallway leading to the basement. The closer they approached the triple-steel door, the more witch-fire, brimstone, and myriad other alchemic odors tickled her nose. And the plain old acidic burning of wood, plaster, and plastic. Thank the goddess, no human flesh. The smells worsened, and Sage cupped her hand over her mouth and nose. She raced the last few steps to the door.

Fruitlessly, she recited a spell to dismantle her six wards, but someone had already butchered them. Only Aspen and Marina could kill her wards under risk of life or death. Either Imelda's people crushed them, or the break from the ley lines had. "Open it."

Rafael drew the chain with his keycard from his belt loop, a permanent fixture on every pair of pants he wore.

The sole keycard bypassed the scanner and code. "Use the eye reader and your code."

In response, she slowly turned to him. He jerked back, a look of terror crossing his eyes. He tried to embrace her, but she stepped out of reach, gripped her crossed arms, and rubbed her elbows. Her fingernails bit into her flesh, and she welcomed the pain. Without peering in a mirror, she knew her emerald eyes had turned solid black, rimmed in silver. A phenomenon that occurred when aether magic trampled her inner elements of fire, air, water, and earth and coiled into one ginormous meld. When her internal magic fought for control, and all lost to the mother magic, something that happened the day she'd met Rafael. Releasing aether magic spelled catastrophe at worst, major chaos at best. A glittery silver aura ballooned above their heads, a safe bubble encasing her magic. Encasing it to unleash upon the unsuspecting.

Witch-fire sizzled off Rafael's fingers. A drizzle and a breeze infused with dust chased it to an ineffectual drop to the floor. "Sage." His anguish dented his forehead. They both put another foot of distance between each other.

"The reader won't read my eyes."

"You can't go downstairs." He reached for her, desperate to touch her, but knew one touch could trigger an avalanche of wild magic. One touch could burst the bubble she desperately fought to keep intact. "You need to calm down. Should I get Aspen? A potion or charm?"

She shook her head. Sage wanted his arms around her so bad, she almost threw caution to the wind. He'd saved her the last time and lived through it. He'd absorbed the magic and more. But he also suffered from the aftermath. The next time she'd seen him, she knew without a doubt he was the one for her. There would be no other, even as she continued to use sex to test new warlocks. How stupid did she have to be to string him along when she'd always known they were meant for each other? Her future included a ton of groveling.

The aura bubble swirled, eddied, and began deflating. "The aether's dispersing." She sagged against the wall across from the door. "Go downstairs and check on everyone. I'll follow in a minute."

"What triggered it?"

She lifted her gaze, the fiery ache behind her eyes dissipating. He closed the distance between them and clinched her hand in his. Aether-tainted fire erupted between them, and he took it, more magic than he'd absorbed from her in years. The shock to his system jolted through his body, and he staggered closer to her. She tried to break contact, but she was too late. Refusing to let her go, his grip was ironclad.

"Why, Rafael?" She stamped her foot on the floor. "It was dissipating."

Pain drew his lips tight. "To disburse it faster, or you'll be without magic for days. We can't afford to lose your magic. Or mine." Loss of magic also affected a witch's warlock.

"Now you'll suffer for days from the aether." She cupped his chin. "Is it worth it?"

He flinched, but he didn't yield. "How can you ask? This isn't our first rodeo." He slanted his cheek into her palm. "To erase your pain, yes. You know I'd take all your aether if I needed to. You know I'd die for you."

To her horror, a tear escaped Sage's right eye, and she slapped it off her cheek before he noticed. Tears were for the weak. She dropped her hand to her side. "Well, now you possess a crap ton of magic. Go do something with it. I'll be downstairs when I'm safe." Using her aether magic would hurt him, yet he'd use it if necessary for any coven member.

"I don't like leaving you alone." Rafael gripped his thighs to refrain from touching her again. Which meant he was suffering too much pain.

She rolled her gritty eyes. "Really? Do you see me? Can you feel me? I can kill with a touch."

He expelled a heavy breath in capitulation. "Did Imelda's threat trigger it?" he asked again.

Her gaze ping-ponged, avoiding direct eye contact. "No clue. She didn't directly threaten me. Must be one of Imelda's black warlocks. Or the entirety of black magic. The whole shitshow."

"Son of a black witch. That's all we need." He brushed a kiss across her lips and spun around. The door clicking open and thumping closed signaled his exit. Leaving Sage alone to deal with the aether teaming inside her, trying to reform and separate her elements into their normal buckets.

A niggling doubt surfaced. She scratched her head as if to spur her brain cells. Who or what indeed triggered her aether to slip out of control? The one other person who'd threatened her the first time it happened was snoozing with earthworms.

Chapter 9

*I*melda's warlocks and witches damn well better be gone. Rafael stomped down the stairs to the fortified basement. A balmy breeze whooshed through the electrified air below, blowing the pungent scent of cut grass and loam to him, the leftover magic strengthening as he approached the main basement space. Air swirled through his hair, lifting from the roots off his scalp. The magic flirted with the residual aether attached to him. Apprehension set up shop in his burning gut. If he used Sage's fire against anyone, he dreaded the outcome due to her aether. This time, the aether flirted and poked holes in Sage's witch-fire. A far cry from the devastation of the aether he absorbed the fateful weekend he'd met her. He'd tried to protect her from another witch who'd bullied and endangered her. The aether almost killed him.

Caerwyn danced across his neck, lightly pecking at his skin. In protection mode, the familiar reacted to Sage's aether, afraid to launch off his body. The owl would never leave him, solidifying his link to Sage, especially in this precarious time with Ethan stalking her. Even familiars held jealous streaks.

The moment he stepped around the corner from the dungeon's entry and through the second door, blown wide open, an ominous silence swallowed the remnants of magic flirting with him.

No battle sounds. No wounded cries or moans. Absolute silence.

The warded circle hit his view, witch-air shrouding it, muffling the coven members stuck inside. He took a head count: Sage's sister Aspen and her two cousins Marina and Brianne, Jessica, and Ben, three other distant relative witches, three kitchen witches, and nine warlocks. The usual suspects who hung around the covenstead and occasionally slept in the common bedrooms or the cottages left over from a former campground. Imelda made sure not to ward thirteen witches together. Thirteen witches might have blasted through the warded circle. Everyone appeared intact, but two people were notably absent who should not otherwise be outside on perimeter security.

A couple of witches shouted at him, evidenced by their mouths and hands trying to move in the mud-thick air.

He held up a finger. "Hold on," he mouthed.

The thick air began to dissipate, and the wards splintered with audible whip cracks. True to her word, Imelda released her spell. He checked the gate cameras on his phone app, and her black SUV drove off down the street. The witch-air continued to dissipate, and voices ascended.

Aspen shouted, "Where's Sage? Is she okay?" She stumbled out of the chalk- and salt-marked circle and fell into Rafael's arms.

The other witches and warlocks stepped out of the circle, shaking off thick air clinging to them like cotton balls. All talked at once, surrounding him. Twins, Marina and Brianne, rushed into the dark crevices of the room and began checking the other rooms in the basement. Looking for something... or someone.

"Where's Eden?" he asked Aspen.

"They took her," warlock Ben growled out. "When I get my hands on that bitch witch, I'm gonna slice her throat." His wife and bonded witch, Jessica Wilde, the girls' mother, also Sage's aunt—her mother's twin sister—put a calming hand on Ben, shushing him. Tears glistened in her eyes. Even though Ben wasn't the biological father of Sage's three cousins, he treated them like his own.

Cold sweat pooled at the base of Rafael's spine. "*Who* took her?"

"Imelda's witches, with Andre. Together," Aspen replied.

"What do you mean 'together?'"

"Whatever spell they used to prevent Andre from using his magic snared Eden."

"Scumbag warlock grabbed her in his arms, made sure she got caught in the spell," Ben said.

Rafael's head muddled, ratcheting up the headache from the aether. Contemplating why Andre had abducted Eden, he scanned his people, checking for any visible wounds on the coven members. Did Andre intend to leverage Eden's witchcraft? To use her like he'd wanted to use Willow? At thirty-two, Eden had been married, cheated on, and divorced. A shit ton of baggage. Why would Andre bog himself down with a half-assed air witch who might, no guarantees, compliment his witch-earth and witch-water? Or was she simply collateral damage?

Questions peppered him, and he explained what happened upstairs, excluding Sage's inability to control her aether. "Sage's fine. She'll be here in a sec. The others secured the wards and are checking the covenstead for Helwig laggers."

Before he continued, warlocks and witches parted

around him, and Sage glided to his side.

"Tell me what happened," she demanded. "How did they capture Eden?"

Rafael took her hand, and she didn't resist. The aether had subsided, and she seemed in control again. Her clammy hand, blanched skin, and pinched lips gave testament to her anguish. Her gardenia scent filled his soul with the sweet, zesty green undertones and a tinge of coconut. Acrid brimstone clung to her, marring his scent of heaven, proof of the dissipating aether.

"Simple. Black warlocks breached the exterior side door, herded us into the warded circle. We watched them break the wards on Andre's door," Jessica said.

"How did Eden get caught in the crossfire?" Rafael asked.

"We don't know. One second, she's running up the stairs, the next she followed a silent summoning by Andre," Ben explained. "It was the darndest thing."

Rafael watched Sage and Jessica trade pained and pointed looks, hiding something the rest of the coven didn't understand. Sage held family secrets from him. It was a given. Even though he was her right-hand man, consort, soon-to-be husband, if he had his way, he understood family secrets were exactly what they implied. By the expressions on their faces, no one else appeared to know this secret.

Brianne and Marina raced across the room and flung their arms around Sage and their mother, pushing him from the group hug. The witches and warlocks were groggy, an expected outcome from such powerful magic, which they probably tried to fight. Magic use and abuse had taken its toll.

"Was Eden physically all right?" Sage gave her cousins a last squeeze and broke up their hug. The aether made her cautious, rightfully so, but her distraught cousins didn't appear to notice.

"She seemed okay." Brianne wiped a tear from her right eye.

"Did she fight the compulsion?" Rafael fought the urge to touch Sage. He wasn't sure the aether wouldn't latch onto him again if her emotions snatched control. "Did she deplete her magic?"

"She didn't use magic," Brianne answered, her mother avoiding the questions while she clucked like a momma hen over her twins.

"We need a plan to snag her, first and foremost," Sage commanded, her spine straightening. Color returned to her face as if she'd received a second wind. "Who else is missing? Any injuries? Did they take or destroy anything? Give me the goods."

A flap of white-and-black wings dove up Aspen's left arm beneath her sweater sleeve and fluttered back to her wrist, its head poking out like a turtle. Seagull. Aspen's weird-ass familiar. What witch let a dirty winged rat choose her? If given a choice, he'd choose a faithful dog. The seagull's odd squawking grabbed his attention.

Aspen slapped a hand over the wavering tattoo. "Quit it, Rio."

Something about the gull tripped unease in Rafael. He stepped forward and pried Aspen's hand off her wrist.

"It's *not* Rio. It's *Rico*." Searching, he slowly spun in a circle. "Where's Marty? He broke your bond." The other missing person.

Aspen cried out and stroked Rico, the bonding familiar which belonged to Marty. "Oh, no. I felt a weird jerk on my magic before they captured us. Figured Marty was screwing up another spell. He's always screwing them up, causing him to push and pull on my magic erratically." Panicked, she drilled her gaze among the warlocks peppering the room and trying to temper the negative magic affecting them. "Their protective ward killed our magic. I didn't notice—" A sob jolted through the witch.

The warlocks all stood at attention and waited for his command. He scrolled through the texts he'd received in the last five minutes from the outside security team.

"Quiet," Rafael shouted and read from his screen. "The perimeter wards are in place and the grounds are secure. Ley lines active and intact. Imelda and her people are out the door."

"Including Andre and Eden." Ben stroked the pistol he always kept in a shoulder holster.

"And Marty," Aspen blurted out on a sob. She cooed at her bonding familiar. "Go find him." She stroked the bird's tattoo head. The gull evolving to its inert tattoo form on her arm was problematic. The fact it didn't budge at her command told a story Rafael didn't want to contemplate.

Apprehension prickled over his scalp, but he didn't plan to burst Aspen's bubble if his instincts proved him wrong. "They let you keep your gun?" Rafael asked Ben, hoping to drive everyone's minds off Marty for a moment.

"Didn't do me any good. I shot through the ward, and the air spun the bullet until it dropped to the floor."

"They knew what they were doing," Sage said like she knew Imelda's plan of attack to the nth degree. "I want three warlocks upstairs with all witches. The rest of you search for Marty and Eden in case they're on the grounds. I want Marina to plan on setting additional wards."

Aspen held up her hand, exhaustion paling her skin. "We need at least three witches at full strength to set a new ward. Or you."

"I don't mean now, sis. I mean make a plan." Sage patted her sister's arm. "Everyone's exhausted. We need to replenish our magic, get a good night's sleep. First, we'll strategize and eat a light meal." She eyeballed the chef and the kitchen crew. They didn't waste any time heading up the stairs to the kitchen.

The other witches and warlocks disbursed, their steps slow and dragging. Rafael turned to Sage, patted Aspen on the shoulder. "We'll find him."

"I think he's... dead," Aspen mumbled, her tears coursing anew. "My bond feels broken. I just don't know what it's supposed to feel like."

"You and Marty weren't lovers. Your bond wasn't strong like a lover's bond," Sage replied. "It might mean nothing."

"I'm heading outside. I want to survey damage firsthand, help find Marty. Will you be okay?" Rafael caught and squeezed Sage's hand, dropped it when she wriggled her fingers out of his grip. Residual aether infused him, pain radiating up his arm muscles. Her eyes had returned to normal, and no one in the room noticed. She'd never let on to anyone else that she'd ever lost control of her aether, a major trust issue for a High Priestess.

Sage lifted on her toes and pressed her lips to his briefly, and he breathed her in again, needing to imprint her on his senses. To know she was okay. "I'll be fine. I want to assess my witches, see what we could've done better." She feathered her fingers across his pectorals. "Oh. Find Ethan, and send him in."

Rafael shot burning daggers from his eyes. "How 'bout I send him home?"

"Rafael," she scolded. "We need to hammer out his proposal. It's obvious we need the Ravenwoods' help now."

"Hammer's not the word I'd use." Rafael marched across the cement floor and up the stairs to the rear outer door, his footsteps reverberating in his ears.

Out of habit, he'd usually play with Sage's magic and light the outdoor candles. He refrained, fearing he'd light the entire forest on fire if he attempted to use her aether-infused witch-fire.

The cool evening air hitting him untied aching knots in Rafael's biceps. He inhaled the fragrant and crisp evergreen air and peered at the indigo twilight sky. Clouds scudded across the moon, leaving a faint glow seeping through the patches, enough to see into the gloom of the forest. A light breeze stirred the cedars and redwoods, filling the air with the cleansing camphora and woodsy, balsamic cedarwood scents.

The moment the Black Tide and the Ravenwoods had crashed their life, their world had flipped into a shitshow on the way to a fuck factory. Rafael slammed the door behind him. The last thing he wanted to think about was those black warlock bastards. He needed to do damage control. Should've killed Andre instead of capturing him.

Except Andre's warlocks would've put a bullseye on the Wilde Coven. "Son of a witch's tit." He gestured to two exterior guards heading his direction along the flagstone path cutting through the lawn. Their somber and pained faces gave half the story.

"You found him." He raked his hand across his scalp, dragging fingers hard through the snarls wind magic left behind. He needed to feel the pain to deflect what he guessed they were about to offload.

Both warlocks motioned for him to follow. The Wilde warlocks were a tight group, and if these two had a tough time spilling the words, it didn't bode well. Silent, he followed them, all three of a similar height. They blocked his view until a cedar grove confronted them, and the two warlocks stepped aside to grant him view of a redwood centered in the grove.

Someone had staked Marty to the tree through his forehead, upper chest, and groin. As his gaze landed on the lowest nail, he flinched. Marty's arms dangled at his sides, scrawny legs swinging free against the tree trunk. Water spritzed off his fingers, Aspen's witch-water draining from his body. Scorch marks circled his neck and extended beneath his shirt. At least someone had closed the young man's eyes, but his mouth hung open in mid-yell. No doubt an excruciating, painful yell from the magic that killed him.

"They killed him with magic, the way he wanted to die." Rafael scrubbed his right hand over his face and reached for a bloodied note stuck in the waistband of Marty's singed jeans. He read it in silence.

Rafael,

If we can do this to our own, think what we can (and will) do to Sage, Aspen, Willow and all the Wilde witches and warlocks. Our determination is only metered by our willingness to take charge of the western covens and accept full cooperation from Sage and the Council. See that it happens. Or Marty's unfortunate fate becomes the fate of all. You won't see us coming.

By the way, thank you for the gift of Andre Charlemagne. We won't forget who drove him out of obscurity and into my realm. It might garner a favor or two. Or might not.

Farewell to Marty. May the goddess favor him with super-warlock powers in the afterlife.

No signature on the note, but Rafael recognized Imelda's tightly scrawled cursive, the same handwriting she'd used on the decree.

The urge to kill grew so strong in Rafael, he saw red.

Marty was Imelda's nephew. Her coven shunned him after they'd discovered he lacked significant warlock abilities, measured by her lofty standards. After the young man's own relatives ridiculed his lackluster abilities, Sage gave him a chance. She'd assigned Marty to Aspen for training, but his training sucked up too much of Aspen's time, so Sage never assigned another warlock to her sister.

Fury surfaced in Rafael like a tidal wave. He pivoted around and bumped into Ethan Ravenwood.

Ethan backed up a step. "Imelda?" he asked, his voice somber and respectful of the dead. A warlock death hit them all hard, whether he was a friend, family, or stranger.

Rafael addressed his warlocks. "Take photos, search for evidence, then take him down and carry him to the basement security bedroom. I'll share the news with Sage and the others."

Exhaustion overshadowed his embattled emotions, and he strode away, his footsteps dragging. He shoved the note in his pocket. "You coming, Ravenwood?"

Footsteps caught up to him, remaining a step behind as if in deference to the somber occasion.

"For what it's worth, I'm sorry," Ethan offered.

"Thanks. It means something. Marty was a good kid. Not the sharpest tool in the shed, but he was present. He belonged to our coven in a way that gave him joy. I enjoyed having him around. He was like a little brother."

And no one screws with Rafael's family. Not even Ethan Ravenwood.

Uncertainty surfaced in Rafael's mind. Should he walk from it all and let Ethan have Sage in the way the black warlock wanted? Or could he abide by a third person in his relationship?

Ideas of revenge against the Helwig coven took control, and Rafael shoved everything else in a box to unpack later.

Chapter 10

A deep darkness shadowed the covenstead. Automatic lights flickered on in the great room, the mood as unfathomable and dark as the occasion. The chef had spread a feast of finger foods on the twelve-seater dining room table that opened to the great room, with only three ornate pillars dividing the space. The coven's witches and warlocks were eating and recovering. Alcohol flowed freely. They needed it, whether or not a buzz dulled their minds and pain further. Imelda got what she'd sought and won the skirmish. Doubtful anything else would happen that night. Regardless, double guards protected the perimeter. They'd also invoked detection spells and were installing additional security cameras.

Although Sage had changed into yoga pants and a loose sweater and sat curled against the arm of a cushiony sofa, her body refused to relax. She declined a relaxation potion and set aside a spelled charm bracelet, needing her mind present to work through the myriad emotions zinging through her body, mired in a swamp of madness she hadn't encountered in her brief reign. She refrained from peering into any of the elaborately framed mirrors that decorated the walls amidst the landscape paintings, bringing warmth and mystery to her favorite room of the house. Nothing about her appearance or the room mattered.

Aspen kept flitting around the room, attending to everyone. "Sis, sit down," Sage demanded, unable to hide the exasperation in her tone. "Quit playing mother hen." Her words softened. "They'll find Marty."

Aspen sagged against the sofa arm. "Can't help it. I need to keep my mind busy. I have a bad feeling." She stroked Rico's beak, and it nipped at her finger. "I wish you could talk."

"Why *can't* familiars talk?" Willow hobbled into the room, Evan on her tail. Crutches clattering to the floor, she lunged for Aspen, and they sandwiched Sage between them in a hug. The age-old question remained unanswered. Witches had tried throughout the centuries, but they had no ability to grant powers of speech to their familiars. The question drew snickering, enough to lighten the grim mood, Willow's intended outcome.

"Evan, please find Rafael and Ethan. It's time we talked," Sage ordered the black warlock. Even though he'd broken their bond, he still belonged to the Wilde Coven.

"Sure thing, boss lady." Evan kissed Willow on the top of her head, patted Aspen's shoulder in sympathy, and headed out the French doors to the backyard.

Sage, Aspen, and their cousins gave Willow the download of the day's events.

"What's our plan?" Willow turned to Sage, her nose scrunching up.

"Revenge." Ben strode over from the dining table and brought plates of food to Aspen and Sage, who took them gratefully, even though their appetites had fled.

The patio door opened, and Rafael entered, followed by Evan and Ethan. Pain shadowed their faces. Their news promised to add more weight to plans of retaliation.

Coven members crammed the room to hear Rafael's update. Gratitude filled Sage that so many were still present, alive, and unharmed. Sounds of eating and forced cheerfulness were reduced to a pin-drop.

Rafael took center stage. "Most of you already know Imelda's people abducted Eden. We found Marty, our youngest warlock, dead in the woods." Gasps and sobs erased the anticipation. "It's clear Imelda had him killed to make a statement."

Sage jerked upright on the sofa. "Her own nephew?" Blasted tears once again stung her eyes, and she fought the waterworks. *No unraveling in front of my people!*

Aspen burst out in sobs, and Willow wrapped her sister in a hug, giving her the strength Sage couldn't in that moment. She needed to keep her head clear for the night ahead and not let grief bog her down. Her bitch switch just flipped to the overload zone.

"Marty's in the security barracks downstairs if anyone wants to pay their respects. Everyone else, head to your quarters, except the inner Council. No one leaves the grounds." Not all the witches and warlocks lived in the mansion or in the cozy cabins in the woods, but there were enough beds for the many overnighters. Sage liked a full house, wanted to provide a haven to any witch or warlock connected to her coven. "The situation's volatile until we understand the full extent of Imelda and the black warlocks' plot."

"Won't the Black Tide go after Imelda? Why would they attack the Wilde Coven *now?*" Jessica asked, her voice quivering. "I don't want Eden caught up in that fight either. We need a minute to recover and plan without them hounding us."

"Jessica, honey, sit." Ben guided her to the overstuffed armchair across from Sage. A wonderful warlock to have on her team, Sage appreciated his thoughtfulness and levelheadedness. After Sage's mother died, Jessica surrendered her claim as High Priestess of the Wilde Coven. The witch was too emotional, didn't always think straight, and zoomed at full throttle without considering the consequences. Ben leveled her, a perfect witch and warlock duo. No one questioned it when Sage inherited the role of the Wilde High Priestess. The coven craved young blood at the helm who'd remain in position for a long while. She never let her emotions dictate her movements, thoughts, and actions. With Imelda poisoning the well, Sage may just hit eight points on the Richter scale.

The other witches and warlocks not on the Council, which only included family members and their warlocks, disbursed, and a tense silence hovered over the room. The retreating clink of silverware on plates and empty glasses lessened the severity of the silence.

Ethan hung back, standing next to Evan and Willow. "Do you want me to leave?" Subdued, he shuffled his feet, a far cry from his previous ego trip.

"No," Rafael and Sage said in tandem.

Sage's eyes rounded, and she tipped her head toward her consort. Had Rafael recognized the benefits of a true Ravenwood alliance? Had he discovered a way around Ethan's insane demand? Surely, he'd never accept the black warlock's terms and conditions.

A kitchen witch brought loaded plates for Rafael and Ethan, who both set their plates aside.

"Thank you. The kitchen staff can retire for the night." Sage rose off the sofa. Needing to busy her hands, she stacked dirty plates and utensils on the utility cart, until Rafael's hands landed on her shoulders, massaging and calming.

"We don't have to do this now. Tomorrow will come soon enough." He kissed the skin beneath her ear, his breath balmy. Anticipation washed goosebumps in waves down to her toes.

She turned, squeezed his hands, and addressed the waiting inner Council and the two Ravenwoods. "First order of business is to negotiate Eden's return." She held up her hand to forestall the rants her Council prepared to unleash. "We go in under a truce. If Imelda refuses, then we go full Ninja on them."

"What will we offer her for Eden's return?" Jessica asked. "Marty's... gone. No leverage there."

"I say no negotiation." Ethan kinked his head to the side, rubbed his temple.

Evan gave his brother a meaningful look not lost on Sage.

"You have a better idea?" Rafael grumbled. "That doesn't involve pilfering another Wilde witch."

"Care to share?" she asked Ethan.

"Can we talk in private?" He stepped toward her, nudged Rafael's arm. "Both of you."

Rafael folded his arm around her waist as if to ward off Ethan's cooties.

"By all means." Sage led the way into the forest room.

Pictures hung askew on the walls and floor. The cyclone had upended every item not bolted or tied down. The door clicked shut on the trio. Ethan's cologne mixed with Rafael's, creating a chaos of sensation inside her senses. One didn't dominate the other, but they complimented each other, stirring up Sage's hormones. She'd dabbled in threesomes before, but never with Rafael. He refused to indulge. Hated that she did. Now her monogamy brought him no small amount of joy. How could she upset their developing bubble of forever together? *Stupid hormones holding my brain hostage!*

"Look, Ethan," she said, "if this is about your offer—"

"No." He crossed his arms, the muscles in his biceps

bunching, and propped his shoulder against the door. "My offer's temporarily off the table. I'll help you retrieve Eden and re-capture Andre free of charge. Afterward, we'll discuss what we can do for each other."

"Does *free of charge* include your entire coven and allies?" Rafael cracked his knuckles, one by one, the sound echoing in the decimated room.

"Absolutely. It's too treacherous to all witches and warlocks, black or otherwise, for Andre and Imelda's alliance. I saw what she did today... to one of her own. Can't happen again to any Wilde or Ravenwood coven member. We're the strongest covens, and she drilled right through the Wildes as if you were human children."

Snow crawled across her breasts, tickling and spearing lust within her. "Well, Marty wasn't exactly one of hers." Sage held her arms over her breasts to subdue the familiar who was ready to launch itself at Ethan. "He didn't agree with her rules, and his defection caused a rift in the family."

"What happens when Marty's parents find out?" Ethan asked.

"Imelda raised him. Stoner dad and mother both skipped out ten years ago. No contact since. I doubt they'd care or even attend his funeral," Sage explained.

"Do we have a deal?" Ethan asked. "We'll discuss the long-term alliance when all is settled."

"What's your return ask?" Rafael gritted his teeth together loud enough for Sage to hear them grind.

"Long term, peace amongst us. Better access to Andre for all witches and warlocks to learn his secrets." He paused, scratched his head. Pain flitted across his eyes. "Short term, I need to quiet the voices in my head."

Sage clutched her neck with one hand. "What? Voices?" She gasped. "You're a psychic warlock?" Air magic aided psychic abilities and vice versa. Air helped connect to the mind, intelligence, telepathy, psychic powers. She always asked every air witch she met if they had psychic powers. Ethan had slipped by her curiosity.

"What the hell?" Rafael's mouth hung ajar.

Ethan sagged against the door and nodded. "It's never happened before, not in my dealings with Andre. I think I have a telepathic link to Andre through a witch. Someone in Imelda's coven, maybe. I don't know. The thoughts are jumbled."

"You're reading our minds?" The sneer in Rafael's tone mimicked his expression.

"No. I can only read a mind of someone I've connected with. I've never connected with another psychic, though." Ethan rubbed his jaw, his hands sliding to scrub his eyes.

Blood danced in Sage's veins, and she eased closer to Rafael, her shoulder touching his muscular chest. A psychic witch, or in this case warlock, could enhance their magical powers and vice versa. She literally felt her eyes sparkle as she gazed upon Ethan in a new light. A very rare and sought-after light. Game changer.

Chapter 11

Sage sent Ethan home with the promise she'd involve him in revenge planning tomorrow. She desperately needed to deconstruct the secret he'd shared and whatever psychic connection to another witch—or Andre—that could give them insider knowledge. Ethan hadn't spelled out what he was plucking from the psychic's mind but said he'd share what he gleaned when he sorted it out himself. Tomorrow couldn't come soon enough.

Rafael finished his security checks and entered their bedroom. His presence calmed her jagged edges. She stared out the window at her domain, once sacred and secured, now breached and nebulous. Strands of fairy lights lit up the backyard, sparkling on the trees and bushes like diamonds. They'd remain on throughout the night for extra security.

Rafael approached from behind, his welcome reflection in her window. She sucked in a breath and a heatwave enveloped her. She didn't even have to turn and regard him in the flesh to appreciate his bare chest, defined abs, and muscular arms. Colorful vines, branches, and flower tattoos twined both upper arms, crawled across his shoulders, and traveled down his back. Goddess, she loved this man who made her desire swell from his mere reflection.

He embraced her, locked his arms under her breasts. She liquified into his hard warmth. His sandalwood, citrusy scent fueled her tank, and she languished in the scent and feel of this god among warlocks. Among men.

He trailed kisses across the nape of her neck to her right shoulder. Witch-fire sparked in her, unimpeded residual magic after tapping out her reserves from her aether overload. The fire hit Rafael, his body bucked against her, and he gasped, his breath fiery against her sensitive flesh. She tipped her head to the side to give him free access to her neck, adjusted herself so his hands now cupped her breasts. He rubbed his thumbs over her nipples, turning them into hard, sensitive bullets. A slow shiver worked its way up from her toes.

"Tell me your secret," he whispered in her ear. Not a question, not quite a demand. "Sounds like I need to know."

The luxurious moment burst, and she pushed out a cry. Just one moment was all she wanted, and he stuck a pin in the balloon. He'd never ask her to vent her spleen if it wasn't for the good of the coven or for her safety. His intuition was impeccable. She had long awaited this day.

Reluctantly, Sage slid his hands off her breasts and wiggled out of his arms. She faced him, sucked in another breath as her gaze raked him up from the fringe of dark hair at his waistband to the five o'clock shadow on his cheeks. She tipped forward and licked his right nipple until it pebbled beneath her tongue. Caerwyn's dappled wings beat against her cheek, and the owl fluttered to Rafael's left shoulder. Sage caressed his toned abs, her fingers reaching toward the waistband of his jeans, the material preventing her from dipping lower. Rafael sucked in his stomach, giving her an invitation, despite his question. Instead, she withdrew her hand and cupped his cheek. "I love you."

"Quit stalling. Tell me what's in the crypt." He tangled his hand in her long, loose hair and tugged her closer, tilting her head back. His lips landed on hers and possessed her. Lips molded tight, tongues tangoing in a greedy dance. His unique reply to her three words filled her soul.

She tasted brandy on his tongue and grew intoxicated from his expert kiss. She was wrong about her earlier thoughts that his kisses weren't new and exciting. Every moment in his presence was an exciting first.

His arms enclosed her before her weak knees dumped her on the floor. His firm lips demanded, and if she didn't give him a rain check, he'd take her to heights that'd kill further conversation, despite his need for answers. And she didn't want him this way. She didn't want quick and angry. They'd both regret their actions afterward. They always had time for a quickie but never let anger in their bed, or on the chair, or in the dozen other places they made love.

She pressed her hands flat against his blazing-hot chest, nipped his full bottom lip, and drew away. Breathless, wanting so much more, she emitted a frustrated groan.

"Your vulnerabilities and strength are love to me. I need to know how to protect them." He picked her up, carried her to his armchair across from the bed in front of the window, and nestled her on his lap to allow her a moment to recover. "Sage," he growled against her head. "Tease." His arms locked her against him, his hardness practically buried in her butt crack, if not for the layers of clothing between them.

"You want in the crypt or not?" She stilled, not wanting to incite his lust further. Time and place. But she needed him inside her to help drive the residual aether out. Sex promised to relax her. The more relaxed, the more she'd return to her normal self.

"That's all it took for your deep, dark secret. Just one kiss?" he said.

One kiss? Did he not know how his mere touch set her on fire, after all these years? His fire, not hers. She truly believed he carried his own brand of fire the way he exercised her witch-fire so effortlessly, like no other warlock. Surely, he jested. She laughed, a full, husky sound that surprised her after the long, horrific day.

"It's Wilde family stuff," she said, preparing him.

"I gathered, or you wouldn't have withheld it." He cleared his throat of the gruffness his desire caused.

"What Ethan said..." she started, and Rafael threw his head back against the chair, growling in frustration. "It's not about *him*, but it's related to his *condition*, so to speak."

"Condition?" He snickered. "The warlock has a condition? What, warts? A pencil dick?"

"Someone's in a better mood." She playfully whacked his arm. "You heard him. He's psychic with telepathy. You know how rare that is?"

"So he says. Hard to believe anything that trips outta that dude's mouth."

"Be serious." Sage pushed up off his lap, drilling her bare toes in the soft density of the wool rug.

"Sage." He knocked his head on the chair's backrest. "I'm just trying to lighten a piss-dark day." His exhaustion emerged in his curt voice. Maybe sex was off the table for the night despite her desperation to feel him inside her. He held out his hand. "Come. I promise I'll let you spill your guts without my snark."

Sage contemplated the daring offer of sitting on his lap again. Nope. Way too enticing... and for what she planned to tell him. She sat in the other armchair, a floral, painted accent table between them. "Your body's too tempting." She stretched out her arm. His large, strong hand enveloped hers, and their witch-fire mated, dripping embers that dissipated before hitting the rug.

She swallowed hard. "Like I said, a witch—or warlock—with psychic abilities is über-rare. Very sought after. Hazardous to many, or a boon to others. Their witchcraft benefits their psychic powers and vice versa. But it's also dangerous to the psychic. Witch powers—their own or from another—can kill their minds. I can guarantee few beyond Ethan's family know about his abilities. No way Andre knew. Him revealing his secret shows his absolute trust in us." She squeezed his hand.

"Still doesn't make me want to accept his offer. I'm not into threesomes. Never will be." Lines etched Rafael's forehead, but a slight smile tilted the corners of his lips.

"No, me neither," Sage agreed. "It makes him a menace to us and the coven. If others know, they'll hunt him down."

"Exactly!" Rafael shouted, his wide grin exhibiting his glee.

"But it's manageable." Teasing him, she pinched his hand between his thumb and forefinger.

"How? If our two covens know, others are bound to know. How is it manageable?"

"Eden is a psychic air witch." Her right eyebrow winged up in challenge, waiting for the bomb to reach its short destination. "Her sisters don't even know."

Rafael jumped up from the chair, snatching his hand out of hers. "Are you kidding me? You didn't bother telling me this important detail about the nature of *your* witches? She needed better protection. We could have staved off this catastrophe with the right security."

Sage cringed but let him get his tirade on the table.

"Damn it, Sage." Rafael stomped across the room, his fists furling and unfurling. "I should've been privy to that particular Wilde secret. I'd have locked her in a steel cage."

He stopped pacing near her chair, glaring down at her, his face softening when he saw tears gather in the corners of her eyes. "Again? You don't do tears. What gives?" He sagged in his chair and turned to her, keeping the table between them as if he needed to protect her from him. "Talk to me, babe. I'll zip it."

"You have no idea how many times I've said the same to Eden and Jessica and wanted to tell you." Sage fingered the stupid crocodile tears from her eyes. *What gives with the rampant hormones lately?* "I agreed to hold the secret, agreed not to treat Eden any different from the other witches. No cage. No coddling. She wanted it that way and accepted the consequences."

"We could've protected her without the world learning her secret."

"Wasn't my secret to blab. I did my best to keep her safe, to withhold her from certain assignments without showing favoritism."

"That's why Ben's always shadowing her when he isn't with Jessica." Rafael tapped his fingers on his knees.

"I compromised. No one questioned him since he's her step-father." She paused, picked at the cerulean polish on her thumbnail. "I planned to use her to glean information from Andre's mind about the black warlocks, his plans, everything. The perfect strategy to gain an edge. What happened today wasn't her fault. It could've been any witch. She merely sat in the crosshairs."

"I disagree. Andre played her. What if he manipulated her from his mind? What if *he's* psychic?"

"I'm pretty sure Ethan's connected to Eden," she whispered, her mind swirling into the new territory psychics represented. "Strange world, two, maybe three rarities in our midst."

"What did Ethan say again?"

"He believes he'd connected to a Helwig witch. Her

thoughts made little sense to him. He said nothing about a connection to Andre. All the witnesses in the dungeon believed Andre held Eden in a witchcraft thrall." The impeccable polish on her long fingernails became the focus of her distraction as she continued picking at them.

Rafael reached across the divide and took her wrist in a loose clasp. "Cut it out. Are you jonesing for another manicure?" Lightening the mood, his smile sent a quiver rushing through her veins. She turned her hand and linked her fingers in his, a perfect meld of strong and delicate, light and tanned skin.

"You know how good you are to me?" she asked.

"Don't you forget it." His grin eased her darker mood, knocked her thoughts sideways.

Wistfulness toyed with her desire. Accepting Ethan's offer threatened to change their dynamic forever. Or kill it. "Never, love." Sage stood, inches out of Rafael's reach, and slipped her yoga pants over her hips. They cascaded down her legs and puddled at her ankles. Her gaze slurped up Rafael's face, his darkening eyes, and lower to the instant erection bulging out his pants. Her slow perusal took in his demanding erection, up his chiseled chest, to his square jaw and full, kissable lips. Caerwyn swooped down his torso from his shoulder and preened for her attention. Tattoo feathers invitingly slithered beneath the waistband of his pants.

Kicking aside her pants, she licked her lips. Rafael groaned and adjusted his tightening pants.

"Are you angry?" she asked, slipping her hand inside her sweater and cupping her right breast, the motion exaggerated through the material.

"No," he said hoarsely, already teetering on the edge. He unbuttoned and unzipped his pants. The sliding rasp of his zipper fed her desire.

"Are *you* angry?" He adjusted his erection in the crotch

of his pants.

"Far from it." She slipped her sweater up and over her head in one fell swoop, revealing her bare breasts, nipples hard and waiting. Desire raged through her, scorching her.

Rafael groaned and shimmied his hips to slip his pants off his butt.

She reached forward, clenched both his wrists. "Let me."

"Sage... I can't hold on much longer." His breathing grew ragged.

"Are you sixteen again?" she queried, everything in her quaking with awareness and expectation.

"I'm whatever age you want me." His lust-laden eyes glimmered with unsated need. "I just need to be inside you."

"We're of the same mind. But I'm in control." She released his wrist, and his ass bucked him up off the chair. Careful of his delicate hardness, she slipped his pants down to his boots. A moment of indecision blasted her when her gaze met his very straining erection.

Before she decided her next move, he grabbed her waist, drew her closer until she straddled him. Fiery skin met fiery skin. Sage wiggled her fingers, sprinkling witch-water to cool them off. Inhaling through her mouth, she lifted up and guided him inside her, and they both cried out. She flung her head back, and he cupped her outthrust breasts, his thumbs working magic on her aching nipples. Four deep thrusts up, down, and he came deep inside her, muffling his savage cry against her shoulder. He bit her neck, licked the skin, and stole her breath when his mouth found hers. She ground herself on him, and her orgasm hooked her hard and fast. She took his panting breaths into her own mouth.

Witch-fire erupted off them, a quick blaze and smoke evaporating in a drizzle of witch-water. The searing intensity spiraled through her, quelling the darkness clouding her day. One last kiss and swirl of her tongue around his and she slumped against him, slick chest to slick chest. His arms locked her in so tight, not even air had a chance.

"I'll never tire of this. Or us," he said. "I will always want you and you alone."

"I'll never give you up, you know," she responded. "We'll find another way."

He pressed kisses to her head, his lips hot even through her thick hair. He cinched his arms even tighter, as if afraid she'd vanish. But when his arms loosened a tad, and he slipped out of her wet heat, a thread of grief took its place.

Chapter 12

Sated and exhausted, Sage had fallen asleep in Rafael's arms on the chair. When she awoke at seven-thirty in the morning, she lay naked in bed, a sheet covering her up to her stomach. Par for the course, Rafael awakened at the butt crack of dawn for his security patrol and commune with nature, or whatever else an early riser did. Sage didn't have the experience. Now she didn't have the luxury of soaking up the new day already creating glowing stripes across the wool rug through the slanted blind slats.

Rich, dark roasted coffee teased the air. Plucking the sheet over her breasts, she sat up, her back against the padded headboard. Just one more moment before she needed to adult. To plan a coup against Imelda and her black warlock clan. No specific rescue plans sprang to mind except the idea of using Ethan's connection to Eden to their advantage. Sage sighed. *Too many freaks, not enough circus cages.*

Rafael nudged open one side of the double doors, two very large mugs of steaming ambrosia in his hands.

"I couldn't love you any more if I tried." She reached for the mug he offered. The ceramic scalded her fingers, joining the fire partying inside her. "Thank you."

Rafael perched on the edge of the bed and planted a lingering kiss on her lips. "Love you too." He drew away.

"Are we secure?"

"We survived the night intact."

She took a tentative sip of her steaming coffee. "I don't know how to confront this shitstorm."

His free hand landed on her thigh, heavy and secure. An unusual unrest and familiar guilt-tinged sorrow squeezed her heart. His silence indicated his agreement with her assessment.

"I've changed. Willow has awakened her magic and joined the coven, and we have a Wilde-Ravenwood alliance to hammer out. I captured Andre first and exposed the black warlocks to the witchworld at large." She defended her shitstorm.

"Maybe too little too late. You've lost witches. You haven't opened the coven to new blood."

His words hit home, a topic they've previously discussed, which she always dismissed. Look where it'd gotten her. "You're saying I'm a freaking failure," she bit out. "My mother would be so disappointed in me." Sage and her sisters had spent their childhood play-acting the High Priestess role, mimicking their mother. Even though they all believed Jessica would inherit the role if anything happened to their mother, they played and trained for it. Their mother died and Jessica passed on the throne. Sage had already proven herself in their coven, had already shown her mental, personality, and witchcraft strength. Her university business and finance degrees also gave her the smarts to run the organization from a business and financial standpoint.

"No, you're not a failure, and your mother would be

extremely proud of the job you've done. You've made a name for your toughness, your empathy, your fairness. A little slide off the rails hurt no one. But you haven't kept up with the times."

"I've let the old ways smother me into thinking my ways remained modern. I've become weak. Screwing every warlock under the sun. Who does that anymore?" She scrunched up her face, feeling the tightness to her eyes.

"You aren't the only High Priestess who practices the old ways, your rightful prerogatives." His grimace proved his loathing of her choices. "You ended all that warlock... business, right?"

She pushed out a heavy sigh, gathered her tangled hair in a bunch, and shoved it over her right shoulder. "Yes, Rafael. I no longer gauge a potential warlock's magic and strength by having sex with him."

Although she'd found pleasure in the sex, it was a chore and a necessary evil. A way to determine an unbonded warlock's strengths and the magic element he may brandish best, by connecting at a core level when most vulnerable during sex. The act gave a powerful witch illumination on his witch pairing based on his potential. Or it would determine that he wasn't a warlock or a good fit within the coven. Sage had to first connect to the warlock in a visceral way. If she didn't connect, then she skipped the step. She certainly didn't sleep with every unbonded warlock who crossed paths with the Wilde coven. And she never had sex with a warlock more than once. These days, they didn't run across many potential warlocks, and she'd left the job to other willing witches in the coven. Or they just took their chances on a warlock. It had been the witchworld's way for centuries, and she excelled at it. However, monogamy with Rafael was too important, too sacred to continue old school ways.

"I haven't sexed it up with anyone but you in two

years," she continued, needing to reassure him. "When the other High Priestesses changed and became monogamous, I might have crawled over the line, but I made it."

"Kicking and screaming." He chuckled.

"The only screaming I was doing was when you were buried inside me." She grinned. "You're the only one."

"Then marry me. It'll show your strength, your willingness to change. Start recruiting powerful witches from outside. Your mother was progressive, and she never gauged a warlock by using sex once she hooked up with your father. She let him co-rule as well." His eyebrows arched. "A warlock ruler? How 'bout that? We can do it too."

Sage groaned, knocked her head against the headboard. "I slammed the brakes on her progression and fell backward to my great-grandmother's era. What have I become? What about Ethan's proposal? We can't advance until we sort it out. I don't know how to integrate black warlocks in my ranks. I refuse to allow them to rule my witches, or any witch."

Rafael angled his face, mere inches from her own. "I just asked you to marry me and that's all you got?" He set his mug on the nightstand, took her mug, and it clunked against his. He caged her between his arms, palms flat on the headboard.

"You did, didn't you?" Sage shied away from marriage. Feared marrying Rafael only to lose him. The devastation would be too great to bear. If she never married him, it somehow might make the devastation less. *As if. What stupid rock bonked me in the head on the way to my life?* She cupped his cheek, and he leaned into her palm. "Can we table marriage talk until we sort out our coven life?"

He slicked his tongue across her lips, prodding them open. "Agreed. I won't wait any longer, though." He kissed her, and she fell into his kiss, which promised everything she'd always wanted. The life she wanted.

He broke away, leaving her desperately seeking air. "How can I refuse when you bring me heaven every day?" she asked. He handed her the mug filled with her favorite French vanilla–laced coffee. "I meant you and your lips are my heaven, silly."

"No, you didn't." He smirked, dangled his legs over the side of the bed. "Ravenwood's on his way. Evan spent the night with Willow, so he's already here." Just the word "Ravenwood" on Rafael's tongue sounded like his coffee had made a second appearance.

"You now see why Ethan's offer is enticing? For the first time in my life, I'm willing to admit help would be… nice."

"We don't need him and his stupid-ass offer. Why does his coven's help come with strings? We help them, they help us. What's wrong with equal compromise?"

"Because he knew he'd get a rise." Contemplative, she sipped her coffee, the caffeine fueling her and easing her encroaching headache.

"Not that kind of rise." Rafael slugged down his coffee.

"I'm sure he believed I was a no-brainer. You know, my lovely, tarnished reputation and all preceding me."

"Nope. You're Glenda the good witch now. He can just cool his jets."

"With Imelda and black warlocks rising from the dead, we need the help," she insisted.

"We don't need his help with a side order of fuckery. We'll beef up our wards, get back in the good graces of the other covens once we discover what Imelda promised them."

"What then? We never leave the covenstead? Black warlocks will always be on the prowl. See how easy Andre attached his spell to Willow for months and possibly connected with Eden. Now Ethan's connected to Eden. I can't overlook the implications. He can help us get her back and hopefully secure Andre, too."

"Remember strings?"

"Rafael." Sage slapped her hand on the jacquard comforter. "He won't insist. His offer's a joke. He already said he'd help us snag Eden, *then* talk long-term alliance. I'll change his mind."

"I can't marry you if you're hooked up with another warlock."

Sage groaned and rolled her eyes. "Stop, will ya? I'm not hooking up with him."

"So you'll marry me? I expect fidelity. I'm just sayin'." Rafael grinned at her, a grin that would've dropped her to her knees if she'd been standing. A grin that caused a multitude of witches to flirt with him over the years she'd known him. A grin she'd missed lately.

A knock thudded on the door, and Willow popped her head in, averting her eyes from Sage's half-naked body. "Time's a-wastin', sis. Breakfast is served, and we have a rescue mission to plan. Ethan and Evan are raring to go. The whole Ravenwood clan is setting up camp outside."

Sage's jaw dropped. "They're here already? We don't even have a plan."

"Not just the Ravenwoods, but other Black Tide defectors." Willow held up her hand to forestall Sage's outrage. "Don't worry, Rafael and Ethan vetted them. Get your hiney downstairs." Willow exited stage left, the door shutting on her butt.

"What's going on?" Sage shifted toward Rafael.

"I get up with the crows. I had time."

"Not what I meant. You didn't clear it with me."

Rafael shuffled his feet. "Really? We're back to you calling the shots. What happened to progress, equality?"

"Guess I need to recruit more witches to put you warlocks in your place. There. There's your evolution, opening the coven to outsiders, fresh blood." Sage shoved the covers aside and stretched out her arms, the kinks in her back and shoulders. Satin shimmied down her naked body, sending goosebumps chasing the sheet. Rafael's wide-eyed gaze chased those goosebumps and landed at the vee of her thighs. She sauntered to him. A darkening shade of chestnut blackened his eyes. When he reached for her, she backed up a step and shook her head, a sly smile belying her inner turmoil. "Sorry, Charlie. I have business to attend to, witches to destroy, black warlocks to castrate."

Rafael winced. "Thanks for killing the mood." He placed his hand over his bulging crotch, as if she was queuing him up for the castration party.

Gliding past him, she thrust out her boobs and slowly licked her lips. He swatted her ass, and the sting shivered up her spine. "By the way, Willow needs her coven initiation."

"She's family. Why? She's always belonged to the coven."

"Formality. To show the coven she's a true Wilde witch, a member of our ruling Council."

"It can wait." He cricked his neck left to right. "Everyone's stoked her magic's emerged. She *is* already a respected member, always has been, even if she didn't know it."

"I'm so glad you never slept with her when you were chasing her around." Sage winked.

"Not even tempted. Not when I have you. Jeez, you asked me to do it to make it look like we weren't so tight, hoping she'd side with me and join the coven."

"I know. I know. Okay, we'll do it during the spring equinox festival." A plan formed in her mind. Dangerous. Lethal. More dangerous than anything she'd ever executed. She needed all her witches on deck, including Willow, despite her sister's untried, emerging magic. All her witches needed to trust Willow. Because if Sage failed and made the ultimate sacrifice, the Wilde Coven leadership might fall to Willow and Evan.

Chapter 13

Rafael reluctantly left Sage to shower alone, despite her suggestive looks and the lingering scent of her. If he joined her, they'd not be quick about it. Lately, quick was all they'd had. He wanted, no, needed, a long night with Sage. No meetings to jet to, no desperate phone calls and texts, no black warlocks to deal with, no distractions.

Her little lap dance last night had to suffice, even though she'd whetted his appetite. No way in hell did he have plans to share her with any warlock, let alone Ravenwood. Ravenwood could plug his blow hole. Sage had more than enough stacked on her toppling plate that already reduced their time together.

Thank the goddess, Willow's powers had finally emerged. Once she finished law school, she'd be ready to accept her rightful coven duties. As coven healer, Aspen had no room for more. With Marty gone, she'll drown herself in her research and alchemy. Now more than ever, he needed to approach the warlock he'd discovered at the compound pharmacy. Fresh blood. And karma had no deadline.

He slogged down the wide, curved staircase, his boots thumping on the stone floor at the bottom. Voices escalated from the great room. Too many voices, and his head already thundered from the aether still creating havoc inside him. Although he'd eaten breakfast, an empty ache refused to abate in his stomach. Unnatural fire rimmed the ache like an intense case of indigestion. Like the one and only other time Sage's aether had awoken something inside his core. As if he possessed his own magic. He rubbed his middle, flinched at stimulating the pain.

Aspen drooped on a cushioned bench in the wide hallway, head clamped between her hands. Her ever-present tote bag containing potions, charms, and other tools of a healer's trade lay on the floor by her feet. Water dripped off the wall and continued dripping off Aspen's fingers, one drop at a time.

"Aspen. You okay? Need anything?" He rested a gentle hand on her shoulder.

She canted her head, her eyes red and puffy, and pulled her silent earbuds from her ears. "Hey, Rafael. Just taking a breather from the chaos."

"You don't need to be here, you know. Everyone will understand."

"Yes, I do. I'm a Wilde sister. It's my duty."

"Aspen." He breathed her name on a sigh. The Wilde witches never shirked their duties, even in the grimmest of times. The residual aether sent a bolt of fire down his arm, and his hand trembled on her shoulder.

Eyes crinkling, she studied him. "Are *you* okay?"

He refused to divulge what'd happened to Sage last night, not sure how much her sisters knew about the aether. Sage's secret to tell.

He shrugged, removed his hand. "Headache."

She searched her bag, produced a small cannister, and

handed him a couple square gummies. He rolled them between thumb and finger. "My newest creation. Gummies for every potion. They'll make you feel better."

"How much better?"

She bumped her shoulder against his upper arm. "For pain relief. Nothing more. They're not CBD- or THC-laced. They taste good too." Her smile fell flat in the grief ravaging her smooth, pale face.

"Did you take some for yourself?"

"No. They can't easily erase my pain." She hid her face behind her hair while she returned the container to her bag and wiped tears from her eyes.

Rafael popped the gummies into his mouth. Cherry burst on his tongue, and he gave her an appreciative wink, trying to lighten the mood. "You killed it. I could eat a handful."

He gave the witch an awkward hug, prolonging it until her final sniff against his shoulder. He composed himself and headed to the great room, Aspen riding his coattails. The entire coven and over a dozen black warlocks filled the room, sitting on every available surface. Separate, awkward groups of Ravenwoods and Wildes stood in corners warily eyeing each other. The noise level rose to the high-beamed ceiling. The morning light poured in from two walls of windows in the room, light settling on the plethora of plants strategically placed throughout the room. Rafael had no clue how their earth witches brought the gardens inside the room and kept it alive and thriving. A fire blazed in the large rock-faced fireplace, snapping and crackling, joining the clamor.

He nodded at Ethan and Evan, noted an older gent next to them. On second glance, he recognized Ethan's father from the photo Evan had shown him. The most remarkable thing he noted was that not one Ravenwood witch had joined the group. Didn't they allow their witches out of the house? Or maybe Ethan's offer didn't include the use of Ravenwood witches.

Before his brain tripped into rat holes, the noise level dropped to nothing, and the light touch of Sage's fingertips landed on the small of his back. As always, she stole the breath from every man in a room, none more so than his own. Her coven gave deference to her as their leader by their obedience to silence when she joined a meeting.

Sage rubbed his back and shifted in front of him. She wore a miniscule, form-fitting, sleeveless dress and thigh-high black boots. He knew this outfit, the cleavage it revealed, and he licked his lips from just visualizing her body beneath the clothes. The outfit represented an ode to her feminine, sexy side. She chose her clothes deliberately, but he wasn't sure why this outfit, this day, unless her vulnerabilities needed a boast. Or she merely wanted every Ravenwood warlock to worship at her feet. In that moment, he didn't mind. Because she was all his. He stifled the urge to touch her, to haul her against his body and wrap her in his sphere of comfort. This was her moment to rule, and he didn't want to show any action countering her leadership.

He didn't know if marriage would change things between them or if she really meant to take the coven in more modern, progressive times under the current witchworld upheaval, regardless of Ravenwood's offer. But he held high hopes they'd share equal footing in their joint leadership.

"Good morning," Sage projected her words to the crowd. "I want Council members to meet me in the forest room, including the top-level Ravenwood warlocks. Enjoy your breakfast and your free time. Rest. Soon we'll have a plan to extricate Eden and Andre from the Helwig covenstead." Sounds of dissent dampened the eagerness to seek revenge. Her coven was raring to go hillbilly apeshit on Imelda and her people. She held up her hand, and the room quieted. "Don't worry, you'll all have a hand in avenging Marty. You'll all have a part to play. Afterward, we'll celebrate our success in grand style."

Rafael couldn't see her smile. However, the return smiles of gratitude provided proof. To have their High Priestess bestow a smile, a glimpse, a touch, with her words and action, fed their people. Goddess alive, he loved this woman with every fiber of his being. He touched his hand to the small of her spine, needing the contact to temper him.

The Ravenwoods remained aloof and wary. Except Ethan and Evan. How many Ravenwood warlocks agreed to join the Wilde Coven? Rafael had a hard time reading their corners of the room.

Sage nodded at the Ravenwoods and spun on her heels. "Where are all their witches?" she murmured to Rafael.

"Wondering the same. Wish I had my own psychic abilities. Glad no one's reading my mind."

She pressed her palm to his chest. "Thank the goddess Ethan can only read a connected mind. You'd feel it if he'd connected to you." The volume in the room escalated to a cacophony. The crowd disbursed, and they returned to their breakfast. An excited jitter permeated the room. A couple Ravenwood warlocks joined a group of witches sipping coffee on the patio.

"Remains to be seen." Rafael fixed Ethan with a laser-like stare, and he voiced choice words in his head to test the black warlock's telepathy. *"Hey, Ravenwood. Before we meet, join Sage and me for a threesome. I'll let you have her first. While I watch. Raise your right hand and slap yourself upside the head if you're hearing me."* Nothing changed in Ethan's demeanor, and he didn't budge a muscle while speaking to his younger brother and father.

"Unless he's made of stronger mettle than I gave him credit for, he can't read me. No man would hit the kill switch on what I just offered." Rafael's lips traveled to her forehead where he planted a chaste kiss. "Let's go plan a revolution."

☪ ☪ ☪

The family witches and a few older Wilde warlocks made up the combined Council. Ethan and Evan sauntered into the forest room behind Sage and Rafael, the older Ravenwood man in tow. Cleaning elves had straightened the room already. Only a missing wall mirror showed evidence of yesterday's chaos.

"I don't believe we've had the pleasure." The man extended his hand to Sage and bowed his head. Ethan resembled his silver-haired, distinguished father. Same gray-blue eyes and chiseled face. "Erick Ravenwood. I believe my late wife was an acquaintance of your mother."

"I wasn't aware." Memories and grief twined inside Sage's chest. "We had no knowledge black warlocks or their witches existed until recently."

"They met at the occult bookstore my wife owned. Consulted on research on and off for years. My wife, Mariah, never disclosed herself as a witch. I'm sure you realize now why we kept our identity secret."

Puzzlement trailed through Sage. Not that it mattered if this woman kept her own secrets, but something seemed off about the Ravenwoods and their secrets, despite vague explanations. "Can we have a private moment?" She needed the matter on the table or she'd never concentrate on their plan of attack. She needed to know who she was dealing with among the Ravenwood clan.

"Sage, maybe later," Rafael cautioned.

"Now. Please. You hold down the fort." She headed to the door, recognized two pairs of footsteps following her, and one wasn't Rafael. "Ethan stays." Continuing along the hall to her office, she didn't wait for a response. Only one set of footsteps followed.

She ushered Erick inside her office, shut the door, and faced him, not bothering to offer him a seat for the few moments she needed. "Do you know what your son offered me?"

"Of course. His offer stems from a great need."

"What do you mean a great need? He said he refused to align with the Wildes unless I accepted his offer to tie me to his bed and bear his children."

Erick flinched. "I'm sorry if he neglected to divulge secrets. He assumed you'd cave."

Indignation prickled through her confusion. "What? That I'd just bend over because he desired me? A *Pretty Woman* deal? Look, it's no secret I have a promiscuous past. Which, I might add, is my prerogative and in keeping aligned with tradition. As I told Ethan, Rafael and I are exclusive. Now what? You Ravenwoods plan to associate with Imelda or other covens?" Did she even want the Ravenwoods to align with another coven? Especially with Evan and Willow's burgeoning relationship. Talk about awkward city.

"Ethan's apprised me of the situation." Erick cleared his throat. "What Ethan offered you wasn't born of selfishness, but desperation and a willingness to honor you, to align with a powerful and beautiful witch and a strong, healthy coven." Erick paused, as if pondering his next words. "What my son left out is that Mariah was the last witch. We have no other witches in our coven. Most other black warlock covens are facing the same extinction of witches born to our families."

Sage gasped, cupped her hand over her gaping mouth. Never giving it much notice, she'd just assumed if the black warlocks had witches under Andre's spell, then they were technically "black" witches. Yet history never really differentiated between black and white witches. They were just witches. She dropped her hand, composed herself. "How—"

"It's like our original extinction on repeat. Without witches born to our warlocks, we will die off again. Whatever happened to our bloodlines has twisted this curse in our modern generation."

"You're not able to bear children, or—"

Again, he interrupted her, and his truth carved more wrinkles around his crow's-feet. "We bear children, all non-magicals. Without fresh blood, this generation is the last of our line."

"Some witches might like to see the end of you," she mused aloud, her brain spinning into an orbit of confusion.

"Yes." He tugged on the sleeve of his jacket, concealing the light brown feathers of his bird familiar. "We didn't think you'd feel the same. You can't imagine our excitement when Evan bonded Willow and formed a true love connection. But they alone aren't enough to keep our bloodlines alive."

"Is this why Andre wanted Willow?"

"A big reason, yes."

"Has he captured other witches?"

"A few, not enough to make much headway. Working with Imelda, she's right where he wants her. If her coven and her ally witches develop relations with Andre's warlocks, they can expand the ranks of the worst black warlocks and witches. It'll snowball, and like dominoes, the good ones will all topple. The rest will demonize the witchworld."

A chasm opened in Sage's chest and filled with dread for the future of all witches on Earth. "Like before the War."

"Exactly. It may take years, a decade even, but it'll become a divisive and perilous time. Black warlocks unleashed on the witchworld, finally out of the woodwork, places every witch in jeopardy."

"They're not fully in the open, though." Sage's heart thundered in her ears. Too many witches already knew of the situation. Word was bound to spread like wildfire throughout the witchworld soon.

"Imelda, Andre, and his people will light the match," he said.

"How do we stop them?"

Erick squeezed her shoulder, and she wanted to fall into his fatherly arms and let him erase the enormity of his news. The memory of her own father holding her when she was hurt and upset fought for space in her mind. It helped her fight the compulsion to succumb to Erick, and she adopted her cold and calculating smokescreen.

"Even if we killed Imelda and Andre, it might not shift the tide. Their people may not automatically surrender," Erick voiced the dire thoughts swirling in Sage's head. "Andre and Imelda have significant forces behind them, including the covens who've veered from the Wildes because of her manipulation. We need a show of force. We need the strongest witches and warlocks on our side. Absent a potent force, we don't have a snowball's chance in hell. There will be bloodshed, but, as they say, only the strong will survive."

Rescuing Eden represented a drop in the bucket.

Perilous ideas swirled once again in Sage's mind and inevitability punched her senses.

Chapter 14

S age and Erick returned to the forest room, and the Council and Ravenwoods hashed out plans to rescue Eden. They discarded idea after idea of potential failures and devastation. Sage avoided Rafael's questioning glances and concentrated on brainstorming. By the time she forced a late lunch break, he pounced. They both needed air and nature to restore balance. Rafael railroaded her to the round, marbled gazebo. Her temple where she communed with the goddess. His refuge when he needed escape from the busy witchworld and wanted to surround himself by nature.

The air was fresh, and a soft breeze rustled branches on the surrounding evergreens. Rafael stomped up the steps of the gazebo and perched on the low marble wall in a curved opening. He crossed his arms. "Spill."

Sage had snagged two water bottles. She handed one to him and brushed dead evergreen needles off a bench in a neat pile. He set the water aside on the railing while she drank a few sips to wet her arid mouth, hoping to loosen the words she needed to utter. A flame erupted from

Rafael's pointer finger, and he lit the pile of dead needles in a slow burn. Sage almost hit the off-switch on her magic but let him have his fun.

"We're in bigger trouble." Not wanting to waste witch-water, she stomped out the smoldering debris and closed the gap between them. "I understand the real reason behind Ethan's offer. It's not as ridiculous and selfish as it sounds."

"Come on, Sage. Don't believe their marketing campaign to slip into your pants. Don't drink the Kool-Aid." Rafael unfurled his arms, his cheeks glowing red. "Evan already spilled the story." He retold what he'd learned from Evan and how he felt in his gut Evan withheld a chapter.

"Wish you'd told me sooner."

"Like last night when I was screwing your troubles away?" He cast a penetrating look on Sage that dipped lower and lower. "Major mood killer."

She nodded, acceding his point, and sipped her water. "You asked where all their witches were. Well, they don't have any. Erick's deceased wife was the last one. That's what Evan left out."

Rafael's eyes widened. Sage explained everything Erick had told her, a man her gut trusted. He'd ceded his position as coven leader when his heart was no longer in it after Mariah had passed. She respected the move, so similar to her mother's twin.

Rafael grabbed his bottle of water and sucked half down. "It all makes sense. But another war against the black warlocks? We may not survive it. Witches were stronger and more plentiful during the first war."

Sage squeezed next to Rafael in the gazebo wall opening, her thigh leaning against his steely thigh. "Agreed. The first war did a number on witches. We're a shell of what we once were. I hate to think what will happen to the world at large, not only the witchworld, if black warlocks gained total power."

"Nothing will happen, because we're stopping them." Rafael's determination fueled her internal fire. Heat simmered between them, and a mist of water cooled the flames. Rarely did she allow her witch-water and witch-fire to mix. In that moment, it offered her confidence. She still worked, despite the rising aether.

"We are? Just you and me?" she teased, sobered.

He clenched his jaw. "I mean, we combine forces with every coven on our side. We'll go outside the West if we have to. Now we have the Ravenwoods and their allies. Evan told me they have hundreds of black warlocks siding with them, and they know more they can approach."

Impressed, she hummed low in her throat. "How many black warlocks around the world on Andre's side?"

"There's the rub. Andre was building an army. Ravenwoods weren't privy to the families who'd joined the Freak Tide. Could be hundreds, could be thousands."

"We need to find out." A perpetually slow thread of unease coiled in her intestines. "We also have to keep our lips sealed or we'll have more than a war on our hands. We'll have every black warlock chasing every witch in sight. Capture, rape, torture. It happened before. We can't go outside with what we now know. We need to keep the narrative controlled."

Rafael kissed the side of her head. "Why did I know you'd say something so fucking awesome like that?"

She turned her head, and her lips met his in a brief kiss. "Have you met me yet? Because we're of like minds in so many ways."

"I guess we should be lucky Andre hadn't started his campaign of terror full throttle."

"He *had* taken his next steps, with Willow." Sage shivered more from the thought than the gentle breeze stirring the trees. "Thank the goddess we kicked his plan to the curb. Thanks to Evan."

Rafael took her hand, fire erupting as their skin touched, quickly doused by witch-water. He rubbed the water off on his pants. "Your magic's amped up today."

She rested against his chest, met his lips again for a lingering kiss of comfort and strength. Mostly love. "You make all my magic sing. You always did. I just controlled it better."

Rafael jerked his head back, eyes wide, and lifted away from the low wall. "I never knew."

"Now you're in the club." Sage straightened her spine until it ached. "You know I can't feed you all my magic at once, nor my aether. It's way too dangerous." She stepped aside, clasped her hands around her bottle. A hot mist dripped off her fingers and mingled with the sweat-slicked bottle. Wrangling in her magic, thoughts boiled in her mind, ideas she hadn't dwelled on in eons. Hadn't needed to. Didn't want the pain and torture of them. "I want us to meet Ethan alone to hear what he's telepathically reading from Eden. I haven't told him about her yet, and I don't want the world to know her secret."

"The world may already know if she's connected to Andre and Imelda gets wind." Rafael stopped on the steps and turned. "For what it's worth, I understand why you kept her secret from me. From now on, please tell me anything that places a bullseye on you or your coven. I'm going to be family, after all." He winked and sidled down the path cutting through the lawn.

"You already are family," she called after his retreating back.

"You know what I mean." He slowed his roll to wait for her response. "Promise?"

Sage sighed. "Yes, Rafael. I promise to spill my guts whenever I have guts to spill." She watched him light a few candles using her fire magic despite the afternoon sun attempting to warm the air. He drew "I love you" in the air with the fire jetting off his finger.

Sage sat on a marble bench, needing a moment to control her magic. Two blue jays squawked nearby, flitting among the trees. The cleansing perfume of pine and redwood did little to assuage the scent of her fears.

Too much had happened over the last couple of days, and she had a hard time keeping a lid on her magic. *What the black hole hell is wrong with me? Is it my aether?* Sage warmed at the implication. Why now after all these years of complete control? Had unidentified black warlocks stalked her the last time she'd lost control? The only explanation she contemplated.

After a few minutes of silent reflection, she reluctantly left her sanctuary and joined Rafael and Ethan in Rafael's office.

Two hulking and gorgeous warlocks any woman could love inside and out waited for her. But she glued her gaze on Rafael. His mere presence lent her strength, comfort, a sense of family and love. Goddess, she wanted children with this man and this man alone. Their children didn't need black warlock genes to be powerful witches or warlocks in their own right.

"Sage." A flush stole up Ethan's neck. "You know the truth now?"

"Why didn't you give up the goods earlier and save the hassle?" A calm vibe framed her words.

"I'm sorry. Without knowing the full story, I hoped you'd be interested. I planned to tell you." He turned to Rafael at his side. "Sorry, man, I was selfish and self-serving. I believed a High Priestess and I would create a powerful coven. And I believed the rumors about Sage's warlock harem." He rubbed the back of his neck. "Didn't realize you two were so tight. After seeing you, I know you belong together without a fifth wheel. Someday, I hope to have what you have."

Rafael grunted his acknowledgement.

Sage smiled. "I accept your apology. By the way, you don't need a High Priestess to rebuild your bloodlines. Any powerful witch will suffice."

"Got anyone in mind?" The furrows in his forehead smoothed, and he chuckled.

"I do. My cousin, Eden Wilde."

"Oh. I was only kidding." Regardless, Ethan's eyes brightened.

Rafael scrubbed his jaw. "Are you sure, Sage? She's not exactly a killer witch. And she's an air witch. Her magic won't compliment Ethan's air. To top it off, she thinks all men suck ass."

Sage frowned. "She doesn't hate men. Well, not all men. She's a potent witch who chooses not to use her full strength."

"Okay, well, you still can't *give away* your cousin. We don't do arranged marriages. You don't hold such power." Rafael scoffed.

"I'm suggesting they explore, Rafael. Jeez, give me a break." She rolled the chair closer to the desk and picked up a crystal security industry award he'd won. He hated it when she toyed with a prized possession. Sure enough, he gave her a glare destined to melt the glass, and she set it down with a gleeful smile, wiping her fingerprints off using the sleeve of her blouse.

"I'm willing to meet her. We might hit it off," Ethan said.

"Good luck getting her to give you the time of day." Rafael's lips twitched as though he wanted to smile. "She's a tough-ass nut to crack."

"You've already met her," Sage said, her voice full of innuendo. "That she's an air witch doesn't matter. If you're a good match, you'll strengthen each other's magic. By the way, witches can birth any elemental witch. My mother was an air witch—" Sage cut off before she betrayed family secrets of the aether kind.

Rafael jumped in for the save. "Willow's fire and water and Aspen's water."

Ethan sat in a guest chair in front of the desk. "Where have I met her? If she's as beautiful as you, I'd remember."

"She's unforgettably gorgeous. You've never met her in person. You've only met her in your mind." Sage examined him for reaction to the news.

Ethan tilted his head to the side, rubbed his fingers against his thigh. "Eden's the psychic? Wow. Okay. Explains her agitation. I never got a handle on her emotions before she moved out of range, so I couldn't tell whose side of the fence she played on."

"Yep. She's a psychic air witch, like you," Sage replied, pleased the idea of a lesser witch or a psychic witch, who had obstacles to overcome, didn't repulse him. After all, Ethan must have experienced the same relationship obstacles. "You'll keep her secret?"

"Of course!" he exclaimed. "As I expect you to keep my secret. Only my father and brothers know."

"You know how rare a psychic witch is. Good."

"So rare, I've never met another." Anticipation glittered brighter in his eyes. "I need to meet her."

"Good. Let's go rescue her," Rafael piped up. His relief over the whole threesome situation was palpable, and a sliver of her own relief sidled down Sage's back. Thank the goddess for large favors... and the potential of Eden Wilde.

"Tell me about her thoughts?" Sage edged forward, laying her palms flat on the desktop. She studied the trio of black opals on her ring, a gift from her mother on her coven initiation day. The ring represented love, endurance, and grace in the face of adversity. Opals were also powerful protection stones, absorbing negative energies and deflecting low vibes from its wearer. Black opals also ground energy while protecting it. It was past time she gave opals to her cousin.

"She was too agitated, her mind overfilled and jumbled," Ethan explained.

Sage kicked out her thoughts about opals. The stones did little to help her cousin now. "Is Andre in her head?" Sage's voice spiked.

"What?" Ethan jerked his head back. "I doubt Andre's psychic. I would've figured it out in our many meetings."

"You so sure about that?" Rafael demanded. "The guy's a tool even to you Ravenwoods, supposed trusted allies."

Ethan bent his elbows on his knees, hung his head a moment. "I don't know. He could've hidden it. I don't believe he ever learned I was psychic or he would've used me differently." He scrubbed his face with one hand. "But I didn't always try to hide it because I was hoping a psychic witch would connect to me."

"Precarious thinking," Sage said.

"Not when you're desperate to escape Andre's machinations without jeopardizing our lives and other black warlocks on both sides of Andre's fence. The asshole knows who butters his bread among his ranks."

"He might know you're psychic. You don't know," Rafael ground out. "What a clusterfuck. How did this one man gain so much power and hardly anyone knew he existed? Why didn't you Ravenwoods come to us sooner?"

"One defection from the Ravenwoods meant genocide to many more." Ethan clenched his fists. "As much as he wanted to build his ranks, he held our lives over our heads. He holds the power and manpower to do it. We're all just gnats on his chessboard. If we didn't toe his constantly moving line, we were expendable. Exactly what he wanted. Dissension weakened him."

Frustrated, Sage held up a hand. "Gentlemen, let's

proceed to our most imminent need. We can talk about the black asshole's role in our society later. *If* we give him a role, that is."

Ethan began pacing the room. "I need to get closer to Imelda's compound, to connect to Eden, get her to project her mind. If Andre isn't connected to her."

Alarm crawled up Sage's spine, and she wrung her hands. "She was in his thrall when they left. No one knows if it was magical or telepathic. We have to be prepared for all contingencies." Sage stood, peered out the window to the verdant front lawns and circular driveway, letting the outside into her soul to calm her nerves. "I'll schedule a meeting with Imelda and add two other High Priestesses who side with the Wildes. On her territory."

Both Ethan and Rafael objected with a loud, "No way."

Sage spun around. Their similarities weren't lost on her, hence the prior weird bafflement of Ethan's now-settled offer. Ignoring their outburst, she continued, "You both will join me as my required warlock guards. We'll post witches and warlocks surrounding her covenstead out of sight and reach of her magic. Close enough to jump if we need them."

"It's a suicide mission." Rafael stomped to her, cracking his knuckles, an old vice Sage hadn't noticed in a long time.

"If she's defected so far to the left of the witch's creed, we'll find out. It'll be to our advantage to entice the other covens back to the fold. There's no way they'll continue to stir the pot together."

"Bullshit. She broke the creed yesterday," Rafael roared, a mad tick pulsing in his jaw. "And they still side with her."

"How do we know? She could've been manipulating them with Andre and the Black Tide's help."

"How will it help us? She won't hand over Eden on a

silver platter."

"It'll get me in proximity of Eden." Ethan gave his two cents. "We have no choice. I need to get closer."

"You can do it outside the grounds." Rafael's gaze never slid from Sage's face, and she flushed from his scrutiny. "If that doesn't work, we'll follow Sage's suggestion. But I need better protection for our covens."

"Her property is too big for Ethan to connect to Eden from the perimeter." Sage became overly interested in her boots.

"She doesn't have ley lines like we do," Rafael argued. "Ethan can find a way in."

"It could take days and put Eden in further jeopardy. We don't have time to lose. The longer this takes, the more opportunity for word to escape about the black warlocks and how Imelda screwed me over."

"People will still find out," Ethan said.

"Not before I regain my position, prove my strength again." Sage met his intense gaze.

"We make a formidable threesome." Ethan's suggestion caused every nerve to hum with a rush of desire.

Rafael cleared the space between him and Ethan in two strides. "Don't travel that road again, man."

"Rafael, love. Calm down." Sage skirted the desk and stepped in the middle of their silent showdown. "We do it my way. Now ready the troops. I'll call Misty and Rebel and brief them, then I'll call Imelda, set a time for tomorrow, to give Misty and Rebel travel time." The two witches were her closest comrades outside her coven. They were the High Priestesses of the Bay Area and Silicon Valley covens, respectively, the two largest Northern California covens, and the closest in proximity to her in California. The three witches maintained a healthy respect for one another. Both witches, in their forties, were Sage's sounding boards when she needed external help. She'd gone to them after Andre had spelled Willow, and they brainstormed ways to rid Willow of the black magic. If she couldn't count on them, they were back to square one. Unless... She let the thought trail off.

"What if Imelda refuses?" Ethan asked.

"She won't."

"How can you be so sure?" He pushed her buttons further.

"Because I'm planning to offer her my position as western High Priestess in exchange for Eden. She won't reject it. She doesn't need Eden."

"Like hell!" Rafael exploded again, sparks dripping off his fingers.

She landed a scowl on Rafael. "I'm not giving it up for real. This is just to subdue her, gain time. She'll have to go through the usual election protocols with majority vote from the other western covens."

"She'll want you to prove your word. With blood, a spell, and whatever else you witches do to prove truth."

"She'll have proof." Sage picked at the singed polish on her pointer-finger. "Don't worry."

Rafael's eyes crinkled. Ethan just stared at her as if every one of her brain cells had set sail on the high seas.

Sage had no plans to give anything up to Imelda or anyone else.

Chapter 15

Sage called the other two California coven leaders and secured their agreement to take Imelda down a notch in a confrontation tomorrow. She didn't divulge Ethan and Eden's telepathy abilities to Misty and Rebel. No one else needed to know. If Imelda or Andre found out, they'd blab it to the whole witchworld, making Eden a bigger prize and threat.

After her tough conversations, Sage called Imelda. She waited on ice while Imelda's lackey who answered the phone fetched the attention whore.

"Sage Wilde, I knew I'd hear from you soon," the older witch said, her gravelly voice rushed as if she'd run to the phone.

"You kidnapped my cousin."

"Collateral damage."

"You can't keep her." Sage remained calm on the outside even though ideas of retribution chilled her internal fire. "How many more rules and laws do you intend to break?"

"As many as it takes to flip the witchworld upside

down." Imelda cackled like the true Wicked Witch of the West.

"Why? You want to instigate another Witches and Warlocks War?"

"To gain absolute control? Absolutely." Another deranged cackle.

Sage closed her eyes for five seconds. The witch was a point short of a pentagram, power hungry, not viewing the full picture. "Andre holds a large faction in the Black Tide. Will he really allow his black warlocks to join your team? Does *he* want to be captain of the witchworld?"

"Offer enough and warlocks will do anything. Now tell me why you called, Sage."

What had Imelda offered Andre to shove the Black Tide in her back pocket and gain his approval for her control? Nothing made sense from what they'd already learned about Andre and his quest for domination. One thing for sure, Sage needed to discover how much power Imelda promised Andre. Too much power could ruin the witchworld. Or Imelda was the mayor of Crazy Town.

"I'd like to meet you tomorrow to secure Eden's release. Misty and Rebel from the Bay Area covens will join me."

Imelda clucked. "Never could break you three up."

"Did you try?" Misty and Rebel already confessed to rejecting Imelda's attempts to gain their votes and covens.

"What High Priestess wouldn't campaign with all the covens in her territory?"

"Can we meet at your covenstead tomorrow or not?"

"Hmmm... I rather fancy a tea party. Yes, yes. I like the idea. Not sure you have what it takes to regain your little air witch, but I'm willing to be amused."

"Rules?"

"One warlock each. No other witches."

"Protocol dictates at least three warlocks for each High Priestess."

"Oh, all right. We'll settle on two." Imelda made a long-suffering sound, but Sage knew the witch was gleeful. "Oh, Sage. Bring that scrumptious Evan Ravenwood. He pleases the eyes. Willow isn't strong enough for him, and I might convince him to stay."

Alarm zipped up her spine. "I'll bring *Ethan* Ravenwood and Rafael. Evan stays out of the picture. You allow us in unwarded, we remain unwarded, and you allow us all to leave intact after two hours, at most. The West covens will be on standby if they don't hear from us within a certain timeframe."

"Don't be silly. I don't eat my guests."

Sage tipped her head back and rolled her eyes. The witch herself might not devour them, but it didn't prevent the rest of her coven from doing the deed. Rules dictated they reach terms and stick to them or suffer dire consequences from the Council. Not like Imelda wasn't already on the regional shit list. "Do we have a deal or not?"

"You drive a hard bargain. Noon. We'll have lunch instead. Three witches and six lovely warlocks. I can't wait." The phone went dead.

☾✦☾

Sage sagged in her favorite bedroom armchair, holding a large glass of deep red wine. Rafael soon joined her after his evening security rounds. He grabbed the other wineglass she'd poured for him, sat across from her, and slugged down half the glass. The taste of his favorite Bordeaux blend didn't even register on his tongue.

"Well, hello to you." Sage sipped her wine, not her favorite, but she compromised for Rafael.

"Eden's not gonna give two shits about him," he said, driving straight past "GO" to the topic *du jour*.

Sage flinched. *Goddess, why is he so threatened by*

Ethan? "It's the best I've got."

"An air witch and an air warlock? Where's the strength? It spells disaster."

"When was the last time you saw a *black* warlock and a witch together?"

Rafael's initial silence was telling. "Let's let the lot of them die off. Problem solved."

Stunned, Sage angled her head toward him. "I understand Ethan and whoever he hooks up with won't single-handedly solve the black warlocks' diminishing population problem, but are you so hot on obliterating an entire magical race? We can be one again." Maybe not if Imelda's plans destroy witch and warlock alike.

"Is that the future you want? Witches controlling black warlocks? Like before the War," he challenged, kicking off his boots with a muffled thunk on the wool rug.

"You'd like that. It's evolution."

"Hardly. I like what I have now. That scenario's kicking us *backward*."

"It could kick us to a new dawn. A different, better world." Sage had no clue what would happen if black warlocks and witches lived in harmony again. Well, not so much harmony since the warlocks called war on the witches once before because they didn't like being treated like second-class magical beings. Had no clue what'd happen if one side threw down the other in another war.

She finished her wine and straddled Rafael in his chair. She started unbuttoning his shirt, wanting to feel his skin against hers. Afraid of what tomorrow might bring, they needed a night alone absorbed in each other.

"Stop."

"No." She continued unbuttoning his shirt, and his erection grew hard against her bottom.

"I mean, stop so I can undress you." He emptied his wine and put his glass down so hard, the stem broke off.

Glass pinged the rug like diamonds.

He scooped her in his arms and carried her to the bed to avoid the broken glass against her bare feet.

"Are you playing the beast tonight?" She smiled.

"You want the beast? Or do you want slow and loving?"

"I want all sides of you." She wanted Rafael to relax. Sex promised to do the trick. She needed him inside and around her. It could very well be their last time together. She forced the thoughts into her mind's crypt.

After a flurry of discarded clothes, and Rafael's mouth all over her naked body, he took her hard and fast, pounding and dominating. Then she flipped the tables and made him suffer, teasing and seductive until they both came in a thunder-and-lightning storm of fire and water. Witch-air dried the sweat on their slick bodies. Rose petals drifted down from the ceiling and dissolved as they hit their bare skin. Every element presented itself, and Sage lay back finally confident in the actions she intended to take.

Caerwyn and Gwyneira chased each other from one body to the other until they settled, Caerwyn on Rafael's chest and Gwyneira's white wings draped across the back of Sage's shoulders, sinking onto her skin in a tingle of feathers and love pecks.

"Your eyes went all silver-rimmed for a millisecond when you came," Rafael grumbled. "Your magic felt different, intense, consuming."

Concerned, Sage peered up at him, still laying on top of her. "Does it hurt?"

"No. Just a ton of magic. Is it your aether?"

"Yes," she replied. "I felt it arising." Rafael shouldn't have felt her magic without her conscious effort to feed it to him, except her naturally granted fire.

"Your magic's changing." He rolled off her and spooned around her body. "We're changing."

She turned in his arms and pressed her mouth to his, stifling a conversation she didn't care to drop yet. He opened his mouth and took her kiss, gave it back with such love and comfort, she about vaporized into a barrel of bubbling wine. His hands gently roamed her body, and her skin shivered where his made contact.

They made love again, slow and languorous. Invoking a dampening spell, Sage contained her magic. She wanted to feel every inch of Rafael, every touch, the feather of his lips without magical enhancement. And their exquisite lovemaking was everything she wanted, everything she needed to fuel her soul and body. They fell in a troubled sleep at the witching hour when the veil between life and death was thinnest, when magic surged the strongest, and Sage's dampening spell dispelled.

Chapter 16

The sun rose strong and took the edge off the chill, normal for the time of year verging on spring. The day of reckoning promised little normalcy, though. Normal was overrated anyway.

Making love with Sage last night never hit the boundary of normal. Rafael never felt more alive, every nerve ending über-sensitive. He'd never grow tired of loving Sage, making love to her, regardless of magic. No two times were the same, and he wanted her more every time he touched her. He brushed his hand over his steely erection, flinched from the lust barreling through him. Maybe they had time for a quickie before heading to Imelda's covenstead. But then, Sage needed to be fresh and energized. "Damn it," he groused, trying to curb his desire.

Rafael finished his morning security tasks, called a few clients who he'd neglected the last couple of days. He waited on the rear patio for Sage to finish her morning rituals with her coven in the witch-house, a fancy name for a retrofitted barn they used for indoor rituals. Another neglected task.

Whenever she lit a candle, his fingertips prickled. Since she'd lost control of her aether, he'd felt more of her magic than ever, including a trickle of all her elements not normally available to him. He'd never much used her air or water magic, mostly fire for protection and defense. He'd only used her earth magic for play. Stories floated around, and he'd seen other warlocks use the elements of their witches. Mug in hand, he sauntered onto the pathway leading into the woods. Checked behind him to ensure no one was watching. Didn't care that Sage would sense the tug of magic.

Eyes closed, he caressed a Lenten rose bud, touched several more, and dipped his hand in the evergreen bush. He recited an earthen spell he'd memorized. He hoped one day Sage would grant him access to all her magic. As the most powerful of her warlocks, he still wanted it all to enhance his own. He needed to use and understand it to help her and keep her and the coven safe. It was a First Warlock's sacred duty. Sage didn't deny him access willy-nilly. Nope. Her aether frightened her. Yet they'd already ridden in the aether rodeo. The magic almost killed him six years ago. Or so she'd assumed. He wasn't sure. He'd felt something in his core he couldn't explain. It scared him. Mostly, it excited the hell out of him. Gave him pause to ponder his nebulous background, the reasons he ended up in foster care at such a young age.

Every bud on the bush opened wide, the muted pink, cream, and green petals angling toward him, preening for his attention. As sudden as the flowers blossomed, they wilted on the vines, and a painful yank on his intestines rooted him to the ground. Sage cut his access to her earth magic.

Hands clapping sounded behind him, and he jerked around.

"What do you want?" Rafael blasted, hooking his

thumbs in his belt loops, the empty mug dangling, embarrassed by his meaningless magic display.

"Checking in," Ethan said. "So Sage has earth magic too. Since when did she let you use it?"

"Not your business." Rafael marched forward, pushed past Ethan. On second thought, he froze and faced the warlock. "Hey, man. Can you do me a favor?"

"Depends." Ethan approached, curiosity blazing in his eyes. Heat threaded off him and triggered Rafael's fire to connect in a friendlier way than the other day. They created a lightning bolt that sizzled above their heads and floated away on a gentle breeze. More a display of color than fire.

"If anything happens to me, I want you to become Sage's First Warlock." Rafael hated saying the words, but the idea of heading inside Imelda's lair shot his nerves to hell. He didn't know if he could contain himself if he fought to the death to save Sage.

"Expecting trouble?" Ethan cocked his head to the side.

"Promise or not?" Rafael demanded.

"If she'll have me."

"She will."

Blunt heels clacked on the sidewalk behind Rafael, and he spun toward the sound.

Sage wore her typical fighting clothes: black leggings, a long-sleeve black silk blouse, and her black, blunt-heeled riding boots. The pants showed off her every curve, and Rafael liquified at the sight of her.

A quizzical crinkle to her eyes passed and smoothed. "You two okay? No fighting, right?" Rafael flicked his hand through the air dismissively. "Let's go, then."

"Are we meeting Misty and Rebel there?" Ethan moved next to Rafael, and they separated to sandwich Sage between them.

"No. I called them off."

"Like hell you did." Rafael spun toward her.

Ethan's angry shock launched marble-size air balls into the dry forest brush, ruffling the dead leaves and debris from underneath.

"I don't want to jeopardize them." Sage hiked toward the garage.

"Instead, you'll jeopardize yourself going in alone?" Rafael took two long strides to catch up to her. "And us too? Are you insane?"

"I can handle Imelda."

"Not if black warlocks cram her house." Ethan's raven familiar cawed angrily in agreement, and he rubbed the back of his neck. "I didn't like the sound of this plan from the jump."

"Then we don't go." Rafael grabbed Sage's arm.

"We have no choice." She kicked a sugar pine cone onto the lawn.

"We'll find another way. I'll get closer to the compound," Ethan rebutted.

"I sent a crew of witches and warlocks over there this morning, and the Helwigs busted them within a mile of the compound," Sage explained.

"Can you connect to Eden from a mile away?" Rafael asked Ethan.

"Not in any meaningful way." Ethan scratched his head, his fingers lingering on his skull.

Sage wrenched out of Rafael's clasp, pinched the strap of her purse slung over her shoulder, and continued toward the garage. "We'll take the warded and bulletproof SUV."

"It's not warded against black magic." Rafael spat out the words as if spitting embers. "Why do this alone?"

She kept walking. "Misty and Rebel weren't so keen about stepping foot on Imelda's territory. They wanted to meet in a neutral public place to avoid an altercation. I told them to stay home and next meeting we'll do it their way."

Rafael and Ethan traded looks of disbelief. "My people are on standby if they don't hear from me every hour," Ethan said.

"Yeah. Same here." Rafael slogged behind his recalcitrant witch, hating when she was in a mood. A stubborn mood that plunked her in jeopardy. Good news, she'd survived every other perilous event. Until Imelda and crew breached her covenstead, the most secure wards in California, severing them as if sliced with a dull sword. Rafael gave Ethan a side-long glance. "Do you still have warlocks inside the Black Tide compound you trust?"

"Absolutely. But they're not privy to Andre's inner circle. They know little, and report to me every couple of days."

"How many?"

"A dozen. Why?"

"Placing bets on our odds. A dozen against how many Black Tide?"

"Hundred or so in NorCal I can ID. We don't know the total worldwide numbers."

"*Wonderful.*" Rafael groaned, hit the remote of the SUV. He darted ahead, opened the rear door, and Sage slid inside.

Her fingers grazed his cheek, and she gave him a tight-lipped smile. "I'm sorry. Don't be worried. I'm not." She kissed his forehead. "You used my earth magic. Why?"

He pursed his lips. "Testing it."

"Don't do it again. It's dangerous if you can't handle it," she admonished.

"How is it dangerous?" He scoffed. "I bloomed a bunch of flower buds. Big deal."

"Rafael." She sighed. "Aether magic is uncontrollable. Once you open the door, you can't always shut it. You saw how the magic affected us both the other day. And that was a tiny thread. If I'd swung the doors wide, you'd be dead."

"Still here, aren't I?" He was referring to the day they'd met when the doors had swung open for the first time. Wide as the gates to hell.

"Don't use my earth magic again. That's an order." Annoyed as all hell by the darkening of her face, she buckled her seatbelt.

What she forgot was that he'd never pulled from her aether the weekend he'd met her. The magic had inundated him of its own volition. Her magic filled every crevice of his being. And he'd lived to never tell her about it. A tortuous crawl of ants worked up his spine as he jogged to the driver's side. Ethan already sat in the front passenger seat, contemplating his navel or something. At least he wasn't flirting with Sage while Rafael still kicked it.

An intense silence pervaded the interior of the SUV, each lost in their own heads. The beefy engine and the highway traffic became soothing white noise.

Ethan broke the silence about halfway to Scott's Valley, a small community between Santa Cruz along the coast and the inland cities of Silicon Valley. The town nestled in the woodsy forests of the Santa Cruz Mountains. Mountains and trees hid much from the outside world. Fortunately, the magic securing Imelda's wards didn't draw from ley lines. The thought gave Rafael no small sense of relief. They could break her wards much easier, if needed.

"What should we expect from Imelda in the way of protocol?" Ethan asked.

"She defies protocol. I have no clue what her intentions are."

Rafael tapped his fingers on the dash. "Yep. You got that right. We're flying into a hornet's nest. Willingly. Like idiots." He had a bad, bad feeling about the upcoming visit... and Sage's unvoiced plan. Oh, he heard her voiced plan, all right. The unvoiced part bothered him like the fiery pits of hell.

Ethan's cell dinged, and he glommed onto it. "Yours and my people are closing in on Imelda's property now. They'll remain out of range of her watchers and magic. Close enough to storm in, if needed."

"What? Who decided on backup?" Sage asked.

"Ethan and I did this morning." Smugness set up shop on Rafael's face. "Did you think we'd go completely alone? Come on, Sage. You're not the powerful wizard of Oz."

She kicked the back of Ethan's seat in a childish show of frustration. "Fine. Whatever. Just keep everyone far enough away to avoid detection. I want them safe. We can't show the outside world we don't get along. We'll suffer sanctions we can't afford."

"Have you had government interference?" Ethan turned in his seat toward Sage, the leather squeaking in protest.

"As long as the covens get along, are ruled by respected people, and don't use magic for ill purposes to gain control of people, businesses, and governments, they tolerate us. A major infraction like Imelda's threatening could end our good standing. What she did to my coven is a major infraction. But she knows I won't tell anyone because it'll hurt us all. Magic will become illegal. They'll force covens to disband, and they'll catalogue every magical being on the government rolls. I've visited with the California governor ostensibly to keep us in check. You can bet your lily-white ass the governments keep tabs on us."

"That, my friend," Rafael said, "is why Sage is a regional High Priestess. She's well-respected and holds an iron fist. You never hear of a major infraction arising from the West."

"Until you're embroiled in one." Ethan faced the windshield again, his spine arrow straight.

"It's why we need to contain this clusterfuck," Sage

replied. "Today."

By the time they approached the wrought-iron gate at the Helwig covenstead, indecision, anticipation, and a mega dose of fear seethed inside Rafael.

The lethally armed warlocks guarding the gate and surrounding the property's perimeter didn't help the doom scalding the walls of his stomach.

C☾C☽C☾

Sage snatched three vials from her purse, handed one to each Rafael and Ethan. "Drink before you get out." Rafael refused the vial, but Ethan took his and uncorked it.

"What is it?" Rafael squinted at the tiny glass bottle.

"Aspen said it'll help against a warding spell and make any warding effect minimal. The potion's effect doesn't last long. Long enough to escape." Sage popped a couple of gummies. "Even though Imelda agreed to no wards, she's snorting crack."

Rafael finally took the vial. "Are you in pain?"

"These are to enhance my power and will allow me to concentrate better."

"Give one to Ethan."

"I'm good." Ethan downed the potion and fake gagged. "Your alchemist might need to learn the fine art of flavor."

Rafael drank his potion and chucked the vial in the ashtray. "Flavor's overrated. I just want her potions to work. Try her cherry gummies someday. You'll eat your words."

"Ethan, are you receiving psychic readings, connections, anything?" Sage asked.

"Hitting walls."

"Can you read minds behind wards?"

"Normally, but who knows what arsenal this witch is working with?" Ethan raked his fingers through his thick hair and scrubbed his head as if to provoke his psychic ability.

Sage stuffed her purse under the seat. "She'll check us at the door. Empty your pockets if you have anything magical on you. And weapons." Neither warlock moved a muscle, which meant they came clean of any accessories. Or not. "Hide nothing. She'll sniff it out."

Ethan reached inside the hem of his polo shirt, ripped the seam apart. He added a vial to the ashtray. "Death potion."

"Who'd you plan to off?" Rafael glared into the ashtray.

"Any enemy who gets in my way." Ethan gave him a point-blank stare.

"Who mixes your potions?" Sage asked, her curiosity helping to kill the heebie-jeebies settling in for the long haul. Witches were the spell makers. She didn't recall hearing about any warlocks before the war mixing potions and casting spelled charms.

"We buy our charms and potions from a trusted local witch, healer. Non-coven affiliated. She works under the radar for select clients."

More curiosity threaded through Sage. She wanted to know this witch, but it wasn't the time to press Ethan for more intel. After all, they'd only declared a temporary alliance.

She slid her spelled opal ring off and handed it to Rafael. Without a word, he stuck it in a velvet pouch with other various charms and stashed the pouch in the glove box. No sense in bringing a conduit of magic inside Imelda's lair. If Sage used magic, she didn't want any restrictions, a conduit, which the ring represented. She'd blast her magic in freefall if needed. The spell on the ring served to either stifle or enhance her magic. And also protect those near her. She hated giving it up.

Already, six warlocks surrounded the SUV, straight-backed and stoic.

"Recognize any?" she asked Ethan.

"Nope."

Sage's mouth opened wide. "You mean they aren't Black Tide? I've never seen them at our usual gatherings among Imelda's people either."

"Like I said, Andre's reach is wide. How they landed *here* is a mystery I want to solve." He rubbed his hands on his thighs, raring to go.

"You and me both." Sage stuck her phone in her back pocket. "Ready?"

The click of both front doors opening provided her answer.

"Stay there, Sage." Rafael shut the driver's door.

Before he reached the rear door, Ethan already had it open. Rafael scowled, and Sage hid a tiny smile she didn't feel.

"Play nice, you two," she said. "We're in this together."

As she stepped out of the tall SUV, Rafael's hand gloving hers, the six black warlocks closed ranks around them. Not a word uttered, but she noticed the shortest of the bunch, a man at least six feet tall, tapped an earpiece.

"Follow us, ma'am," he drawled. "Mrs. Helwig is waiting for you. She appreciates your timeliness." He searched behind them. "When shall we expect the other two witches?"

"She'll speak to Imelda, not you, runt," Rafael replied. He was a mere two inches taller than the black warlock. He and Ethan flanked Sage, both so close to her, she prepped for the heat they projected to combust her.

"It's okay." Sage squeezed his hand, drawing strength from him and steadying her nerves. "The other witches will not be joining us. You can lighten up on your gate security detail." The black-clad warlocks stood along the fence at consistent intervals that probably encompassed the entire covenstead. Fun times ahead. Would they make it out alive?

Ethan scoped the grounds and said under his breath, "I don't recognize a soul."

"Doesn't surprise me," she replied. "We're heading into a perfect storm."

"Let's cut and run." Rafael abruptly stopped.

"And leave Eden behind?" Sage captured his hand to get him to move.

"We'll find another way. I wished you hadn't called Misty and Rebel off."

They approached the double front doors, cement gargoyles perched atop the pillars flanking the black door. A modern medieval revival house, castle-like in appearance. Perfect place for a showdown. Not so much if the house boasted a real dungeon. Very few green plants decorated the front yard and empty planters edging the foundation of the house. Black mulch covered the dirt. Empty planters sat along the driveway and porch, except a few held dead, brown flowers. Imelda taking drought water restrictions to an extreme? Or trying to prove a point? Or a witch's earth magic had spun out of control. Whatever. Death fit the austerity of Imelda's world.

Chapter 17

The front door opened as they approached. Imelda's warlocks trapped them in a no-escape zone. Rafael squeezed Sage's hand and let it go in case she needed to direct her magic. Three witches and three warlocks ushered them into the foyer and wanded them for weapons. A second wand detected magic charms and potions. The wand detected no magic contraband. *Go freaking figure.*

"Nice detector." Sage reached for the wand a plain-Jane witch held, Imelda's second niece who wielded water magic. A very powerful witch who could drown them in a typhoon. "May I?"

"Sorry, no. Trade secret." The witch shoved the wand in the console table drawer. She warded the drawer with a silent spell and a waggle of her fingers.

"Whatever floats her sinking black boat," Rafael uttered, the bright flecks in his eyes devouring the drawer. As head of security, he was always on the hunt for the newest and best security tool.

Imelda's witches and warlocks led them along a dim

hallway, white-veined, black marble floors and light gray walls providing monochromatic decor. Bright watercolor paintings depicting dragons, gargoyles, fairies, and all kinds of fantasy beings broke the severity and lent the hallways an odd cheer.

"She set no wards." Rafael dipped his head for Sage's ear only. A tiny spark touched her wrist.

Sage's heart rate ramped up another notch. "How do you know?"

"I feel your magic," he said. She saw his shrug from her peripheral vision.

Shock locked her knees. "Since when?"

"Since always?" He scratched the pink heat blossoming on his cheek.

"You never told me." Sage took a cautious step forward, stopping in front of an oil painting of fairies flitting through a dark forest under stars and moon glow. She clutched his arm.

"What's the big deal?" he asked.

"The big deal is that regular warlocks can't feel or sense magic unless your witch opens the door to you," Ethan replied. "Only black warlocks can."

"Exactly." Sage drew her gaze to the painting's forest scene, trying to quell her mixed emotions about Rafael's bombshell. Had he gained more lasting power from her aether? Might explain how he'd easily used her witch-earth earlier when her aether forced her door open.

"Admiring my artwork?" Imelda said from the doorway of a sparsely decorated room. The black-and-gray theme continued, but no colorful artwork decorated the bare gray walls. Their escorts ushered them into the room and departed. The meeting room held a round table and ten black leatherette padded chairs on wheels. Three warlocks bound Imelda from behind, and two others guarded the door. Assorted bottled beverages nestled in buckets of ice on the sideboard. A tray of sandwiches and side dishes sat beside it. Several packaged salads also dotted the sideboard, as if Imelda had lunch catered.

"Help yourself, then we can discuss business." The witch gestured toward the spread.

"I've given Rafael and Ethan instructions not to eat or drink anything." Sage smirked. Imelda could have spelled or laced the food and even unopened bottles.

"Suit yourself. I assumed as much, but I didn't want to host lunch and not serve food."

"No offense, Imelda. You wouldn't eat at my table under the circumstances."

"*Touché.*" Imelda cackled. "We're a lot alike, Sage Wilde."

"Hardly." Sage wrinkled her nose.

Rafael surveyed the minimalist room, and Ethan pulled a chair out for Sage. "Thank you." She sat rigid and on guard. The cold of the seat bottom seeped through her leggings. Her witch-fire could not fight the chill attacking her from all corners of the room.

Rafael and Ethan positioned themselves, one at each side of her, off center from the door. She hated sitting with her back to the door. Bad karma. She tested the room with a small exploration of magic. Imelda had indeed set wards, but Sage found a tiny breach to her left. Thank the goddess for Aspen's potions, which Imelda had no way of discovering sloshing inside Sage's belly. Ethan tapped and dipped his head sideways at her, which meant the magic wards didn't impede his psychic powers.

Gwyneira didn't budge from her disconcerting spread across Sage's shoulder. She didn't like the static owl, but the wards in the room prevented all their familiars from coming alive. Too bad the potion she took didn't help Gwyneira.

"We'll get down to it." Imelda sat, queen of her

roundtable. Her warlocks waited, silent and immovable behind her. The real deal, since the wards killed any glamour magic. The witch appeared stronger, more refreshed than yesterday. But Sage sensed an illness she hid behind good old-fashioned medicine and sleep.

"I'll not leave today without Eden," Sage began, her tone calm, collected, demanding.

"By all means. I hadn't meant to take her, but Andre grew infatuated and refused to leave without her."

Despite Sage's curiosity, she seethed inside. "What type of infatuation?"

Imelda wiggled her fingers. "Oh, you know, love at first sight or some silly nonsense."

Love, my ass. "Is she okay? Is he locked up? Did you lock them together?" Sage jabbed her finger on the table with each question.

"He's free to roam within boundaries. He has visiting rights," the witch parried.

"What the hell does *visiting rights* mean?" Rafael demanded. Sage winced.

"It means, Mr. Reyes, when Andre wants to see Eden, I grant them time alone."

"What about what Eden wants?" Sage jumped up, palms on the table, leaning toward the witch. Imelda's warlocks stiffened, and their hands went to very manmade guns stuck in shoulder harnesses under their arms. She eased out another feeler of magic, watching Imelda for a sign of awareness. The breach in the wards widened, and Imelda's mask remained blank, except for her freaking ego dancing across the wrinkles and crags of her weathered skin.

"I don't need to force the little air witch. She's all too happy to visit with Andre. They're kindred souls or some such, according to Andre." Imelda fiddled with the long sleeves of her black tunic, slowly turned them up at the wrists and folded them in. The deliberate act jogged an indistinct memory. "I admire what you two have become since the fateful solstice gathering when we all met Mr. Reyes for the first time. Especially how far you've grown, Sage, from that wild, loose, and rebellious nothing of a witch who didn't earn the crown as the youngest High Priestess ever. We all thought you'd destroy the western region."

The memory finally blasted apart the knot in Sage's brain. A Helwig High Priestess at the fateful solstice gathering who'd bullied and challenged Sage for her position, for Rafael, for everything she held dear. Same witch who, without knowing it, forced Sage to grow up and become a leader. The very dead witch. The incident toughened Sage and forced her to prove a point to all the other covens that she could handle the role bequeathed by her mother. When everyone made fun of her for being a child, threw their warlocks and alcohol at her, she threw it all back in their faces over the years, ditching her rebellious ways in the only way she knew how. Cold, tough, calm, and collected, even when she seethed inside.

"You plan to throw that in my face the rest of my... or *your* life?" Sage asked, her calm draining away. "I didn't kill your sister."

"Tsk, tsk. Now, who said you killed her?" Imelda batted her sparse eyelashes at Sage. "My sister was her own woman. Her actions destroyed her. No one accused anyone of outright killing her." Imelda's gaze landed on Rafael, oh so accusingly.

"Don't pin that on me," he said in a cold and low voice. "She raised magic against Sage first, trying to *kill* her. I defended my witch." Rafael had just learned he was a warlock, didn't even know what it meant to be one, and he still defended Sage. Renewed pride rushed through her bloodstream.

"If I recall, you belonged to no one, but my sister had set her sights on you first."

Rafael scoffed. "I wasn't for sale or free for the taking."

"Are you sure about that?"

"Enough of this!" Sage exploded, fighting the aether stirring and popping in her veins. "It's all water under the fucking bridge. Can we return to the issue at hand?" She narrowed her eyes, wracking her brain for any tidbit from Eden's life that left her wanting to associate with the evilest black warlock alive. Unless he'd glamoured her... or read her mind.

"You know you can't keep Andre." Sage tried another tactic to flip the conversation around.

"Andre is where he wants to be."

"The Black Tide will destroy your coven if you ally with them. Worse than before the War. Our numbers have declined, and we don't know how many black warlocks exist. Do you want another war?"

Imelda waved away her question with a slant of her hand, her thin, craggy fingers and blunt fingernails a flash in the air. Thick air surrounded Imelda—an air magic shield. Imelda used a spell or potion to maintain her own magic in the warded room. Sage was sure her other witches and warlocks were free to use magic in whatever little bubbles surrounded them against the wards. *Shit on a stick.*

"Numbers are irrelevant. Everyone will fall to the strongest leader," Imelda replied emphatically, as if she'd already stolen the top dog position.

"*Right.* Does that mean Andre and the Black Tide need your numbers? Or what did he offer you?" Did Andre want to align with her, or had Imelda seriously kidnapped him? Chaos demanded answers in the ache forming in Sage's temples.

As if voicing his name channeled his appearance,

Andre sauntered into the room, unfettered, unguarded. The guards in the doorway made way for him. He sported expensive black dress slacks and a long-sleeve dress shirt. A leather band tied his long hair back in a loose ponytail. Didn't appear a prisoner. Hard to tell.

Rafael's hand touched the side of hers. Magic radiated from her to him, he flinched, and gave her a curious sidelong glance. She cricked her finger at him to duck down and whispered, "It's working." He gave a curt nod, and they both reverted their attention to the asshole of the hour.

"Sage, my pretty." Andre nodded at Rafael, and Rafael literally bared his teeth at the warlock. "Ah, my boy, Ethan." He clapped his hands once, the sound reverberating to the ceiling. "Are you here to join my power brigade? Didn't I tell you we would prevail?"

"Not my idea of prevailing. You said nothing about controlling the Wildes, joining a witch's coven, or kidnapping a witch. I thought you wanted to earn everything. Far as I can tell, you haven't earned squat. This is downright stealing." Ethan's anger whipped around Sage.

"I didn't *steal* a witch, to mimic your crass term. She came willingly," Andre replied.

"Bull. Shit," Rafael shouted, his rage knocking him against Sage's shoulder, and she winced. "Return Eden Wilde now or there will be consequences to the Black Tide and the Helwig coven from the national level."

"What do you want in trade for Eden?" Sage asked, ignoring Rafael's outburst.

"What I've always wanted," Andre replied, a smile stretching his thin lips wide. He sauntered to Imelda, placed his hand on her shoulder like a father doting on a perfect daughter.

"I wasn't talking to you." Sage scanned their faces for any resemblance. Found nothing that tied them by DNA.

He wasn't old enough to be Imelda's father. "Imelda? This is our meeting. Why are you aligning with this trash?"

Andre smiled wider. A cross between irritation and triumph cloaked Imelda's face before indecision flashed across her eyes. The witch swallowed hard a few times.

Bingo! Sage could work with the hag's indecision and nervousness. "You're his bitch, Imelda."

"Whatever he promised is nothing more than a ploy to sucker you into his realm, to get witches under his belt. He needs you more than you need him," Ethan finished for Sage, and she was glad he held a better understanding of Andre. "Without witches, the black warlocks die off."

"Dear boy," Imelda mimicked Andre, "do you think I don't know that? Why would we witches let the black warlocks die off? Better to hold your enemies closer, as they say."

"My dear," Andre pressed a palm over his heart, fake sorrow tugging his mouth down, "I'm hurt."

"Enough with this tug of war!" Sage stamped her boot on the floor, half rising from her chair. "What do you want for Eden? I don't give a flying fuck if you're enemies or lovers." She sank down, her back so rigid against the padded seat, it felt like steel meeting steel.

The two traded knowing smiles, and Imelda said to a witch standing at the door, "Bring in Eden Wilde."

An anticipatory silence descended upon the room. Hatred for Andre and Imelda ignited a fire in Sage's chest, not even close to witch-fire. How dare the two collude together to stomp on her coven?

As if Eden waited nearby, the door opened. Sage jumped up to greet her cousin. The witch meeting her sight bore little resemblance to the vibrant and cool Eden Wilde. A dead void posed in this pale version of her cousin. Someone had straightened her long brunette hair, something Eden never did. The guise lent her an evilness

Eden never expressed... unless directed at her ex-husband. The epitome of a witch as ignorant outsiders characterized them. Despite the zombie personification, Sage rushed to her cousin and embraced her. Eden didn't return the hug and became a rag doll in Sage's arms.

Bereft, Sage dropped her arms to her sides. Ethan coiled his arm around Eden's waist to haul her to a safe distance to prevent her from joining Andre. Recognition flitted across Eden's eyes before extricating herself, shuddering hard as if fleas invaded her. After all, she didn't know him from Adam, except maybe from her mind. Sage prayed to the goddess the two had established a mutual psychic connection. Eden didn't flee the room like a raving lunatic, so hope floated.

Sage spun on Imelda and Andre, her eyes burning from the fire undulating behind them. "What did you do to her?" She quashed her inner magic to prevent it from going wild and attacking the pair. Rafael laid his hand against the small of her back. The simple touch hauled her back from the cliff's edge.

"I'm fine, Sage." A frog seemed to have landed in Eden's throat. "I'm where I belong. This is the place in the witchworld I never believed I'd have." The words were rote as if spoken from cue cards, no heat, no emotion whatsoever.

Sage didn't face her cousin. She wanted to *see* Imelda answer her question. Eden wasn't fine, and Sage didn't trust a word rolling out of her mouth. "Well, Imelda. I'm waiting for an answer."

"You heard the witch. Why do you think she came so willingly when my savior rescued me from your prison?" Andre replied, his smarmy smile not extending to his eyes.

"You're a sandwich short of a picnic. You've spelled her," Rafael said softly, dangerously. "She'd *never* voluntarily side with your covens. She's a Wilde true and through."

"You heard my warlock," Sage said. Rafael got ahead of himself a lot. Yet, in this case, they were in sync. He also deliberately mixed up his metaphors to suit his own thoughts. *True and through* fit Eden. She deserved a trustworthy warlock. Did Ethan represent that man? With a trustworthy warlock, Eden might return to active duty instead of sitting on the sidelines watching the world go by and letting her hatred of her lying, cheating ex-warlock, ex-husband eat her alive. Sage should've eviscerated the warlock instead of merely banishing him from joining any western coven. *I digress while I try to figure a way out of this crapfest. And why the hell isn't Imelda responding?*

Sage scanned Rafael and Ethan. They each waited for a pointy-toed shoe to drop. However, she noticed a book of information speed through Ethan's eyes. Had he connected psychically to Eden?

"Imelda, what do you want? Whether or not she wants to, Eden's returning to the Wilde Coven with us. Today." Sage maintained a neutral expression and tone.

A gash of a smile graced Imelda's red-lipsticked lips. "We're keeping Eden here while you give us everything we want." She paused for dramatic effect. And paused and paused.

Oh, holy goddess. This woman will be the death of me and mine. Alarm bells clanged in Sage's head. "Which is?"

"*Who,* is the proper pronoun," Andre dropped his lethal iota in the conversation.

It dawned on Sage. Who Andre wanted all along. Willow.

Rage hammered the alarm bell, breaking it into a million pieces. She fisted her hands to contain the external explosion. The telltale pain mushroomed behind her eyes, exacerbating the sting of her eyeballs. *No. I'm so screwed! My brain's going into an aether-induced lockdown.*

"May I have a moment with my warlocks?" Sage choked out, gasping from a sudden lack of air. Dipping her head to shield her eyes, she drew in air before she saw red.

"By all means." Imelda shooed everyone out, and the door shut with a definitive click.

"Don't say a word aloud," she said. "The room's probably bugged to the nth degree." She kept her face hidden from prying cameras and her eyes hooded. Horses thundered through her head, and flames enveloped her entire body. Air and water magic did little to soothe it. Air fanned the flames, and the water dried up like an arid desert. Gwyneira's wings fluttered a skosh against her shoulders, coming alive, despite the aether and despite the wards. *Interesting... the rising aether gave my familiar life in a warded room.*

"It's happening," Rafael affirmed rather than questioned. Fire coiled on his fingers, and he clenched his fists as if to contain the magic from leaving his flesh and bone.

"What's going on?" Ethan mouthed, hands shielding his lips.

The wards fragmented further. "He still wants Willow," she murmured. Rafael tried to touch her, but she backstepped. "And Eden."

"Makes sense. A dog with a bone," Ethan replied, his awareness of the wards breaking widening his eyes. Threads of air magic glowed on his fingers.

"What is Eden saying to you?" More power ascended inside her, pulsing through her every fiber.

"What's wrong? Who broke the wards?" Ethan reached out to touch her, withdrew as if scorched.

"Her aether's rising." Rafael turned to her. "Did you incite this? It's too soon after last time."

Rafael knew her too well. "I tried to stall it longer. But..." She flicked her hands in the air. "Black warlock threats seem to trigger me." She rubbed her scratchy eyeballs. "Both of you make excuses to get out. I don't know what will happen. I'll stay behind while you ostensibly go get Willow."

Ethan wagged his head. "I'm a black warlock. I can handle it."

"No one can," she insisted, stamping her foot on the floor. "Just do as I say. Now freaking tell me what Eden said."

"They've spelled her," Ethan continued to whisper. "Alarmed at first, then excited to connect with me. Andre's not psychic, as far as I can tell from her. They're keeping her in a warded room in what she calls the tower on the third floor. I can see it from her mind's eye. She wants to return to her tower. Senses something brewing here and doesn't want to be a part of it."

"Eden's been too much a loner the last two years. She needs a good warlock to tow her from her doldrums. To rejoin the living." The hint didn't go unnoticed in the flush working up Ethan's neck. "At least we know where we'll find her."

"Well, she's intrigued by me," he replied. "She wants to know me better. She's torn since she understands I'm Imelda and Andre's enemy." Excitement burned red spots on his cheeks. "I'm definitely intrigued."

"Where's Andre's room? I can't tell if Imelda imprisoned him and all this is a ruse or if they truly planned this coup together." Rafael kinked his neck right to left, prepping for a fight.

"Andre comes and goes as he pleases," Ethan explained. "It's all I can tell from her mind."

"Try to sway her. I need her to want to come home, to snap out of this," she said. "Either we leave with her now or send her back to her room. I don't want her involved if this mess goes sideways." The aether dimmed and settled, and she peered up at Rafael. "How do my eyes look?"

"You're good. They won't notice anything." He pulled her into his side, flinched, but held on. "What do you mean *going sideways*? What are you planning?"

"To get us all out alive." Sage straightened her blouse, patted down her hair, avoiding Rafael's gaze. "Call Imelda back in."

Ethan opened the door, and the room again filled with Imelda, Andre, and their entourage. Not Eden.

"Where's my cousin?"

"We sent her to her room. You saw that she's okay." Imelda smiled, took her customary seat.

"What do you want, Andre?" Sage gritted her teeth, had to mentally prevent her hands from wringing his scrawny neck.

"I think you know," the black warlock taunted. "Two things I—and Imelda—want." His gaze raked over Rafael in a weird, lustful way, settled on Ethan, and shifted back to Rafael.

Sage froze, rooted to the spot. Did he want the Ravenwoods too? "You can't have Willow."

"Then you can't have Eden," he replied. "It's a good, sensible trade. Willow's still learning her magic, but Eden knows her stuff. You're getting the better end of the stick."

"No deal," Sage countered. "I don't barter with my witches as pawns in your game."

"We keep Eden, who is very willing to stay." Imelda paused. "And you will suffer the consequences of not joining the right side of this skirmish. All we want is peace amongst witches and black warlocks. We want to work together, right, Andre?"

"Of course, my dear." He patted her shoulder.

"With you at the helm, I suppose?" Ethan swept his arm, taking in the devious pair. "Thought you worked alone, Andre."

"Oh, my boy. It's what I always told you Ravenwoods. Only a matter of time I'd find a worthy and willing witch to join my cause. Since the Wildes weren't so willing, I explored elsewhere. You know we need to align with witches to grow our future."

Imelda's spine straightened against her chair. The witch assumed she was Andre's first choice. Sage cataloged the information for later perusal.

"What else?" Ethan encouraged the man to speak when Sage wanted him to concentrate on Eden.

"Well, you know I'm always on the hunt for black warlocks, especially ones who've been on my radar for years." Silver flecks lit his dull gray eyes from within. "To beef up our ranks. Remember the special ones I've told you Ravenwoods about."

"Give it up, man." Rafael pressed his fists on the table. "We don't have all day."

Andre remained silent, a Cheshire-cat grin plastered on his face, his gaze slurping Rafael up as if he wanted to eat him alive. The gaze holding a million secrets.

A deadly light bulb flared brightly in Sage's brain, ready to detonate if Andre uttered one more word. His words and his gaze explained so much, but not near enough. Hell would freeze over ten times before she caved to the asshole. *Holy crap on a cracker.* Her mind spun out with his unspoken ask.

Chapter 18

The ache behind Sage's eyes returned with a vengeance. All her natural elements of magic filled every crevice inside her. The magic melded, creating a chaotic storm of aether. Fog clouded her eyes, and Sage felt them darken to black, the silver rim blasting out a sparkling light. Andre gasped, and Imelda clutched her moonstone pendant, her mouth hanging ajar. The chain on the pendant broke, fell to Imelda's lap, and her fingers clutched air.

"I'll relinquish my position as High Priestess of the western covens," Sage said. "It's all yours, Imelda." She stalled to give the magic leeway inside her, to build and coalesce. Gwyneira stirred on her shoulders, rapidly flapping its wings, readying for takeoff.

"What's happening with your eyes?" Imelda stuttered. As she scooched back in her chair, she jammed her elbow against the table and stifled a cry of pain.

"Forget my freaking eyes," Sage ground out. The magic pulsed inside her, waiting for her command. "I'll convince the region to let you lead. Just give me my cousin. Forget about Willow... and anyone else in my coven. The four of us hit the road now. Deal?" The lies rolled off her tongue. Any remaining wards in the room collapsed under Sage's rising aether.

"Sage?" Rafael's muted voice carried from a distance. His hands touching her from behind sparked and nearly ignited. Holes singed her blouse where he made contact.

"No deal," Andre said. "Take him." He gestured at a group of warlocks who'd slipped through a hidden door in the wall to Rafael's right. They surged inside the room and surrounded Rafael and Sage, shoving them apart. Sage's hip hit the table, and she winced. Her familiar emitted a loud hiss. Rafael bellowed, a dull roar in her ears. Baseball-size fireballs levitated off his palms and died instantly. Six warlocks caged him in a cocoon of impenetrable air. Three caught Ethan, held him in his own witch-air bubble, and floated him to the far corner of the room. The wards so thick his angry shouts sounded like whispers.

No one possessed the ability to approach Sage. Magic encased and protected her. Aether in its highest form, impenetrable, dangerous, and indestructible. Lightning bolts erupted off Sage, almost striking Imelda and Andre. Stars shot up to hover beneath the ceiling and began to fall as more replaced them. They landed around Imelda and Andre, not touching but creating an inescapable curtain. Fireballs formed and rolled off her hands, burning the floor, the table, wherever they landed.

The warlocks ferried Rafael kicking and shouting through the hidden door. Although she felt his ineffectual tugs on her magic through his warding, she controlled what she dished out, didn't want him touching her aether. She'd think about how he managed it later. The one other time he'd touched her aether in its most intense and purest form nearly killed him. She refused to risk him again. Yesterday's small slippage didn't count since she'd constrained the magic from going hog wild.

Horror tugged Imelda's eyes and mouth wide, a caricature picture of doom. Terror deepened in Andre's wide eyes, but his excited shock fueled her magic. Sage ignored the others in the room. Except Ethan. Weaving his magic, he knotted threads of light in his air cage and his lips moved as he recited silent spells.

Sage recalled what he'd said about black warlocks tolerating aether. Could she safely use him as a conduit, an aid to get them out alive?

"Sage, what is your intention?" Imelda found a shaky voice. "You've broken through my wards. You've defied protocol during our friendly meeting."

"Screw you and your protocol. You agreed to no wards. I'm merely dishing out what you served first." Sage fought through the pain in her skull, the fire consuming her every cell. Fire encapsulated her, wind fanned the flames, and water cooled her. Earth remained ready and willing to aid the other elements. Sage unleashed the aether in waves, like a tsunami, a hurricane, a firestorm, and a cyclone all entangled in one. It was intangible and touched nothing in the room. But the magic killed every ward, killed every other iota of magic for blocks, maybe miles. Gwyneira flew off Sage's shoulder, developing to owl form. Using her wings and feet, the familiar guided the magic around the room. The owl pulled aether from one corner of the room to the other like a tent.

Ethan's air shroud dissipated, and he fell toward the floor. A thread of glowing aether whipped in front of him, and he caught his balance against the table. The magic knocked him back, unharmed, but zapped his ability to use his own magic. Imelda, Andre, and the Helwig witches and warlocks sagged to the floor, eyes wide, mouths moving soundlessly. Hair haloed around their heads, and their clothes fluttered against their bodies. They twitched and bucked against the floor. Embers burned holes in the hardwood, black sizzling spots among the variegated brown wood.

In slow motion, Imelda shoved through the magic and tried to thrust Sage's witch-air back at her. Air met air, and a cyclone danced on the table. Sage's hair swirled around her head in a golden halo. She raised her arms toward the ceiling to temper and direct the magic outward. The aether controlled her, and she succumbed to its authority, unable to fight it any longer. The magic snapped and flashed like lightning, scorching the walls, table, and chairs. Waves of water washed the fire into a murky, black mess of ashes.

Ethan regained his air magic and joined the maelstrom. He centered the cyclone above the table until it diminished to a gentle breeze. Since he wasn't bound to Sage, he couldn't use her aether, and for that she was grateful. Yet the aether didn't affect his magic after her initial whiplash. If it was true black warlocks could weather an aether storm, why had Andre fallen like a sack of dried bones?

After what felt like hours, the magic abated inside Sage. It ebbed and flowed and remained as powerful as if she hadn't spent a boatload. A gush of water and an avalanche of earth ascended above Andre laying prone on the floor and poured across the room—Andre's magic. Sage jumped onto a chair, and Ethan followed suit to avoid the mud.

Three angry panthers slithered off Andre's body, proof that he still contained magic despite the aether. The felines surrounded Imelda and pounced one at a time on her, teeth bared, roaring and growling. Sage turned her head to avoid watching them rake Imelda's body with their long claws and bury their fangs in the few fleshy parts of her thin body.

Sage tossed sizzling fireballs toward the panthers,

trying to stop them from killing Imelda. Dozens of large rats soared off Imelda and attacked the panthers, biting them until the felines retreated, shaking off the offending rodents—Imelda's familiars. Another few seconds flew by, and the rats evaporated. Imelda's final current of magic. A powerful death outpouring unaffected by Sage's aether.

The panthers gave Sage and Ethan long looks and bobbed their heads at Sage, in deference to the magic now defining her and positioning her as one of the most powerful witches in the world. The panthers slunk to Andre, still incapacitated on the floor, and his skin re-absorbed them. Why had she waited so long to allow the aether to rule her once again, instead of always dribbling it out or battling to bury it?

"Sage? Can you hear me?" Ethan's voice escalated with each word.

Slow and steady, her arms dropped to her side, and a warm pulse of magic shivered over her. The ache behind her eyes tapered, and her head thundered. A calmness overcame her. Her familiar flew to her shoulder, cooed in her ear, and her skin re-absorbed the owl.

"Imelda's dead," she choked out. Her magic may have knocked the witch out, but if Andre's panthers killed the witch, their allegiance was far from perfect. He'd ordered the killing, which meant he never intended to ally with her. "Bind Andre," she ordered Ethan. "Let's snag Rafael and Eden and get the hell out of this dead zone."

"What about Imelda's witches and the other black warlocks? They won't let you leave alive." Ethan scratched his head, air spitting off his fingers and ruffling his dark locks, leaving his hair in a ruffled, albeit a gorgeous, mess.

Her gaze slurped him up, viewing him in a new light. The man was as gorgeous as they came. Any witch would be lucky to have him. But she no longer felt any lust toward him, just a friendly fondness and excitement to have such a strong warlock at her side. He was a good man, and he'd make a welcome ally to the Wilde Coven.

She appreciated how much she desired Rafael, the other half of her soul, her future. Too much time had elapsed while she'd sowed her stupid, wild-ass oats, playing her given High Priestess role to the hilt. She'd not waste another day to be with Rafael in all ways. Marriage, children, old age, death, you name it. But was he okay? Panic clamped her heart. She welcomed the pain, used it to spur her next steps.

"If any are awake, they'd have to shoot me. Their magic's incapacitated. It won't last forever, and they'll suffer the affects for a few days." She soothed Gwyneira with a few finger strokes and thanked her familiar. "Let's go." She waved her hand toward Andre. "Spell him." She tossed orders to Ethan as if she ruled him. Without a second thought, he recited a spell to subdue and ward Andre.

Andre rose haltingly and took small, slow steps like he was sleepwalking. Although his brain controlled his arms and legs, he was as pliant as an obedient child.

"There'll be black warlocks who didn't succumb." Ethan tweaked the knot on his warding thread, a silky, ghostlike thread floating in the air. "I'm still standing. Still practicing magic."

"Did my aether hurt you?" Concerned eyes landed on his red, exerted face.

"It's killing me." Sweat dripped off his temples, plastered his hair to his head. "Hampering, not killing, my magic. Please don't tell me it's permanent?"

Another vise pinched her heart. "No, it's not." She laid her hand on his arm and squeezed. "I'm sorry. I have pain potions in the SUV."

He patted her hand. "I'll live. But damn, Sage. I've never seen the like. I'm not sure you can even bond me if we traveled down that path. A black warlock's magic might be too strong for your aether. We could end up killing each other. Except... what Andre implied—"

"That Rafael's a black warlock," she finished for him. "How would Andre know?"

"Decades of research. Like he said, he always hinted there were secret black warlocks who didn't know their true identity."

Pronounced an unmanageable child, Rafael moved from one foster home to another. He'd never known his bio parents. If he was truly a black warlock, no wonder no foster parents could ever handle him. No one helped train him to use and control his magic. Therefore, his magic never manifested correctly, or at all, and caused a ton of internal strife within Rafael. *Holy black hell, is it true?*

"Why did Andre succumb to my magic blast?" She diverted her attention off Rafael's frightening potential.

"He's a weak black warlock. More bluster than bite. His familiars do his dirty work."

They cautiously strode out of the room, and a static silence greeted them. Witches and warlocks littered the floor, fallen where they'd waged war. Sage crouched and checked pulses on two witches and a warlock. Relief softened a knot in her shoulders for each pulse beating against her fingers.

"Are any of these black warlocks?" she asked.

"A few I recognize. Apparently, weaker warlocks can't handle your aether."

Standing upright, she continued walking behind Ethan and Andre around the bodies. She searched inside her core for a tug from Rafael. Nothing indicated where he might be or if he was even alive. *Goddess, strike me now if I killed him.* She didn't think she could live without him. The guilt alone promised to eat her alive.

Buried in her own head, Sage bumped against Ethan's

back. He'd come to a standstill in a deserted hallway. Not one body blocked their way. "What's wrong?"

"Eden." He held up a finger for her silence. "There's fighting at the base of the tower. She doesn't understand why they won't leave her alone."

"She's brainwashed." Sage pushed at his back. "Go. Do you know the way?"

"She's feeding me directions. I told her I'm coming to put an end to it so they'll leave her alone." He halted again. "She's asking about Andre."

"Tell her you're bringing him to her." What kind of mind control had Andre used on her cousin? Was Sage capable of ending it? Or would she have to kill Andre to disconnect them? Would she also kill Eden in the process? "Oh, joy."

"What?"

"Too many dodgy variables. We need to get Eden and Rafael to the covenstead. We can deal with the ramifications later." She felt Rafael tug on her fire magic, and a new thread of relief slithered down her back.

"I have an experienced healer who can help if they're compromised," Ethan offered, his footsteps quickening. Andre's zombie shuffle picked up speed, as well.

"I might need all the help I can get. Aspen's good and learning more every day, with great ideas, but she's young without the experience a long-time practitioner can bring. Nothing like my mother. But Mom trained her well." She digressed, her stride increasing. The closer she walked to the "tower," the more prominent Rafael's tugs on her magic plucked on her core of aether. Panic flared up in her chest and created a new fire.

The ache behind her eyes soared, and grit coated her eyeballs. A flash of power almost hit Ethan, and he stumbled from the backlash. "I'm sorry. My aether's rising. I think you need to leave. Take Andre and go."

"I told you I can take the aether. Didn't I just live through it?" He nudged Andre forward. "I'm not leaving you alone."

They hugged the walls of the living room, working their way to the other side of the house. They approached the base of a literal round tower at the end of a hallway to their right. A battle scene unfolded, and Sage jumped backward out of view. A dozen witches and warlocks lay on the floor in various poses. Six black warlocks remained standing.

"Do you see Rafael?" She tried to peek around the corner again, but a warlock peered down the hall, and she hugged the wall next to a compliant Andre ensconced in his shroud. "Damn it. I need to see him." Although Rafael was now pulling from all her elements, she couldn't discern what he was doing with the magic.

"He's blocking them from the stairs and Eden."

The aether crammed into every fiber of her being again. Her head thundered, and she ignored the pain. "Stay here with Andre," she commanded.

Ethan grabbed for her, but she jumped out of reach and pointed to a witch's circle painted on the floor in the room next door. "Can your raven build a ward around Eden?"

Balthazar materialized on Ethan's shoulder and launched into the air. Like a torpedo, it flew straight up the stairs of the tower. The familiar carried glowing threads of air in its beak, already woven for Ethan's spell.

"Already spelled my familiar to protect her," Ethan said.

"Thank you." Appreciation spilled from Sage's voice. "Now build a protective ward around you and Andre."

"Sage. Don't do this alone."

"I won't be alone. I have Rafael."

"You don't know what your magic will do to him." He

rubbed the back of his neck, scanning the hallways.

"Build the ward. Now." She stepped into the entryway to the hall where the fighting ensued. Without another thought, she cloaked an air-tight shield around Ethan and Andre for protection. Ethan's furious yells faded the thicker the shield grew.

Various familiars from cats to frogs to birds scurried, hopped, and flew, respectively, around the room. She knew deep in her core they wouldn't hurt her. Again, it seemed they deferred to her in a similar vein as Andre's panthers.

Magic bounced off her. Three warlocks surrounded her, and she let their magic capture her and hold her in temporary stasis. The other three continued to fight off Rafael's blasts of magic. The magic he displayed wasn't anything Sage had ever seen. Air, fire, water, and earth all rolled up in one. But with no direction or command, ineffectual balls that hurt but didn't impede the warlocks. Something else tinged his magic. Another magic. Not hers. Not one discernable element. Something all Rafael. The aether meld and this foreign magic was the reason his defense gained him no ground. He sorely needed training.

"Stand down, Rafael," Sage commanded. "All of you, stand down. I'm in command now."

"The hell you are," a tall warlock with a craggy face yelled. His spiky blond hair stood on end, more from a jar of gel than magic. "We only take orders from High Priestess Helwig."

"Sage." Rafael's rough voice cut through the heavy breathing in the room. "What are you doing?"

She ignored him. "Imelda's dead. I *am* the regional High Priestess and in command of the Helwig coven now. You'll obey me or you'll die. Take your choice." She stretched out her arms, and two ravens, an eagle, and a hawk landed on them, careful not to dig their talons in her flesh. Another eagle alighted on her right shoulder. A black cat crept closer and sat on its haunches near her feet, and three large frogs leaped up and clung to her legs. All black warlock familiars.

"Choose wisely." Her smile promised to kill.

The aether inside her roiled and gurgled. No need for a mirror. She knew her eyes had turned obsidian, ringed in a silver so intense, the reflecting light glowed on her cheeks.

The three warlocks who'd surrounded her strengthened the holes in the shield their familiars created. Her aether blasted it apart as though their magic was child's play.

Stupid is as stupid does. The warlocks surrounding Rafael joined the three converging on Sage. Their familiars quaked, uncertain who to obey. Not one moved away from Sage. Gwyneira cooed and made soothing sounds from her throat to calm the agitated familiars.

Rafael advanced toward her from his position at the bottom of the tower staircase. "Sage?" He held out his arms. "Give it all to me. We can walk away from this alive."

And she knew in that moment he *could* accept and use the aether. Would it be enough to hinder the six warlocks and allow them both to escape to safety?

Chapter 19

Rafael's eyes pleaded with Sage to turn on the spigot to her magic through their bond. He comprehended her magic, even tainted with aether, knew how to use it. During his fight with the black warlocks, he recognized his difference from the average warlock using white magic. Something all his life led him to believe so, but he could never shake it out. When he'd first used Sage's aether before they'd bonded, he recognized he was no ordinary warlock. But to have survived Sage's powerful magic now twice, it made sense. What that prick Andre wanted made sense. Even though said prick could eat shit and die before he got what he desired.

It was clear now. Rafael had been born a black warlock, possessing his own magic. Untried and inexperienced, buried beneath Sage's magic. He'd always realized something dormant lay beneath her magic, in *his* core. It defied a name or definition. Her witch-fire and aether had been too strong to allow his magic to emerge. Until this day of reckoning.

Despite the air blanket, the black warlocks, and the

familiars surrounding Sage, he made direct eye contact with her. The love in her eyes nearly sank him to his knees. Instead, he strengthened his stance, preparing for the next battle. Shock shook him to the core when a tiny thread of Sage's aether hit his nucleus of magic.

"Where's Ethan?" he asked suddenly.

"Safe," she mouthed.

"If I don't make it out alive, I want you to accept his offer."

The warlocks grunted. The blond said, "Don't worry, lover boy, we'll take care of your witch." He grabbed his crotch and made a thrusting motion into his hand.

A pounding began in Rafael's ears, and his vision clouded. The unnamed magic thrust off his fingertips and zapped the blond warlock upside his head, knocking him to the ground, unconscious or dead. Rafael didn't give two shits. A smirk traversed his face, and he prepared to blast another warlock. *Way too easy now. Game on.* Magic danced inside him like never before, illuminating him from the inside out, granting him strength, both magical and physical.

Six more warlocks rushed the hall, filling the space. Pale and haggard, a couple limped, survivals of Sage's magic blast. Rafael raised another hand, poised to thrust aether-tinged fire. Lightning, stars, and fireballs aided his magic, creating a magic storm between Sage and the warlocks.

Wide eyed, Sage signaled him to stop. Although he held his ground, he'd never quit defending her, not until the day he died. He just hoped fate hadn't planned his death that day.

"The rest of you want more of *that?*" she asked the target of Rafael's fury.

"We're not afraid of your magic," a short, bald warlock said, one of the original six. "We're here, alive, lived through both of your best attempts."

"Are you sure I displayed my best?" Without waiting for a response, she tipped her head at Rafael and released another stream of aether to him along their bond. It hit him, and he staggered. The magic fizzed inside him before joining the strange brew of his own magic. He recovered quickly and gestured for her to drive more toward him.

Tiny crow's feet bracketing her eyes stretched taut. Slowly, she complied, ensuring he could accept each stream she cast to him. Each thread hit him harder, and he lurched as the aether stuffed every crevice inside his body. His eyes went wonky, blurry, expanding the thundering ache behind them. No normal warlock could take this much magic. Not that he was stoked to find out he was a black warlock, but he loved the power it afforded him. At least he'd do good with it and not play an evil minion of the man who wanted to rule the world.

Their magic meld took a few seconds. Almost like he truly brandished a breed of aether encompassing all the natural elements, already melded together, but also with the ability to separate and use each element.

The black warlocks surrounding them appeared as though they waited for Andre and Imelda's recovery. Maybe they were rethinking their allegiances after witnessing their familiars jump ship. Their contented familiars, a multitude of birds, clinging cats, frogs, rats, mice, and even a lizard, converged upon Sage's body. Each familiar she drew toward her broke another hole in her warded shroud. No one else noticed. *Keep waiting, assholes.*

"What'll it be, gentlemen?" Sage asked.

"You two come with us willingly, or we have our orders to take you down." A tall, burly authoritative warlock, one newcomer, bowed to Sage. Not mockingly, but in deference to her station. Didn't matter. The magic roiling on the warlock's right hand spoke another language. An implicit warning to Rafael's partner, his witch, the woman he loved more than life.

Sage's magic shattered the warlock magic encapsulating her, air exploding in puffs of smoke and sparks. The familiars all jumped, flew, or crawled off her, but surrounded her, guarding her from her adversaries. It gave her hands and arms free rein to use her magic. A black lab lopped to Rafael and pressed himself against his leg. He took a second to pat the dog's head, gaining a sudden, strange affinity toward the lab.

The warlocks uttered various objections and coercions to their familiars, all to no avail. The men were toast in the eyes of their precious right hands.

"One last chance. Back off or suffer the consequences." Sage remained calm on the outside, yet her rage in their connected magic quivered through Rafael's body.

"High Priestess Wilde, please stand down. You've broken the rules of a witch's parlay by raising your magic against us on our territory," the lead warlock said by rote. May as well give his name and ID number too.

Sage snorted. "Drugs addling your brains? All rules are off, thanks to your leaders. Is that your final answer?"

Before Sage could blink, three warlocks leaped at her, all magical guns blazing. Sage blasted out her own full-frontal assault of aether. Magic screamed in the air. Electricity encircled her, knocking all the warlocks out of the circle. They floundered backward, stumbling and scrambling to catch their balance.

With one assessing perusal, the love in her eyes thawed him, and she went full medieval on the warlocks, the hall, the entire house, and the extended grounds. His one final thought before the magic slammed him was the safety of Ethan and Eden from the direct onslaught of what felt like all the magic under the sun. Sage was doing her job, and he trusted her. She'd never jeopardize Eden or

Ethan, let alone the Helwig witches and warlocks, never permanently.

Magic inside Rafael pushed the aether attacking him, but he used it to drive back a new horde of black warlocks descending upon them. Sage rushed to his side, their backs to the stairs. Their magic fused in front of them, a storm of air, water, fire, and earth of cataclysmic proportions. Every warlock fell, shock on their faces, their bodies bound with invisible threads morphing into tangible thick vines. The vines grew and wrapped around the warlocks, rooting them to the floor, stopping short of suffocating the men. Familiars fled to parts unknown. The black lab remained glued to his side.

Fireballs and lightning strikes boiled up in the air and crashed to the floor, spreading electricity across the floors. Sage erected a shield to keep the magic from hitting them. Didn't matter. He hauled in her magic and poured it out, and his body became a weapon of invincibility. Joy surged through him. Grinning, he accepted the flood of aether, the waves knocking him against the stair rail.

Until it became too much. He lost control and could not sever his bond to Sage in time. Losing the ability to redirect Sage's aether, he began to absorb the magic, whereas seconds ago he held it at bay. Somehow, some way. This time was different. Pain lanced Rafael's head as though his skull split in half, and he cried out. Horror widened her eyes as she took in the catastrophe.

Arms flailing in the air, she shut off the tap to her magic.

Too late. He lost control of his limbs and hit the floor. Magic crawled all over him, sizzled around his body. The black lab licked his face, whined, and lay beside him.

He had a hard time discerning where she'd gone; her words were muffled, and a gray cloud obscured his vision. She touched his shoulders and jerked away as if acid corroded her flesh down to bone.

"Sage," he tried to croak out, but the word never left his mouth. One final lancing pain struck him full force, broiling his every cell. Air fanned the flames. No witch-water or witch-earth chased it to douse the fire. The world blackened and flung him into an abyss mirroring the depths of hell.

Chapter 20

Rafael!" Sage lunged forward, almost taking a header from the vast magic permeating the room. The vise pinching her heart tightened. She fell upon his prone body, caught herself on her elbow and sucked up the pain.

No need to worry about anyone attacking her. She'd knocked out every magical being within the vicinity of the covenstead. Thank the goddess she'd instructed her coven to stay at least two miles off the grid.

Fingers against Rafael's neck, she hunted for his pulse. Couldn't find it. Tears welled, and she swiped them away before they obscured her vision. "Come on, baby," she whispered, her fingers seeking a sign of life.

The black lab skulked out of hiding and laid his head on Rafael's arm. The dog gave her hope that Rafael lived; otherwise, the familiar wouldn't be there. Or maybe the dog was just a dog. Who knew? Inane thoughts crowded her mind until her fingers struck gold. A faint pulse, beating slow but steady. "Thank you, goddess." Despite the pain of their melded magic lingering on their bodies and creating a fiery friction begging to fry her alive, she hugged Rafael.

"Sage?" Ethan said behind her. "Is he—"

"He's alive. That's all I know. We need to get him and Eden home." Fallen warlocks littered the room. "How are we going to get them out? Depending on how your shield worked on Eden, I may have conked her out too." She could barely lift her own arm, but she'd power through to carry Eden and Rafael out before Imelda and Andre's crew awakened. They may not have magic for a few days, but there were enough Helwig witches and warlocks to physically hamper their escape.

"Can you raise witch-air? You zapped my magic even behind the ward." Ethan helped her straighten Rafael's bent legs. "Wrap them in air and float them out."

Sage concentrated, waggled a finger, shot off a puff of wind. "Not enough for an adult body."

"We'll have to carry them out." He headed toward the stairs, slow and wary. "I'll get Eden."

"Hurry. I don't know how much time we have before the effects wear off."

"Oh, I think we have plenty of time." He chuckled wryly. "Your magic breached my ward. My circle broke apart toward the end." He continued ascending the stairs.

Panic danced up her spine. "Where's Andre?" she called.

"In the protective circle, and for good measure, I tied his wrists to his ankles with drapery cords."

"Perfect." Relief skated across the knots in her shoulders.

"This is why we need each other. We make a good team." His voice drifted off as his footsteps faded up the circular staircase.

She let his dig slide. Not the time, not the place.

"Rafael, love, can you hear me?" She pressed her mouth to his cool lips, imparting the heat of the fire they created when they touched. He gave no sign he'd heard. No sign that life beat inside him other than his faint pulse.

Tears finally cascaded down her cheeks. The fire and air on her skin dried them instantly. Witch-water soothed the sting. She stroked his face, his arms, his chest, trying to let him know she lived, and lived for him.

She surveyed the devastation her magic, no, hers and Rafael's magic, produced. Not merely the bodies littering the floor, but anything not nailed down was laying in pieces on the floor or in piles of ashes. Charred marks scarred the walls, and water and earth turned the floors to a wet, muddy mess. A thin layer of mud covered some of the fallen warlocks. All the familiars returned to their warlocks, which meant the warlocks were alive. Another knot untied in her shoulders. She wasn't hellbent on a killing spree. They'd deal with the covens in a more political, non-violent way. If it came to war, so be it. But these people had followed orders, just like she'd expect her witches and warlocks to follow, whether or not they liked it. Maybe she'd gain some new members for her more modern, progressive coven after the current mess shakes out.

Ethan's footsteps sounded on the stairs, heavy and slow. He tramped into the room with Eden flung over his shoulders like a sack of dead bones.

"Is she alive?" Sage caught her breath.

"Yes." Ethan gently laid her on the floor near Rafael, where mud hadn't reached. "I couldn't get her legs and arms to cooperate to carry her like a gentleman should. She fought me even in stasis. Cursed me out in her head too."

"That's Eden for you."

"And you want me to consider her a partner, the mother of my children?" He grinned his devastating grin that had set her hormones in a tizzy the day she'd met him. Goddess, it seemed forever ago.

"She'll come around." Sage stood on unsteady legs.

Ethan snaked out an arm, and she grabbed it for support.

"Do I need to carry all three of you out? At least Andre's able to move." He slid his arm around her waist, bracing her until she gained her balance. The heat of his arm added to her exhaustion, but she welcomed the momentary brace, wishing his arm belonged to Rafael. Only the goddess knew if he'd live to grant her such wish.

"Thank you." She freed herself from him and stood on noodle legs. "Who first?"

"Leave Andre in the warded circle. I'll take Eden to the SUV."

"What if she wakes up and tries to leave?"

"I'll secure her." His brows drew into a vee between his eyes. "It's all I got. I can't take them both at once."

"I'm sorry I'm useless." She kicked at a shard from a decimated ceramic vase. The piece skittered into a pile of black-and-white silk flowers flapping in witch-air infusing the room.

"You're as far from useless as a lab full of AI engineers."

She mustered a smile. "Go. Before—" Sage readied a paltry fireball. Three black warlocks entered the room, hands in the air, their magic palpable.

Ethan pivoted on his heels, ready to secure them in his paltry air magic, weak glowing threads already forming off his hands. "Kyle, Cody, Chase," he exclaimed. His threads of air disintegrated. "What the hell are you doing here?" He closed the distance to the one he called Kyle—who appeared older than the other two by a couple of years—and they hugged it out like long-lost bros.

"Followed Andre's sycophants here to work from the inside once we discovered Helwig had snagged him," classic tall, dark, and handsome replied. "He called us here, so it worked perfectly. Unless we were his guinea pigs all along."

"Man, I'm glad to see you." Ethan addressed Sage. "Second Ravenwood cousins. Bow to High Priestess Sage Wilde," he tossed over his shoulder.

"No need. Just help us get away," she replied. They complied anyway, lights gleaming in their very teal eyes as they offered her the customary greeting for a High Priestess. They could be brothers to Evan and Ethan, except for their exceptional eye color. "By the way, how'd you survive... the magic?"

"Saw Ethan shielded in a circle and did the same," Kyle replied. "Lady, you've got some powerful magic. I'd hate to get on your bad side."

"Do you trust them?" she asked Ethan, impatience trickling inside her.

"Implicitly. They covered for me when I escaped Andre's compound after you captured him."

Lady Luck delivered the help they needed. Ethan and the three brothers carted Eden and Rafael out to the SUV while Sage guided Andre behind them, wanting to push his compliant, walking-dead gait to force his feet to move faster. On the way out the front door, Sage grabbed the security wand from the console drawer and shoved it in her back waistband. An easy grab and present for Rafael. Her magic had rendered the ward on the console drawer useless.

The black lab hopped inside the cargo hold where they'd laid Rafael and rested his head on Rafael's chest.

"You want Shadow in or out?" Kyle asked.

"Fitting name, if clichéd. Leave the dog. Who's familiar?" Sage asked.

"Shadow never became a familiar. She was the house pet."

The cool afternoon served normalcy to Sage. She breathed deeply of the pine rich air to temper the magic refusing to subside inside her. Eden slept onward next to

Rafael in the cargo. Sage caressed her cousin's cheek, pushed a shock of brunette hair behind her ear. She squeezed inside and nestled Rafael's head in her lap, sifting her fingers through his wind-blown hair.

How long would it take for the magic to wear off? Would either Eden or Rafael ever visit normal again? So many questions, so few answers. History and medical books didn't exactly contain anecdotes for getting hammered by aether magic.

She called Aspen and gave her a heads-up and then called the witches and warlocks on road duty with instructions to head home. The siege had ended, but the war cry had sounded with first shots fired.

Chapter 21

Ravenwood and Wilde vehicles converged upon the covenstead, cramming the driveway as Ethan drove the SUV close to the front door.

"Secure Andre in the dungeon," Sage ordered the witches and warlocks waiting for them. "I want all hands on deck, triple wards, and double perimeter patrol." She entered the house, inhaled the familiar cinnamon-and-apple scents of home, her sanctuary. "Let me know when Andre shakes off the effects of the magic restraints."

The three Ravenwood cousins helped Ethan carry Eden and Rafael into the infirmary, a place that suited her sister's needs to a tee, including a two-burner gas stove, oven, and sink to create her potions and charms. A myriad of herbs and potions, both sweet and bitter, rode the air. Sage tweaked her nose to halt a sneeze.

Aspen gasped when Sage entered the room behind the men. "Your eyes. They're so dark."

Sage waved her sister off. "It's my aether."

"I've never seen that happen." Aspen gathered supplies and headed to the two twin medical beds in the adjoining room.

"Because you've never seen *anyone* exhibit the power your sister blasted out today." Awe and appreciation tumbled from Ethan's voice.

"She knocked out everyone not in a protective ward and killed the magic at the Helwig covenstead," one of the three nearly identical brothers said. Sage needed to straighten out their identities. Later. The present involved too much for her brain to comprehend much more.

She followed Aspen to the other room and shut the world out. "Ethan can call his healer if you need."

Aspen scoffed. "Please. At least let me work *my* magic. I do have mad skills."

"Sorry." She listlessly patted Aspen's arm. "I didn't mean it like that. Just two heads are always better than one."

"I know. Just kidding. Give me a few minutes. Can you leave the room while I do an initial assessment?"

Sage's gaze raked over Rafael and Eden. Both appearing asleep, their faces exhibiting too much pain and horror as though nightmares plagued them. "I'd rather not."

"Sage." Aspen huffed out a breath, alternatively scratching the backs of her hands. "I need to concentrate. Your magic's interfering. It's affecting me."

"What?" Sage folded her arms around herself. "Are you in pain?"

"Prickles." She swatted at the cloth cubicle panel partially separating the beds. "It's affecting Rafael and Eden too. See their faces? They keep twitching. Their eyeballs are moving, and I doubt it's REM." Aspen left to sort through the labeled potions and charms in her floor-to-ceiling medicine cabinet. She separated them on a tray she carted into the room.

Rafael went full-on twitch. Not quite a seizure, but

enough to realize it landed too far from normal. Erratic friction played along the strange new bond connecting her to him.

"Sorry, sis, you need to leave."

Sage's feet were rooted to the floor, unable to tear her gaze from Rafael or stop the fleeting glimpses at her cousin.

"Sage!" Aspen shouted. "Get out! You're not doing them any good standing there. I need to know what I'm up against."

Hands gently clenched Sage's shoulders from behind. The burned-citrus scent of Ethan's magic tickled and annoyed her senses. "They'll be okay without you helicoptering."

"I can't leave him." Giant tears welled in her eyes. *Again with the freaking waterworks!* Another spasm hit Rafael, and he bucked on the bed, proof of her unwelcome presence. She pushed back against Ethan, fled into a hallway jam-packed with witches and warlocks. Avoiding their questions and words of comfort, she headed toward her bedroom. Ethan remained on her tail.

By the time she'd reached her sanctuary, annoyance took a spin at her. "I don't want you here. Rafael did this because of your stupid-ass offer, trying to prove that he and I were a force to be reckoned with. That we didn't need a black warlock to strengthen our bond."

Ethan lifted his hands in capitulation and backed away to stand under the threshold. "I'm sorry. I know you don't mean to blame me. If it makes you feel better, take your best shot. I might add that you now have a black warlock strengthening your bond."

"We don't know for sure! I need proof. Rafael will demand proof." She spat the words out.

"What more proof do you need? Your aether filled him, he used it along your bond, and he lived through it. Black warlocks didn't conk out from your first aether attack, and neither did Rafael. By the second blast, you'd depleted their magic, knocking them all out. I only retained my magic because I was in a protective circle. Otherwise, who knows what your aether would've done to me? Rafael took it all until shit went sideways in the end."

"I need to know his lineage." A semblance of calm claimed her before she tripped off the rails to no-man's-land. Her knees crumpled and deposited her on the padded bench at the foot of the king-size bed she shared with Rafael. She hated the idea of sharing her bed with any other man. She'd never shared it with another warlock since she'd kept her more promiscuous side out of their sanctuary.

"I'll get the proof you need."

Eyes clear and bright, she peeked up at him. "Will you, please? Can you do it now? Rafael will want to know after he awakens. He's always desperately wanted to know the identity of his sperm donors."

"Okay. Can I get you anything? Send someone up to hang with you?" He approached, sifted his hand through her hair, almost fatherly. He withdrew his hand as if singed, leaving strands of her hair floating. "You're radioactive."

"Great." She pounded her fist on the padded bench. "All hail the radioactive High Priestess. Everyone, bow to my imminence or I'll zap you to dust."

He laughed. "Don't sell yourself short. You may be the highest of the High Priestesses after today." He backstepped. "I'll send up lunch since we missed Imelda's grand gesture of packaged crap."

She closed her eyes for a moment, opened them, softened with gratitude. "Thank you, Ethan. For everything. I couldn't have done this without you." Exhausted, she tipped back, her elbows on the bed, unable to rouse her languid legs. "We'll cement our alliance when we get through today's trauma and drama."

"Oh, I know we will. Even if the offer has changed." Chuckling, he left the room.

Lethargic, Sage wobbled to her dresser and peered at herself in the mirror above it. Her hair looked like rats had nested in it, and it had unraveled from the clips she'd used that morning. Ash smudged her right cheek, and her berry lipstick had faded. Her eyes were a dark sapphire blue on their way to normal. The silver ring had vanished. Closing them, and with her mind's eye, she scoped out her internal magic. The bond to Rafael, although faint, existed, but it was different. It sizzled against what little magic she contained after having expended most of it. The makeup of the bond, although weak because of depletion, felt stronger, more secure. And conferred him access to her aether without her spoon-feeding it to him. *We're freaks of the witchworld. In a stellar way.*

"A black warlock bond." She opened her eyes again. How had Andre known?

Her relationship with Rafael would never be the same. Not if he truly was a black warlock. Using his own magic, he didn't need her. He'd have all the power he'd always craved and the motivation to leave. After all, she was too high maintenance as a regional High Priestess, despite that he always loved her status. On the flipside, he could lead his own coven of warlocks once trained. They certainly didn't have time to waste if the Black Tide and the Helwig coven and their compatriots took swift action against the Wildes and Ravenwoods.

"Rafael can't hold it against me. He can't walk away because of Ethan's proposal." Frustrated, she gritted her teeth and threw up her hands. Yet she'd let him go if it was the only way to save him. From her, from her aether.

She buried her face in her hands. No tears. Just recriminations and grief gushing through her. No more stupid tears while a witchworld waited for her to prevent a war. But she needed her anchor, her destiny at her side.

A knock sounded on the double doors. "Come in." She stood tall and erect, despite her aching back and wobbly legs.

Jessica carried in a tray with a diced chicken garden salad and ice tea, the tea dark and bitter the way she drank it. Her aunt set the tray on the small table by the windows.

"Did Aspen lace the tea?"

"No. She won't until you tell her what you need." Jessica approached. "Eden's waking up." She said nothing more, and the lack of an update on Rafael didn't go over her head.

"How is she?"

"She'll be okay. Aspen thinks it'll take a few days for her magic to recover. Ethan's protective ward helped prevent worse damage. Eat, take a shower. Come see for yourself."

C★C★C★

After a few bites of salad and a short but hot and cleansing shower, Sage allowed Evan and Willow to escort her to Eden's bedroom on the other side of the second floor.

"Why are you two playing my guards, gimpy leg and all?" she asked.

"Rafael's out of commission," Evan said, sounding so much like his older brother.

"And?"

"Dude, you've scared everyone else into the hills." Willow tossed a spray of sparkles she wouldn't normally be able to do into the air. "Yeehaw."

"Am I hurting you?" The aether still fizzled on her skin, within her muscles, even though she couldn't light a simple candlewick.

Willow faltered a step, kept on leading the way, one hop at a time. "It's tolerable. Fun times, though."

"You know how you get a slow burn in your gut if you eat super-spicy shit?" Evan asked. "It's like that, but head to toe."

"*Wonderful.* My magic makes me a pariah." Sage slowed her roll to distance herself from them.

"Not helping." Willow snickered. "Come on. Get your ass in gear."

"Yes, task master. You plan on taking over the coven?"

"I will if I need to," Willow said matter-of-factly.

Sage gasped. "You're serious. Were there plans afoot?"

Willow turned on her sister. "Serious as I'm standing here. We had backup plans in our pockets. You didn't think we'd let you throw yourself to the wolves without Plan B, did you?"

Sage closed her eyes a long moment, opened them, walked the last few feet to Eden's door. Evan and Willow took up guard on either side of the door. Willow could bash someone with a crutch if nothing else.

"Why doesn't Eden have a guard?" Sage asked.

"She refused," Evan said. He pointed to the ceiling. "Cameras are active and someone's always a few feet away, hiding in the trenches."

"Better than nothing, I guess. Can I go in alone, *mistress?*" Sage knew how much Willow hated the old-fashioned salutation.

"Sage." Willow waggled her head. "You're still in charge."

"Will she let me in? Will I hurt her is what I'm asking?" Sage glowered at Willow and her snark.

"Yes, and yes." Willow tugged her sister forward. The contact caused a smoldering chafing against their bare skin, and she twisted her hand from Willow's grip to save them both from the pain. "She knows the scoop. Aspen gave her a pain potion and a charm chaser to extend it." She dug into her jeans pocket and produced a vial. "Take this. It'll help your own pain."

Sage nudged Willow's hand. "No. If you're all suffering, I'll suffer too."

"Be that way." Willow uncorked the vial and drank half the potion, smacking her lips as she shoved it into Evan's hand to drink the rest.

Eden was one of the few witches Sage allowed free rein to roam without a warlock. Eden had her reasons, and Sage refused to fault her for them. When your ex-husband, ex-warlock cheated multiple times, and impregnated another witch, he soured the stomach. When said ex told his wife he'd rather live with his mistress, well, that soured the mind, heart, and soul. Eden never told him she knew about the affairs from day one since she read it in his thoughts, something she swore she'd never do, not that he ever knew. He'd exhibited classic cheater attributes she refused to let slide and gave herself the liberty of infringing upon his mind to validate her suspicions. Sage was happy to kick the cheater out on his ass. She never liked him from day one.

Eden sat in her over-stuffed armchair in front of the window with a view of the deepest parts of the forest. Moonlight cut through the forest in swathes of luminous light. Sage always found her cousin alone, chilling from the mundane and crowds of the house or reading her favorite cozy mysteries.

Without moving a muscle, Eden said, "I'm sorry I'm such a burden."

Stunned, Sage rushed forward and fell to her knees, clamping her thighs for safety when she wanted to embrace her cousin. "How could you ever think that? That raging dipstick kidnapped you, manipulated you."

"He wouldn't have if I didn't have psychic abilities."

"Eden! Do you know how rare you are? I know of two

of you in the world. And you're both in my house."

"Ethan Ravenwood," Eden said thoughtfully. "Yeah, we connected a few times."

"Without that connection, we would never have found and secured you."

"Is Andre still manipulating you?"

Eden shook her head. "Your aether blast eventually killed his spell." She gestured to the other chair. "Get off the floor, silly."

With creaking and sore knees, Sage lifted off the floor and sat in the chair. She noticed empty vials on the table, the spelled wooden bead bracelet on Eden's wrist. "Are you still in pain?"

"It's fleeting. It'll pass." Her gaze raked Sage from her hair to her sneakers. "Your magic's palpable."

"Sorry. Has your magic returned?" Hope clogged her throat.

"It's returning in dribs and drabs."

Sage breathed again, treaded lightly. "Can you tell me what it was like being coerced by magic?"

Eden wrung her hands. "Andre latched on to my mind. It was like I'd lost all control of my body."

"How'd he do it?"

Brighter spots of red bloomed on Eden's cheeks. "I tried to ferret information out of his mind, to learn things from him. I ended up opening a hole for him to use his magic."

"He's not psychic, is he?" Unease gnawed at every fiber of her body, and she sat straighter in her chair.

"No. Just strong manipulation skills."

"How did he use magic in a warded room?"

"Happened after Imelda's witches destroyed the dungeon wards."

"If you were in the warded circle, how'd he breach it?"

The spots on Eden's cheek widened, and perspiration dotted her upper lip. "I was leaving the dungeon with his cannister of familiars at the time of the attack. I hid in the storage room at the top of the stairs when they breached the room. They eventually sniffed me out."

"Why take the familiars?"

"To separate them from Andre."

"Oh. Nice," Sage uttered, surprised Eden thought of it in the chaos. "Can you read Andre's mind?"

"Yes. But I won't again until we determine how to prevent him from attacking my mind with magic."

"That won't happen again." Sage folded and unfolded the hem of her oversize long-sleeve T-shirt. Baggy clothes dampened her need to feel powerful, sexy, and in charge when she felt anything but.

"Imelda will return. She's all about power, control, and revenge."

"No." Sage fought the sorrow creeping in her chest. "She's dead."

"Oh. Well." Eden pushed off her chair. "One less evil witch to contend with. What else happened while I was squatting useless in a tower?"

A long, weighty pause filled the room. "I'll tell everyone together. For now, what do you think of Ethan Ravenwood?"

Eden sneered. "I heard about the offer. Are you considering it? Rafael will crap all over it."

"He's presumptuous. And Rafael will not only *not* like it, he'll take a hike."

"Why the offer in the first place?"

"Because his mother was the last witch born to a black warlock in our region, maybe one of the last in the world. Their witches have dwindled to nothing. They want to align with strong witches not only for an allegiance but to carry on their legacy."

"Oh." Eden released an unconscious blast of air in Sage's face, fluttering wisps of her hair. "Whoops. Sorry.

Magic's coming back, but hard to control."

The door opened, and Willow popped her head in. "Aspen wants you both to get some sleep. *Pronto*."

In no mood to argue against sleep Sage knew would never arrive, she rose from the chair, her sore body screaming in protest. In the doorway, she turned to Eden. "Think about Ethan."

"What do you mean?" Eden touched her fingertips to her lips.

"He could be good for you, to you. I can't think of a better warlock for you. You have a ton in common." She pointed to her head. "You could lead a powerful black warlock coven together."

"Oh, hell to the no." Eden shook her head with such ferocity, Sage feared it'd spin off into the Pacific. "Are you so ready to kick me out?"

"I'll never kick you out. But you'll never have to worry he'll learn about your telepathy and desert you due to it." Sage left her cousin pondering an intriguing future.

Chapter 22

Aspen and Ethan waited for Sage, both pacing separate sides of her office the following morning. The sight of them didn't bode well as Sage sidled into the room. Myriad herbal scents wafted off her sister and sprinkled the air. More than normal. Sage shot out a puff of air to disperse the smell in her path forward.

"Can I see him?" Sage asked. Clouds filtered dim light through her windows, blotting out the sun, ratifying her lousy mood.

"No," Aspen replied. "He's still in extreme pain. Your aether's causing it, and your bond's making it worse. His vitals are stable, but he won't wake up. The coven doctor is clueless. It's magic, pure and simple."

"Apparently, there's nothing simple about it." Sage wanted to die on the spot but held herself erect, cool, and confident... on the outside. Inside was an entirely opposite story. "What are your next steps?"

"A circle of thirteen is trying a healing spell as we speak."

"If that doesn't work, I'm calling my healer." Keeping

his distance from Sage, Ethan stopped pacing, crossed his arms over his chest. His raven familiar vaulted onto his shoulder, nodding its head before slinking back under his collar.

"Call her now," Sage and Aspen said in tandem.

A moment flew by, silent, all lost in their own minds. Ethan made the call and summoned his healer.

"Any danger to the coven?" Sage changed the subject when all she wanted to do was hold Rafael and give him all her strength.

"No," Ethan replied. "My cousins returned to Imelda's covenstead to play their part among the Helwig and Black Tide allies. They're sending me intel."

"Who's leading the Black Tide?" She propped her shoulder against the door for support before her knees crumpled.

"Andre's second, a bastard son, Marcos Charlemagne. Imelda's oldest daughter has taken over her coven. According to Kyle, they're all licking their wounds, regrouping. Magic is slow to return to them."

"Was Mika Helwig on the covenstead earlier?" Imelda's forty-year-old daughter lived in San Francisco, keeping the Helwigs bound to both sides of the mountains.

"No. She drove in after the bloodbath."

Sage flinched. "How's your magic?"

"Effects are tapering off."

"Glad someone's healing." Sage stood straight again, hated using the door for a crutch. "I want to see Andre. Ethan, will you accompany me?"

"Not a good idea, sis. Not until your magic tank's full." Aspen pointed out the obvious.

Sage pushed her damp, loose hair behind her ears, and flung up her arms. "Argh! I need to do something."

"Pray and plan," Aspen replied. She headed to the door, stopped at a small accent table, and touched a bowl filled with dried lavender. Water filled the bowl and boiled, leaving a strong, soothing scent drifting across the room, enough to diffuse the other herbs.

Ethan wanted to remain with Sage, but she didn't want his distraction. Nor did she plan to foist him off on Eden yet. Her cousin needed time to recover and gear up to the idea of a warlock, a black warlock to boot.

Finally, left alone, she hefted book after book from her shelves, some as old as dirt. She hunted any spell or potion with the potential to save Rafael.

Hours flew by, and the clouds obscured the sun, lending the room an early twilight. Nothing concrete sprang off the pages to help her warlock. Her magic was leveling out to normal, not that normal existed anymore. The aether remained on the fringes, and she believed it might never abate.

Aspen had installed a camera in Rafael's room, so at least he remained visible to Sage. Excruciating pain masked his pasty face. Occasionally he'd thrash on the bed, not once opening his eyes. After a while, she closed the app. Her inability to help him tortured her. The weight of her grief grew unbearable as her vigil continued.

Her aunt, cousins, and sisters summoned her to a dinner Council meeting, forcing her to vacate her office and adult. Sage expected the inevitable summons. She'd always remained transparent with her Council. On the subject of her aether, she'd been less than. They now deserved to know.

While they ate, Sage regaled her Council of everything occurring at the Helwig covenstead, and most of all about her aether magic. They'd always known she possessed aether, but never knew the full extent of it. Aether in a witch was rare and typically skipped generations. Her grandmother possessed it. They'd all waited for the day of its emergence.

Historically, no documentation existed proving that any black warlock ever possessed aether, but Sage told them it may be possible in Rafael. The thought rolled through Sage's mind, and the idea emerged that Rafael may never use *her* aether whether or not he was a black warlock. The idea didn't sit well. Since his true colors had painted him and he'd proven himself, she wanted him to have access to all her power. He'd need it in the days to come.

"You can rule the witchworld," her aunt announced.

"I know," Sage replied, unable to think upon the crazy-ass idea. "Tell me what you've learned from the covens who fled to Imelda's side."

"They've come to their senses. They recognize your power," Jessica said. "Imelda's staunch allies are sitting on the fence, probably waiting to see how power shakes out. All idiots, if you ask me."

"What about the black warlocks?"

"Evan said many will defer to you and Ethan as coven leaders if you forge an alliance. You scared the crap out of them." Willow smirked. "Evan and I scare the crap out of them too." She butt-danced a jig of joy in her seat.

"Not the Black Tide, right?" Sage squinted.

Willow shook her head. "Just the black warlocks who're adrift and some who temporarily sided with Imelda. Ethan can ID them."

"Another war's coming. The Black Tide won't let Andre go anywhere. He's too valuable to them. They won't quit targeting witches to beef up their ranks and breed baby warlocks," Sage ruminated aloud. "We need to blast out a communication to every coven to remain diligent."

"Already done," Jessica said and flinched. "Sorry, we didn't wait. We needed to alert the covens about what happened at the Helwigs', about the Black Tide and their lack of witches. You have a lot on your plate. Ethan helped with the messaging. Everyone needs to remain diligent."

"Well... okay." She took a second to adjust to others doing her unspoken bidding. "I appreciate the forethought. I want to put out a call for every coven in our territory to take sides."

"Your allies are pouring in, scared you'll attack them next." Willow grinned. "You have no idea how many witches and black warlocks will be at our beck and call worldwide."

Despite the weight of their conversation, Sage laughed at her sister's newfound exuberance. "You're sure taking this new role of coven witch to heart."

A deep flush stained Willow's face. "Sorry it took me so long."

The door burst open, and Aspen flew inside the room, panting from her flight from the infirmary. "Ethan's healer's here. She examined Rafael and wants to talk."

A crackling shiver of excitement crept through Sage. "Can I see him?"

"She wants to see his reaction to you, so, yeah, hit the infirmary." Aspen jetted out of the room, leaving behind the scent of camphor.

Sage followed, her steps light and quick. The rest of her Council tailed her, remaining at a discreet distance to avoid the aether she still radiated. They'd suffered enough in the dining room even from her position in a corner.

Two warlocks guarded the infirmary. Others following Sage, took up their posts outside the door. With Rafael out of commission and after the attacks, the Council dumped the extra guard detail on her. No use complaining. Rules were rules.

Sage eased quietly inside the infirmary. She stood just inside the threshold. "Sage Wilde." She held out her hand to the older witch, withdrew it after realizing she was still a pariah.

Flattering white strands streaked the witch's dark hair. The minimal wrinkles on her skin put her about fifty. No more than five feet tall, she was slender as a rail. "Oh, stop." She grabbed Sage's hand, squeezed, and let go. "A little aether won't hurt me. Marjorie Magellan, of the Magellan coven."

Sage's mouth dropped open. "The Magellans? I didn't think you were still around the region."

"A few. We remain impartial. We help the Ravenwoods and a few other covens. The Ravenwoods have always been good to us. We like to reciprocate."

Every nerve buzzed with anticipation. She wanted to see, touch, and hold Rafael more than ever. Magic seesawed on their bond, unnaturally and spotty, but she reveled in the existence.

"How do we heal and awaken Rafael?" Sage didn't mince words.

"Your sister's a talented healer. She's tried every magical charm, potion, and spell in the book. There's nothing I'd do different. Your medical doctor examined him and pronounced Mr. Reyes stable."

"But he's in a coma?"

"It's a good thing. Otherwise, the magic attacking him would drive him there. I've never seen a black warlock, or any warlock, bonded to an aether witch. It's unheard of. The magic is simply too strong."

Sage clutched her arms over her middle. "What's next?"

Marjorie cleared her throat as if about to deliver an uncomfortable truth. "I'll tell it to you straight. He won't awaken until the magic subsides."

"Then we give him time. The aether's already diminishing."

Marjorie smiled grimly. "Hon, it needs to happen sooner rather than later. The longer he stays under control of the magic, the higher chance of permanent damage or permanent loss of his magic. If he's a black warlock, which I understand you've just discovered, his awakening magic could have a profound and detrimental effect on him, both physical and mental. And he may never handle your aether or his own magic, black warlock or not."

Marjorie's pronouncement cruised the fringes of Sage's prior revelations. Hearing the words engulfed her in grief so strong, she almost spewed out the few bites of the lasagna she'd crammed down. Rafael suffering any longer, or even losing his magic, his new magic, especially when he'd always wanted more power, made her tortuous decision easy.

"I need to break my bond to him." Her matter-of-fact voice competed with the maddening anguished tumble of her heartbeat.

"I'm sorry. Until you do, we have no treatment options."

She shoved all the emotion from her mind into a box when she wanted to dissolve into a puddle and let the earth absorb her. "Will he suffer?"

"Only while you're in the room. He might experience pain when the bond breaks. It'll be short-lived. I'll give him traditional pain meds upfront."

"Let's do it now." Sage mentally tallied the items needed for the ritual.

"Let me give him an injection. Give it twenty minutes to work." Marjorie squeezed Sage's arm gently and turned aside.

Sage backstepped, straight against Ethan's solid mass. "How much did you hear?"

"Enough." He embraced her from behind. "I'm sorry."

She pushed out of his arms, didn't want to touch any man but Rafael. "Changes nothing. I'm still off the table." She faced him, grim reality tugging the skin around her mouth and eyes.

"I know, Sage. You were meant to be with Rafael alone. I have evidence he's a black warlock." He tapped the phone in his pocket. "He'll survive, and you'll be stronger together than ever. I accept it."

To divert her mind, Sage listened to the proof Ethan found on Rafael's lineage. His words slivered through her in a hopeful storm. What Andre had done to Rafael spurred her next words.

"I want an alliance with the Ravenwoods. You can have any *available* witch in my coven who accepts you. I prefer you pursue Eden if she's open. I think you'll make a perfect pairing with your psychic abilities. Think of the possibilities."

"I've thought of nothing else since I carried her down the tower stairs." He gave her a quick smile, and the flecks in his eyes brightened. "She may deny it, but our connection is strong." He held out his hand. "We have a deal."

Sage shook his hand despite the aether sizzling where their skin made contact. "The Ravenwoods and Wildes." She towed him in for a hug and kissed his cheek. "Thank you for everything you've done to help us."

"After what I saw, I'm not sure you needed our help." He chuckled. "Thank you for giving the Ravenwoods a chance and a future to look toward."

"Eden will fight you. Don't say I didn't warn you." Sage gazed into his blue eyes, wishing for a new day with Rafael sailing in the blue waters of the Pacific.

"I'm up for the challenge. There's something there."

A rustling behind Sage forced her to separate from Ethan. She turned to find Marjorie grinning.

"I trust you've struck an alliance?" Her eyebrows hiked up to her hairline. "It's about time you Ravenwoods got off your asses and found a good coven of witches." Solemn, she inspected Sage. "Five minutes. Are you ready?"

No, she wasn't ready to cut her bond to the love of her life, the man of her dreams. Why had she waited so long to truly understand everything he meant to her? And now she was on the verge of losing him, losing it all. She had no one to blame but herself.

To save him, she'd forego him completely and grant him the world if he asked for it.

Chapter 23

Marjorie preceded Sage inside Rafael's room. Serenity flitted across his face, alternating with pain etching lines around his eyes, then smoothing out. The black lab lay in a dog bed someone had placed beside Rafael's bed. A filled water bowl and empty food bowl sat in the far corner. The lab gave a friendly thump of its tail on the floor. Sage set her tote on the bedside table.

"I doubt he's in much pain, but the door's nudged open, and it'll open more in a couple hours as the meds wear off." Marjorie checked his vitals. "Do you want me to stay?"

Sage shook her head. "I need to do this alone. Please remain close just in case."

The healer headed out, clenched the molding around the door. "This will help him immensely. I'm sorry about the bond. Other ways exist, you know, to be together." With her hopeful words, she departed.

The words didn't help, though. Breaking her bond was akin to a slow, tortuous death. Maybe not his. Hers, definitely.

She watched pain flash across Rafael's quivering lips. Leaning down, she kissed him, his lips rough, cold, and she wanted to impart all her warmth. With all the fire and aether dancing between them, his icy skin shocked her. They were indeed in uncharted territory.

Perched on the edge of the bed, she twined her fingers in his left hand. She rubbed her cheek against his hand, wanting him to feel her and know she was present. Familiars danced across her skin, excited and waiting in anticipation. Caerwyn peeked out from the top of Rafael's T-shirt, the white ruffle on its head erect. The owl dipped down as if hiding from the forthcoming consequences of breaking the bond.

The dog sat up and pressed closer to the bed. Watching, waiting. Protecting Rafael. From her.

"My love," Sage said. "You know this is for your own good. I hate it with all my might. But I loathe seeing you in pain even more, and I can't allow it to continue. Two healers and an MD all say the same. You need to awaken. I need to stop the aether from attacking you, causing permanent damage. Cutting our bond is the only way." Her voice hitched. "I love you. I will always love you. Nothing changes. You're still my number-one warlock, always will be, in life and in death." Tears trickled down her cheeks, and they wet his hand. The sensation of his fingertips pressing against her skin skipped her heartbeat. Had he heard her?

No time to dwell, she laid his hand on his chest and yanked her tote bag closer. She snagged a small golden cord, a used black tealight—no time to let a pillar candle burn out—a pair of scissors, and arranged them in an orderly position on the rolling cart. Fighting the blasted tears stinging her eyes, she tied the ends of the cord together and visualized the bond she meant to break. The witch to her warlock, her guardian, her right hand. Rafael by her side in all ways.

"Warlock bond," she repeated over and over, ensuring the spell broke only her warlock bond and not their natural bond of love.

"Ignite." A flame erupted from her pointer finger. It rolled off her finger, sputtering from aether. The candlewick caught and flamed bright. Her hand hovered over the scissors, afraid to touch them. She kissed him again. "Nothing changes," she said.

Sitting upright, she gripped the scissors and passed them through the flame, envisioning the fire as her desire to be free, empowering the blades. A hard-fought task when she didn't want such freedom.

Reciting the hateful spell, her tears streamed anew.

> I cut the cord, the ties that bind us
> Intertwining warlock life to witch life
> With love, I release what is tied to me
> With love and thanks, I set us free
> With gratitude for all that we shared
> The ties are now released
> As the candle perishes
> Release this bond
> As I cut the cord
> Release this bond
> We each are free from the bond tying us together
> By the Goddess's will, so mote it be.

She cut the cord in half, buried it in a black cloth bag filled with dirt from the garden, and shoved it back in her bag. She'd bury it for real later, a necessary part of the ritual to stick. While she waited for the candle to burn out, she wiped the drying tears off her cheeks and sat on the bed beside Rafael. Already, the bond receded, emptying her soul, her body, and tugging on the strings binding her heart to him. Caerwyn moved from beneath Rafael's T-shirt in tattoo form, and the white owl landed on his shoulder, ready to launch into the air. Somber eyes glared at her, reconciled to its fate.

The moment the flame on the tealight sputtered, the bond separated and whipped inside her, unable to wait to break in half, mocking her and everything she represented. The flame winked out, and a puff of smoke rose from the tealight cup. Magic slipped into thin air, and the ties that bound them left a massive crater in her heart, body, and soul. Cold spears of grief and regret pierced her with jagged edges, rocking her back and forth on the bed.

Caerwyn launched off Rafael's shoulder, landed on the back of Sage's hand, and slithered up her sleeve in renewed tattoo form. Gwyneira cupped its wings consolingly around the bonding familiar, who'd feel as lost as Rafael.

Sage gently cupped his chin. Already peace smoothed his features, even though the residual aether still attacked him.

"I'm sorry, Rafael. I didn't want this." She kissed him again, her lips lingering until a light touch tapped her shoulder. "I'll always be yours, and I'll be here for you."

"Is it done?" Aspen asked.

Not taking her gaze off his face, she nodded.

"Oh, sis, I'm so sorry." Aspen tried to hug her, but Sage jerked aside.

"Don't," she ground out. "I can't have anyone touch me."

"You haven't lost him, you know? He'll never leave you."

Sage spun on her sister, fire drying her tears, a gust of wind cooling her. "You know a witch breaking her bond to a warlock is permanent. I can never bond him again."

Aspen's eyes misted. "I meant that he still loves you. You don't need to be bonded to be together, to love one another."

Grabbing her tote, Sage hugged it to her middle. "You've never experienced this kind of bond." She spat the words out like ice crystals. "You don't know what it's like. How I feel like the world has ended." She headed for the door. "When he awakens and is safe to move, please transfer him to the East guestroom. I don't want him recovering in this dreary medical cubicle. He deserves better. He needs to see the sun rise every day."

"Do you need anything for pain?" Aspen reached inside her medicine cabinet.

"No. I'll share my pain with Rafael."

"What about for your heart?"

"Nothing on Earth will cure that pain." Sage stepped over the threshold.

"What about the dog..." Aspen's voice trailed off.

Sage held her tote to her stomach and pivoted around. "What?"

"Where'd the pup go?" Aspen looked under Rafael's bed. "He's gone."

Sage's gaze landed on Rafael's bare forearm. "Oh. My. His arm." She pressed her fingertips to her lips. The black lab, in tattoo form, chased its tail on Rafael's arm, hogging the entire length of his forearm.

"Holy hell in a handbasket. What the what?"

"Forgot to tell you," Sage said. "Rafael's a black warlock. Guess he found his familiar."

"Well, well, well." Aspen clapped once. "Better late than never. And I was starting to like that pup. Glad she's sticking around."

Sage left her sister watching over Rafael. Three warlocks followed her at a safe distance. Far enough that she didn't blast them with aether. Two of them were bonded to her. Neither had found another witch to bond. They didn't want her to break their bond until they found a witch to love for life. Sage wasn't it.

Since Rafael was no longer bound to her, it eased a path for him to split if he so desired. After everything that'd happened in the last few days, after everything she'd put him through with the other warlocks, with the aether, she couldn't blame him if he ran for the depths of the hills.

Instead of heading to her office, she hightailed it to the backyard. Passing the gazebo, she held her vigil ambling along the paths cutting through the evergreen bushes, the rose garden awaiting spring, and along the paths her parents had cut through the woods for hiking, meditation, and contemplation. She needed the cool air to temper the fire of magic and anger within her.

A meditation bench in a clearing enclosed within evergreen trees beckoned. She held her hand up to hold the three warlocks at bay. She sat, mulled over the events of the last few days, avoided thinking about Rafael, until her thoughts landed on Andre Charlemagne. *That son of a bitch.* She jumped off the bench so fast, the three warlocks charged her, searching for invisible peril.

"I'm going to the dungeon." She plowed between two guards.

"Um, Sage, not a good idea," Ryan, Rafael's second in command suggested, jogging to catch up to her.

"I'm not asking your permission." She loved Ryan's watchfulness and loyalty. He was a good warlock and wielded her fire well. He was a better lieutenant to Rafael than he was a lover, not that they'd gone beyond the one-time hookup prior to her bonding him. No one ever really compared to Rafael. Too bad he and Eden or Aspen never hit it off.

The three warlocks didn't utter another word as she ran-walked toward the house and tromped down the back stairs to the dungeon. By the time she hit the basement floor, she'd gathered a trail of witches and warlocks, including the ones guarding Andre's room. A few grimaced and groaned from the aether magic attacking them.

"How bad is my magic?" she asked the room.

"Tolerable. Just prickly," Eden said, scratching her arms to prove a point.

"Why are you here? You should be resting." Sage scowled at her cousin.

Eden tilted in, said in Sage's ear, "So I can read Andre's mind."

"Are you getting anything?" Sage whispered back, inhaling the scent of Eden's apprehension and a new lavender-vanilla perfume. Supposed to be a calming influence, lavender didn't seem to work too well at the moment.

"Bits and fragments. Things are making a little sense about him, the Black Tide, his compound."

Excitement swamped Sage's anger. "Okay. Don't tax yourself and keep your mind safe from him. Don't even get close to giving him an opening."

"The good news is my telepathy works without magic. His coercion doesn't." Eden uttered a wicked chuckle. "The other good news is that he doesn't know I can read his mind!"

Sage rolled her eyes. "Keep it that way. Jeez, you're in a good mood." She continued to whisper when she wanted to shout it to the world. She hadn't seen Eden so animated in years. Maybe the lavender perfume was working magic. Or a dose of happy gummies did the trick.

"I think I have a new lease on life." Eden tapped her fingernails on her phone. "Something knocked sense in me during this whole debacle. I feel needed."

"Oh, cous, we've always needed you." Sage bumped shoulders with Eden. "Are you sure it doesn't have something to do with a warlock named Ethan Ravenwood?"

"No freaking way!" Spots flushed Eden's cheeks. "Don't

even go there. He already wants to talk." She flinched and shook her head, but Sage saw through her. Ethan intrigued Eden as much as she did him.

"So, talk."

"I will… just about Andre and the Black Tide. We'll trade notes on our," her voice dropped again, "respective abilities."

Sage couldn't ask for more. She'd count on Ethan and Eden in their coven's fight against the black warlocks if their world shifted. The two psychics promised to turn the tide in Sage's favor with their abilities to ferret out secret information. Another reason for keeping Andre alive when she'd rather kill the cretin.

Approaching the door to Andre's cell, she said, "I'm going inside. Alone."

"Absolutely not." Ryan barred the door.

Sage slid him a withering glare and hurled a fireball at the warded wall. It scorched a tiny hole in the steel-reinforced cement wall. "Are you testing me, Ryan? What would Rafael say?"

"He'd say hell to the no. Wouldn't matter. You'd still do you," Eden butted in. "Let her in. With her newfangled powers, she can use magic against a ward. The prick won't approach her."

"I go in beside her at least for brute strength." Ryan negotiated as if Sage wasn't standing there. Two other witches unlocked the multiple locks on the door, both physical and magical.

"Fine." Sage flung out both hands, flinging witch-air and cloaking Ryan in a protective ward. "The wards in the room will kill your magic."

He swung his arms to test his motion range. "Are you sure the wards won't knock out your magic? I need to know what we're up against."

"Nope." She gripped the door handle, bolstered her

nerves spinning out, and opened the door. "Stay behind me to the left." And she marched straight into the lion's den.

Andre perched on his chair. "Sage Wilde, my extraordinary jailor. A pleasure to see you again."

Air circulated down from the ceiling vents, not enough to clear the stench of despair and anger. "Cut the crap, Andre." Sage strode to the closed door and entwined Andre in air ropes, tying him to the chair. Spots of rusty dried blood spotted the cream-colored walls. Sage almost wanted to paint the walls with Andre's blood.

His eyes bulged. "I'd heard snippets about your coup at the Helwig compound. You are indeed extraordinary. It appears I set my sights on the wrong witch."

Too bad she hadn't gagged him. The enticing idea amused her, but she curtailed her smile.

"Why *did* you cozy up to Imelda?" The need to know burned a hole in her mind. "She's small fry compared to other covens."

"Because she had such other covens joining her," he mocked. "Because she *was* small fry and easy to manipulate. And she was dying. Cancer. Her daughter doesn't have the ambition to rule a coven, so her people would've fallen into my web."

Her chin quivered. The diagnosis explained the pain she'd seen on Imelda, the gaunt, ravaged mask aging her faster than time alone allowed.

"I did her a favor, ending her pain." Andre's voice splintered, and his eyes watered. "We both ended her pain. Assisted suicide."

Sage's mind returned to her own part in Imelda's death, then buried it to dwell on later. To grieve later. Despite Imelda's actions, she deserved a proper sendoff within the witchworld, like any High Priestess. Sage corralled her rambling thoughts.

"Here's what I want, Andre. Call off your black

warlocks. Witches will allow all black warlocks who surrender to us the right to join the new witchworld we create. We'll allow any black warlock who joins us to pursue a willing witch for a love match or mutual and equal bond, and we'll all live in harmony once again."

Andre smiled. "Never believed a Wilde witch would stoop to kidnapping. You can't keep me in this dinky room forever."

Sage bristled at him dodging her non-negotiable offer. "You're a war criminal, you treasonous bastard. I can incarcerate or *kill* you. Your choice."

"What war? What crimes?"

Sage tapped her mouth, her scraggly fingernail clicking on her bottom teeth. "Oh, let's see. You plonked an illegal black spell on Willow, attempted to kidnap her, used an illegal coercion spell on Eden, and *did* abduct her. I'd even say you raped them with your black spells. I'd call your list of crimes an act of war."

"Even war criminals get their day in court."

"Oh, believe me, it's coming. Or I can just kill you now?"

"This conversation is tedious. Just get it over with." Red stained Andre's face. "Give me my familiars so they won't bother you any longer."

Her witches had recaptured his familiars, which included an unfortunate full-body cavity search. "There will be a full regional Council trial. Don't fret, Andre, dear," she mocked. "You'll have your day in *our* court. We might even give you a break if you relinquish control of your black warlocks and hand all your information to us. I might consider moving you to a more comfortable cell including atrium access for fresh air and exercise. You'll eventually love it here."

Andre continued smirking at her. Minutes crawled by while she waited.

"So be it." She turned her back on him, at ease knowing her magic worked in the warded room.

"He's mine now," Andre crooned. "Rafael and all the black warlocks... are mine. They'll never belong to you or any witch."

Chapter 24

The midnight moon illuminated the clouds, creating ghostly shapes in the night sky. Sage lay in bed, unable to sleep. Her phone rang, and she scooped it up.

"I've moved Rafael to the guestroom," Aspen said. Sage's relief barely made a dent in her angst. "It worked. He's better. At least something good came of your severed bond."

"Is he awake?" Every muscle stilled.

"In and out." Aspen yawned loudly. "He's out of the woods, and he's asking for you during his lucid moments. Oh, I've sent Marjorie home."

Aspen forbade her to see him or come near his room on the other side of the house. Another reason she'd put him in the East wing, as far from her bedroom and office as possible without having to leave the house. She almost relocated to a cabin on the fringes of the property. Overkill, Aspen had said, so she stayed put.

Two full days escaped after the phone call. She'd kept busy contacting the covens in her region. They'd all learned about her aether power surge. It scared them enough to re-affirm their allegiance, even the covens who'd stupidly sided with Imelda. Even Imelda's daughter, who'd temporarily taken over her mother's coven, until the Helwig Council elevated her to High Priestess. The black warlocks who'd sided with Imelda and Andre left licking their wounds. No one identified where they holed up. Andre knew. Apparently, he'd housed the Ravenwoods and select other black warlock covens in a different location. Andre knew who buttered his bread.

Sage was positive the Black Tide wasn't gone for good. Not with Andre alive and kicking under her dominion. A potential war hovered on the horizon. She refused to rule it out or drop her guard. For now, she needed to tidy her own house. First, heal Rafael and sort out their new unbonded world. High Priestesses just didn't have unbonded warlock guards, lovers, or husbands. The Council would demand she bond a third warlock, as rules dictated. She may have no choice in choosing Ethan.

Sitting back in her chair by the window, she sipped a steaming green tea to calm her nerves. The sun set, and bands of indigo and purple twilight streaked the sky. The forest trees swallowed the rest of the natural light. Landscape lights glimmered on, dotting the gardens, the woods, and the cabins nestled among the trees. A welcome sign of normalcy. Her gaze bounced to the scattered tables on the patio, expecting to see the candles lit. Lit from Rafael playing with her witch-fire. The candles remained dark and bereft of life, joining the cold sadness inside her.

The aether had receded, and she almost felt normal, well, maybe a new normal. Another couple of days and the residual effects will have gone like the dearly departed. Regardless, the aether languished ready inside her core, more than ever before. More magic than she'd ever housed. As she waited for Rafael's recovery, she worked on control of her new magic. Thankfully, her efforts paid off. The witches and warlocks she'd asked no longer felt the magic. They may still shrink from her, but at least she wasn't hurting them. "Fear was good. Kept everyone in place," Rafael liked to say whenever she cracked the whip on her coven members.

Soft classical music played in the background, and Sage set her cup on the table. Her eyes closed of their own volition, and she drifted off for one of her cat naps since deep sleep had eluded her for days.

A scratchy but gentle hand touched her face. In a panic, she vaulted out of her chair, half asleep. A fireball rose off her palm and floated in the air. Her eyes flew open and widened. The fireball fizzled out in a puff of smoke.

"Rafael." Sage breathed out his name. She wanted to leap into his arms but feared hurting him. "Aspen released you?" After not eating for days, he was pale and gaunt. The sight of him in baggy sweatpants and a black hoodie soothed her sore eyes.

He dug his hands in his jacket pockets. "Not really. They wanted me in a wheelchair when I demanded to see you. I needed to walk on my own two."

"The Council and Nurse Ratched refused to let me see you. I would've carried you here myself if forced to." She gave him a tentative smile, unsure of his emotions, unsure if she should touch him, despite her desperation to feel him under her skin. He showed no emotion whatsoever. "Are you okay? Is my magic hurting you?"

"Been better." He raked his hand through his bed-head hair, trying to smooth it down. "I feel your magic—more of it—it's different. Doesn't hurt."

"Good." Sage could dine on the small slice of relief. "Are you hungry? I can get—"

Silent, he shook his head, paced a few steps. Sucking in air from exertion, he halted before her, too far to touch.

"Did you break our bond because of Ravenwood?"

Sage gasped, her mouth dropping open. "Is that what you think?"

"I don't know what to think. You said you'd *never* break our bond unless I wanted out," he lashed out. "And I sure as hell *didn't* want out. Now... not so sure."

"Rafael, you're not serious." Irritated, Sage stamped her bare foot on the thick wool rug. "Didn't Aspen or anyone else tell you what happened?"

"A little. Little made sense. I heard some of what you said... I heard the spell. I never wanted to wake up after that bullshit." His pale cheeks pinkened with his ire, fear, every other emotion flitting through him. "All I know is that I woke up, and you weren't there, nor was our bond. The severing cut me in pieces. It about killed me to discover your magic gone. You know severing a bond is permanent, right?"

"Of course I know. Hello... I'm the witch here." She stretched her hand toward him, and he lurched back. "Rafael, I didn't do it for Ethan." She wrung her hands. "Love, it was the only way to prevent my magic from destroying you. I had no choice." She told him all that'd happened since he'd gone down at the siege on the Helwig covenstead. By the time she finished reciting the events, he'd drooped in his chair and dropped his face in his hands.

Exhaustion bogging her down, Sage sat on her knees between his legs, looking up at him. "Do you understand why I did it? To save you and your magic. Nothing else was working." He refused to look at her as he absorbed what'd happened. "It killed me to break our bond. Still kills me. Worse than burying my parents."

He lifted his head, his mouth a grim slash. "Believe me, it kills me too."

"Changes nothing between us."

"It changes everything. You'll have to bond a third

warlock. You can't function without a trio. That's one more person in our life. If we have a life."

She sniffed. "Don't you dare go there. We have a life, regardless of the bond. I would love you even if we weren't magicals. And it's not like our life has been mutually exclusive all this time and not a freaking open book. We'll figure it out, find the right warlock."

"It damn well better not be Ravenwood."

"Don't worry. Ethan's enamored with Eden."

Rafael shook back his head and emitted a snigger that didn't reach his eyes. "Good luck with that. He's gonna need it."

Sage rubbed her hand along his inner thigh, stopping short of the danger zone. "She's open to talking to him."

"You're kidding me?" He stopped her hand moving on him, gloved it within his own. His touch was electrifying in more ways than the separate magic they created.

"It still changes nothing between *us*. And there is an us." She squeezed his hand.

"I'm no longer your First Warlock. That changes, and I hate it with everything inside me."

"But you are my number one everything. And you *are* a warlock." She eased her hand from under his, jumped up, and retrieved her phone.

"God, please don't tell me Andre's my father." His skin turned ashen, and his hands trembled.

"Hell no." She scrolled through her documents and handed the phone to Rafael. "It's confirmed. Your father was a powerful black warlock, who contained fire and water magic. He belonged to the Black Tide. Your mother an air witch, who died after you were born, like you already knew. Your real father escaped Andre's clutches and took you with him. To hide you from Andre, he placed you with a family who in the end couldn't deal with your magic, even as a toddler. That's how you ended up in foster care, name change and all." Sage took a few deep breaths, filling her soul with the clean soap scent of Rafael, and continued, "Andre eventually found your real father and killed him when he wouldn't divulge your new name or whereabouts. Your father was just trying to save you from the Black Tide. Things went sideways."

Rafael rested his head on the chair, eyes closed, silent for the longest time. He handed the phone back to Sage. "It explains the magic inside me." He opened his eyes, new flecks of silver brightening them as though touched by the sun.

Sage squinted at him. "What do you mean?"

"Did you read about my mother?"

Sage skimmed the bio on his mother, her eyes widening. "Oh. She was an aether witch. Like me." Her heartbeat broke into a trot, and she took his hand in hers, twining their fingers together. "Do you think you have aether magic?"

"I don't know. My magic's a jumbled mess. Doesn't it explain why my magic never manifested until now?"

"Absolutely. I manifested early, but it's because my mother trained me. She recognized the aether in me at an early age." Sage tapped a fingernail on her chin, her manicure nearly decimated. "I think you caused my aether to flare when we first met, and again this week. My reaction to strong black warlock magic. Our magic clashed, even though you didn't know it. Explains a lot, though."

"I need help with this. I don't know what it means to be a black warlock." He straightened in his chair, excitement bringing new life back to his eyes. "I'm stoked about it, though."

"Agreed. We need to learn how to separate our magic so we both don't destroy the world!" She laughed. Pride flooded her with his admission that he needed help. "Evan and Ethan are raring to mentor you. You're way behind the eight ball."

"Guess I need them now that you've struck an alliance. Right? We have the alliance without you accepting his offer." Without waiting for her answer, he patted his lap. "Get the hell over here. I've missed you."

Grinning, she eased onto his lap, twining her arms around his neck. "Yes." She rubbed her cheek against his slightly damp hair. "We have an alliance. Ethan will not be in our bed."

"If you don't kiss me, I may have to bail. Now that you don't hold my strings any longer." Their lips met, reticent at first, then his hands dug through her hair, and he drew her head closer. Their kiss filled all the voids inside Sage, drove out all her fears. When they drew apart, Rafael gasped, sagging into the chair, his strength zapped.

"I'm sorry." He buried his face in her neck, soaking in the scent of her skin.

"Don't be. We have all the time in the world." She stroked his shoulders. "I have one final question before I put you to bed."

"Bed sounds good." His lips traveled up from her neck to her ear, leaving a trail of goosebumps. "Shoot."

"I may not hold your strings, but do I still hold your heart?" She held her breath.

His lips found hers again, and he just pressed them together, breathing in each other. And he nodded, her lips moving with his until their mouths parted, and he deepened the kiss, signifying a new bond.

Chapter 25

They lay tangled in each other's arms, the only "bedding" Sage allowed in Rafael's weakened state. She told him about all the activity and conversations he'd missed. Everything.

Sage reached inside her nightstand drawer and snagged the titanium wand she'd stolen from Imelda's house. She laid the magic detection device on Rafael's chest. "A present for you. Reverse engineer it so you can replicate it."

Rafael scooped up the cylinder for closer inspection, stroking it lovingly. "Damn, woman, you melted my heart again."

He introduced her to his new familiar, Shadow, the black lab. The pup frolicked around Rafael's body, exhibiting classic traits of an exuberant puppy.

"Did I tell you I'd always wanted a dog familiar in the coven?" Sage feathered her finger over the lab's swishing tail.

"Fate had your back." Rafael set the electronic device aside and gathered Sage in his arms, spooning her from behind. "Man's best friend." The lab never stopped moving, until it sensed Rafael needed rest and stretched out on his arm, and they all slept.

A text message dinged, waking Sage the next morning, and she slipped out of bed to read it without waking Rafael.

See the book I left for Rafael outside your door, Ethan texted.

Barefoot, she retrieved the book, an ancient text of black warlock magic. A book missing from her own arsenal. The perfect instruction manual for Rafael.

She sat in her chair, the book on her lap, and leafed through the old, delicate pages.

Rafael groaned in bed and rolled over on his back. "What now?"

"Another gift for you." Her eyes alighted on a chapter. The words undid her, like all the spells and magic spelled out in the book. "Rafael. Check this out."

He crawled out of bed, padded over to her, and kissed the top of her head, the heat of his breath warm against her messy hair. "Despite our broken bond, I feel more connected than ever."

"The power's gone to your head. You always wanted my witch powers for real. Now you have your own."

"Don't you feel it?" He peered at the book over her shoulder.

"You're always inside me. Bond or not." She pressed his hand to her heart. "Always here. But if you really want to know, yes. I still feel connected to you. I experienced a moment of total loss where I thought I'd go insane. I think you're right. You hold aether magic, and we're connected by it. Aether to aether."

"What's the book?" He reached down, and she extended it to him over her head.

"From Ethan."

Eyes widening, he accepted the tome reverently,

holding it close in both hands. "Wow, black warlock instruction, spells, and history." He grinned a soul-stealing grin. "Guess he's a nice guy after all." He sat and leafed through the book, turning the pages with due respect.

"Told you so. He wants you to learn what's inside you the right way."

"Oh, hello sunshine." He grinned wider. "Did you read this? I can block your aether."

"Oh, nice, but we already know that. The warlocks at Imelda's managed it. The first time. Second time, not so much, but you'll get a handle on it." She smiled, her heart so full of joy, the excitement pounded against her ribcage. "Read page fifty-two."

Rafael leafed ahead, careful not to bend the pages. It took a moment for him to read the scrolled cursive. His gaze lifted, and his smile was like sunshine, stars, and moon all wrapped in one package. "This is insane. I can separate out all elements and use them individually?"

"Yep. All the power you always wanted. You're just a little behind the learning curve. Like modern witches and black warlocks of old, you'll need to find your niche and your most potent powers. Go chill outside and read. But rest. I want you all to myself tonight."

His grin widened, crinkling the skin of his eyes. "You'll get me." He stroked his hand down the length of his erection. Sage trailed her fingers over his hair and left him to devour his book of black magic. Not sure his hard-on was for her or the book. She'd place her bets on the book.

C⋆C⋆C⋆

From a flame dancing off her finger, Sage lit candles on the mantle, turned the gas on the fireplace, and shot out a couple fireballs until a fire danced and crackled in the ceramic logs. She poured two glasses of ice-cold champagne. They may not have a full trough of things to celebrate, but Rafael's recovery and discovering his true identity was more than enough.

Sage luxuriated in a long, fragrant bath and wore one of Rafael's favorite lacy bra and panties set covered by a silk robe. No use killing the man before his recovery.

She didn't have long to wait before he jogged into their bedroom, the precious book in his hands. "Babe, you have to read this." He practically shoved the book under her chin.

Laughing, she stepped back. Her eyes lit up, and a flutter rolled in her middle. "I've never seen you so excited."

"Like a kid finding buried treasure." The delight on his face transformed his brooding warlock mask.

"Yes. *You* are the treasure."

"My life, my body, everything makes sense for the first time. Like long-barricaded doors have opened, and I've finally entered my real life."

Sage hugged his arm close to her. "I'm so happy for you." She squeezed him and let go. "What did you discover?"

"You won't need a third warlock." Humming with excitement, he showed her a spell in the book.

Sage read the words, tried to absorb the implications. Thoughts zinged in her mind. "Don't know why I didn't think about this when grief wracked me and I was drowning you in my tears."

"It's not the progression you wanted, but it solves our problem. It brings back the old traditions. Doesn't matter that you broke our bond. It can still work."

"Traditions of black warlocks dominating witches that started the war." Distaste framed her words. "It's just not done." But Evan had bonded Willow. Why hadn't Sage thought a way existed around her severing their bond?

"It won't be like that. *We* won't allow it. You're still my witch, and we still live in the modern witchworld. Can you imagine you being bonded to a black warlock, Evan and Willow, and maybe even Ethan and Eden bonded, what it signifies to the world? It'll prove that witches and black warlocks can co-exist peacefully again." He bounced from foot to foot. "Think of the power we'll each have. We'll be unchecked, unstoppable. We need this. My job as your warlock is to protect you." He hooked a finger under her chin, forcing her gaze to lock on his. "My job as your consort is to love you."

"What's your job as my husband?" Sage asked, never breaking eye contact.

Just like that, the idea of *Rafael* bonding *her* shoved everything else out of her mind. Did it matter he was bonding her and not the other way around?

"Sage? What are you thinking?" A black cloud stormed his face. "Nothing changes between us. *Nothing.* I swear. Andre doesn't own me. The Black Tide doesn't own me. I belong to you, to the Wildes, until I die."

She took the book from his hands, shut it, and carefully placed it on the table between their chairs. "I'm thinking that I love you more than life. I'm thinking I've never loved you more than in this moment. I'm thinking I might like this equality thing with you."

He enclosed her in his arms, his arms trembling in exhaustion from a long day of studying and practicing spells when he should've been resting. "Is that a yes?"

"Only if you marry me like you promised." She pressed her lips to his throat, nibbling and planting kisses up to his chin.

His eyes glistened. "You never said yes."

"I'm saying yes now."

His lips met hers for a long, leisurely kiss, his arms tightening until air whooshed out of her. He swept his tongue over her lips, sealing their kiss, and said, "I love you, Sage Wilde. Everything I have is because of you. You represent faith, family, love, everything missing from my life when I met you." He punctuated his words with quick kisses. "Sage Wilde, will you marry me?"

"Rafael Reyes, yes I will." She punctuated her words with lingering kisses. "And will you become my First Warlock again?"

"*Au contraire*." He snorted. "Will you, Sage Wilde, become my first... um... witch? Is that a thing?"

"I'll be your first everything." She leaned into his kiss to solidify their vow and pushed against his hardness, vowing to be careful making love to him that night, even though she wanted both fast and rough and slow and sensuous, what they did best.

☾⋆☾

They toasted to their good fortune and for their future good fortune, drinking most of the champagne as if thirst ravaged them. In reality, Rafael needed to be inside her more than anything. He needed to know their lovemaking hadn't changed between them.

"I've found my forever in you, Sage Wilde, witch, lover, and wife." Eyes twinkling, he set their champagne flutes aside.

"You've always been my forever. Known it the day you flew into my web." Sage seductively peeled aside her robe to expose half her left breast. Rafael licked his lips but didn't hinder her from doing the same to the other side. He always tripped out on her strip-teases.

"Took you long enough to admit it." He playfully slapped her butt before he cupped her ass cheek. He led her to the bed and drew off the robe, sucking in a sharp breath. "I've missed you." Rafael needed to claim her in all ways, the beginning of his life with her, finally with a more permanent defined role, not just First Warlock or consort. What he'd always wanted.

Her mouth parted to stop him, but she didn't curtail his fingers from stoking the smoldering fire between her legs. Growling, Rafael's mouth crushed hers, and she accepted the thrust of his tongue against hers, a velvet sword staking its claim. Fire ignited in the core of his body, both innate magic and the fire of his longing. He nibbled at her lips, and she bowed against him. She deepened their kiss, pressing closer, like she wanted to dissolve into his body. His kiss demanded everything from her, and she didn't disappoint.

They made love, unhurried and intimate, the most intimate he'd ever experienced with her. Since she'd changed her tune about marrying him, everything had changed. He no longer held back. Now that he recognized his identity and the new secure place he held in the Wilde Coven, he'd been reborn with aether roaming at ease within his body.

Before Sage killed him with her tongue, her lips, her touch, his orgasm hooked him, and Sage's orgasm chased his own, her shudders rocking through him. The friction caused a pained pleasure, forcing him to pull out of her wet heat. Fire erupted off his fingers, singeing the bed covers, sending smoke spirals wafting in the air. Chest heaving, he sprawled spread-eagle on the bed. Panting, Sage leaned back on her heels, her need vibrating her body. Bracing her hands on Rafael's muscular shoulders, she stretched out on top of him.

"I love you. You'll always be mine and mine alone." Rafael feathered his lips over hers. She moaned into his kiss, and his tongue tangled with hers. Soft and slow, he kissed her, so tender and evocatively, tears welled in her eyes, and he thumbed them off.

Rafael released her mouth, and she whimpered. "You

never cry, tough witch."

"I've shed more tears this week than in my entire life."

"Over me?" He kissed her again, and her heart thudded against his chest, in sync with his own. "Vulnerability is powerful."

"Say the bond now before I recant."

He joggled his head. "We don't need to do this now."

"Say it," she demanded. "Are you backing out, warlock?" The teasing lilt of her voice undid him.

"I need a white candle." His gaze lit on the mantle of plenty. "I can't weave yet. What if the spell doesn't work?"

"Hang tight. I'll get the candle." Sage untwined her arms and legs from his, and cooler air skimmed over his bare body. She glided across the room, her body glistening from their lovemaking, her long, blonde hair tangled from his hands sifting it. Her gorgeous, luscious body made him hard again. He tamped down his lust and sat up in the bed, leaning against the padded headboard.

"Ethan and Evan will teach you to weave. But you don't need to weave magic for all spells." Sage handed him a half-burned white candle and a lighter and straddled his lap, the candle between them.

He lit the candle, the amber flame dancing between them. Voice roughened, he uttered a bonding spell he'd memorized earlier that day, binding them in more than magic, as warlock and witch, but also binding him to her in every way possible.

> Oh brilliant fire, which I hold in my hand
> By the air that I breathe, by the breath within me
> To Sage Wilde, bound together for life I wish to be
> I give you the magic of my body, my heart, my soul
> Eternal, true and steadfast
> I open my body to your magic
> Call upon all my magic as if it were your own

I'll not ever use my magic or yours against you
I will guard your powers as I guard my own
Link us together
Take this spell and make it be
As I will, so mote it be.

Sage voiced her part of the oath and added one final line, "I will protect your mind, heart, soul, and body to the death. So mote it be."

Fire burst off her and sizzled over his body. He tumbled in an inferno threatening to implode into his core of aether. A cloud of their mingled fire hovered over their heads. Air, earth, and water held it in check. A healthy dose of all four elements melded, glowing ropes of aether fringing the mushroom cloud. Sparks showered the room, like a diamond exploding in the night sky into a thousand scattered shards. Air whooshed through the sparks, sprinkling multicolored glitter to blanket the room. Magic threads weaved above them in different colors. Rafael waved his hand, and the threads followed his fingers. He directed them to spell out, "I love you" in rainbow colors.

Caerwyn flew off Sage's arm in a tingly wash and sank onto Rafael's neck. Right where the familiar belonged. The owl tattoo rolled over Rafael's neck and skittered across his shoulder intermittently sinking under his skin and vaulting off. Caerwyn showed a newly formed black lab bonding familiar how to leave. The tiny black lab bounded off Rafael's left pectoral onto Sage's shoulder and began chasing her owls.

"Oh, my goddess." She pressed her hand to her chest. "Is this what I have to look forward to with a dog familiar? A really cute black lab, I might add."

Rafael's eyes popped. "Guess now we're officially bonded. You have my—"

"Bonding familiar?" The new tattoo visibly sizzled on

her skin. "Shall you name it... um..." She tapped a fingertip on her chin. "Raven because it's black?"

"Hell to the no. There will never be a raven in our relationship." He mock gagged.

Sage busted out in laughter. "Good thing your familiar wasn't a raven."

"Do you remember that black warlocks only have one bonding familiar we give to the witch we expect to spend forever with. To the witch I intend to bond for life," he said. Her eyes softened. "How about Onyx? In some legends it symbolizes protection."

The lab licked Sage's arm, and she stroked the tattoo. "Onyx it is." Tears glistened in her eyes. "I've missed our bond. It's incredible. Different. Stronger, more of... everything. Your aether is zinging inside me. Thank the goddess it plays nice with mine." She touched the glitter puddling in Rafael's belly button and brushed her fingertips over his lips. "Rafael Reyes, I accept your protection and your love. I continue to accept you as my First Warlock. And I will be your wife and love you beyond reason. Today, tomorrow, forever." Rafael caught her hand and kissed her palm. "You are your own master. This is an equal partnership."

"Damn straight." Rafael set the candle on the nightstand, and they rolled on their sides to face each other. "You have the protection of my body, my heart, and my magic. You own me. Always."

Sage's eyes softened and she said, "The goddess blessed me with you." Magic shivered through Rafael, and Sage's pull on his magic was so sweet and pure as it joined with hers. "Jeez, we're full of saccharine romance vibes tonight!"

"I promise it will always be like this." He nuzzled her neck. Powerful new magic emanated off him, both his own and the full body of Sage's aether. Testing his new powers, air billowed from him. "And you are my forever, my lifeline." Air tickled the vee of Sage's thighs.

"Hey," Sage berated teasingly. "I'm still the ruling witch of the Wilde Coven. I make the rules."

"Evolution. Equality. Work the words in your new motto." Rafael grinned again, and the last few days vaporized into the atmosphere.

Their new future beckoned.

BLACK CURSES BREWING

Wilde Witches – Book 3

Read Aspen Wilde and Lucky Lorenzo's story in *Black Curses Brewing*, Book 3 of the Wilde Witches series.

ABOUT THE AUTHOR

After lamenting the lack of young adult books to read, award-winning and *USA Today* best-selling author, Erin Richards, wrote her first novel at the age of eighteen hoping to shift the tide. But the only tide she shifted was moving from high school to college. Then everyday life took its toll on her writerly dreams until she couldn't ignore the writing bug any longer. By then, she had immersed herself in reading adult fantasy and romance novels. Writing suspenseful paranormal and fantasy romance was a no brainer and she went on to publish two adult romance novels and hasn't stopped since. But her muse wanted to give that YA writing gig another chance, and Erin finally realized her lifelong dream of publishing a YA novel with the debut of *Vigilante Nights*.

Erin lives in California. In her spare time, she enjoys reading (of course!) and perpetually landscaping her yards, even though she hates digging holes...unless she's burying fictional bodies! She also confesses to a fascination with American muscle cars... and reality TV shows!

Visit Erin Richards online at:
www.erinrichards.com

Sign-up for her newsletter at:
www.erinrichards.com/connect.htm